THE UNSEEN

Lisa Towles

9MM Press
New Zealand
9mmPress@zoho.com

Publisher's Note: This is a work of fiction. Names, characters, places, and incidents are a product of the author's imagination. Locales and public names are sometimes used for atmospheric purposes. Any resemblance to actual people, living or dead, or to businesses, companies, events, institutions, or locales is completely coincidental.

The Unseen/ Lisa Towles. — 1st ed.
ISBN 978-0-578-42267-1

For Lee

Acknowledgements

I would like to express my heartfelt gratitude to the following people whose care, love, and support helped me during the development of this book:

To my amazing parents – thank you for your constant love, support, and encouragement. Through your example you have taught me how to dig deep, listen to myself, be gritty in the face of challenge, and reach for the stars

To my sister, my most treasured confidante – you're an amazing talent who brings strength, wit, and grace to everything you do

To Olivia and Cassidy – thank you shining your radiant light on my world

To Bob and Bev – thank you for your support, encouragement, love, and understanding

To Gail, Missy, and Kadi, my awesome readers - thank you for your attention to detail, great questions, encouragement, guidance, and friendship

To Rachel, Natalka, Tiffany, Toni, Mary, Denise, and Majdah – thank you for your strength, courage, stories, friendship, and inspiration.

To the brilliant and gifted engineers, writers, designers, architects, and innovators I'm so lucky to work with every day - you are my greatest teachers

To Kelly Wendorf - thank you for being a light in the darkness, and for helping me find my muse

To Beth Barany, my writing coach - thank you for your savvy advice and guidance

To Paulette Burns, thank you for the precious fourth grade reading circles and for making stories come alive for me

To Leo Bottary, for providing the beautiful office where I wrote the ending of this book - thank you for your friendship, guidance, and inspiration

To Arthur Conan Doyle, for giving me the version of Sherlock Holmes that lives in my heart

To Jayne - thank you for your awesome editing expertise, support, kindness, and patience

And most of all to Lee, my beloved, whose constant cheerleading, deep talks, tireless humor, sage wisdom, and depth of understanding bring me the greatest happiness of my life, I love you

You are all a part of my family and my village,

Thank You

Vision is the art of seeing things invisible.

– Jonathan Swift

Prologue

MAY 1, 1970, DUBLIN

"Why do you always know what I'm going to say?" Rachel Careski stared out of the living room window of her third-floor apartment with her arms folded.

"You know why."

She sighed, wondering if she'd ever win this argument. "If you really knew me, you'd know why I was going."

"You're running again, this time from the best opportunity of your life."

Rachel looked on as her brother moved around her room, examining luggage, unfolding and refolding clothes in her suitcase.

Soren Careski put his palms up. "Okay, just tell me why it has to be now. This fellowship will be offered only once, not to mention you're the only woman to be a recipient, ever. Tell me you really don't care."

"Academia bores me," she said pointedly, over-enunciating each syllable.

"All for some old paper stuffed in a jar in the desert."

"Don't even try to be dismissive about something like this. Deny it if you want but you and I care about the same things. You know damn well why I'm going. Besides," she sighed, "someone's contacted me."

Soren stopped. "Who? Contacted you how?"

Rachel Careski set down the thin pants she'd folded and crossed her arms. "Someone's been contacting me. For three months."

"Who is it?"

She shook her head.

"Let me understand this," Soren said quietly. "Someone you've never met is sending you on a secret mission five thousand miles away for the purpose of …?"

Rachel stared, brows lifted.

"Come on, give me something here! You're the only family I have on this continent. I'm very selective about …" the words caught in his throat. "I'm worried for you."

"Because I'm a woman? Grow up, Soren. I thought you knew me better than anyone."

"We don't know anything about that world."

"You mean you don't. It's the same world, countries are just divisions. Besides, you know my curiosity about the Middle East."

"You're gonna travel alone by, by—"

"Ship and rail car."

"For God's sake. To find what?"

"A papyrus. Buried in ceramic jars in a cave, which is how they used to be preserved. You know this."

"Preserved? You mean hidden. And why were they hidden? To protect them because of their power to inspire death and destruction, mass murder."

"They're paper, Soren. It's people who give them power."

"What prize do you hope to get if you find them?"

Rachel shrugged. It was a fair enough question. "Surely discovery credit at least."

"And why doesn't your benefactor—"

"He's old. He's dying and too weak," she interrupted.

"So he says," Soren replied. "Will you be paid?"

"Everything's taken care of. Tickets, lodging, transport, private guide."

"Do you trust this man?" he asked softly and put his hands on Rachel's shoulders. "Just tell me that. Do you trust him?"

"I don't know how many thousands of people have died to protect this artifact, I want to make sure no one else does."

"You didn't answer me."

"So far ..."

June 10, 1970
CAIRO

"Tea, Miss?" asked a well-manicured man with an English accent. Tea, Rachel thought, seemed at least ten worlds away from this place of blinding sun, blowing sand, and camels. The two chairs and tiny table outside the café were baking along with her unprotected skin. She lowered the brim on her hat and thanked the man and glanced carefully behind him as she moved her bag to the other shoulder to grasp the delicate bone china teacup and saucer. Two men in Western dress, no turbans and somewhat lighter skin than the locals, stared openly at her fingers grasping the cup. Returning her gaze to the young tea server, she smiled and laughed suddenly, pulling her fingers away.

"Hot," she said under her breath, "caught me by surprise."

"This special tea, Madame," the server explained, "will cool you down from inside."

"Not that, it's the cup that's too hot. You must have just brewed it, though I notice there's no tea on the menu. Do you live nearby, or work in another café, perhaps?"

Obviously stalling, the boy stammered, with a tentative half-turn toward the lurking observers huddled two feet behind him in thick, woolen suits. "I ... yes ... certainly, miss. I am most happy to share every detail with you but first I ... must—" The boy halted his train of thought, jerked his gaze behind him at the two men, then dropped the tea tray in a shattered pool on the cobblestones and took off down a wide alley between two buildings.

Rachel calmly watched the scene unfold; first, the two men walked steadily past her toward the boy, then turned back to look at her and ran after him. She set the cup down and followed, far behind and walking slowly, but still in their direction because somewhere, up ahead, was the answer to the burning question in her mind - who wanted her dead on her first day in Cairo?

June 17, 1970

"Sabik, here, closer to the pillar," Rachel directed her Bedouin guide. The boy, less than seventeen, had a smooth, sculpted face, offset by hands more belonging to a lobster fisherman. Without viewing the map her silent benefactor had sent, it was impossible to tell if they were in the precise location, but the risk of holding the map out in the open was too great.

Strange country, strange customs, and already an attempt on her life within the first forty-eight hours after her arrival.

She stood awkwardly at the opening of the cave, gazing down at the vast, empty valley, far better than a boring fellowship at Cambridge. A sound jerked her head to the right - some small rocks rolling downhill. A goat, she saw and laughed, watching it scale the rocky ledge as though it was feeding comfortably on a grassy pasture. Without taking her eyes off that ledge, though, she carefully pulled the map from her pocket, slid the folded page up her sleeve, pulled her purse to the front and lowered the map into the main compartment, opened it and let her gaze fall on the hand drawing. Sixteen paces in from the opening, five paces left, 1.25 meters down.

"Ma'am!" With the sound of Sabik's voice came the unmistakable clank of metal on stone.

"I'm right here, keep digging," she said in an oddly calm voice, still staring outside, down the ledge, up, and on each side. While her eyes saw nothing but tan, chalky powder, some other part of her sensed him. Her benefactor? One of his agents? Someone.

Rachel knew she must, at some point, leave the ledge and attend to what was decidedly her excavation, her find. And some part of her knew the moment she vanished from sight, the jackals would circle.

Nearly thirty years ago, seventeen other sites in this region of Egypt had been excavated, spread out among fifty-two caves as she'd read from magazines and her subscriptions to obscure archaeology newsletters. All discoveries so far had been credited to two tribesmen from the al-Samman clan, and all from within the cliffs of Jabal al-Tārif. But none had focused on this particular cliff – close to the other sites but far enough away to not arouse suspicion. It was a brilliant idea, but how had her benefactor known of this site without having been here himself? My bones are far too old now to be scampering around on my hands and knees in a dusty cave, he had written in one of his letters.

"Ma'am, come quickly!"

Rachel trekked the twenty-five steps into the dark cavern away from the ledge toward the digging site, ignoring the voice in her head. Sabik looked like an old man the way he hunched forward, his hands wrapped around something large.

"Is it heavy?" she asked, to which Sabik laughed aloud and raised the ceramic jar two inches, then lowered it with a clunk, panting.

"Jesus," Rachel's eyes widened, scoping the shape and dimensions. "Where's the opening?" she asked.

Sabik looked to the right and lifted the mouth of the jar twenty-five degrees. Rachel lowered herself till prostrate on the dirt floor and shone the small flashlight inside. Rough-edged papers, yellowed, papyrus-like if not actual papyrus, at least fifty sheets, were loosely rolled and coiled along the shape of the container. Several smaller sheets, loose in the middle of the stack, seemed within her reach. She edged her right hand into the center and touched the edges of the smaller forms. The paper's edge felt sharp, almost shiny, and pulled easily toward her, separating from a larger fold of the smaller-sized forms in the smaller stack of loose papers. She pulled, slowly, one inch at a time. Someone, a long time ago, had very carefully decided what to pack into this vessel and arranged them in some pre-determined order of importance. It felt unholy, somehow, almost grotesque to grope at them like this. The piece in her left hand was the tenth sheet - she'd counted. The more important question: what was on the first sheet? Was this one less important, historically, culturally, to the owner of this vessel and these papers? Had they been stolen? Belonged to a library, or privately owned? And by whom? And what was at stake if they had been discovered thousands of years ago?

Sabik set the vessel down and moved to her side to view the single page. His young face beamed with hope and anticipation, and frankly, she felt grateful for his companionship.

"Can you read it?" he asked her.

She unrolled the page and instinctively scanned right to left, blinking dust out of her eyes to assess the shape of the letters and the position of each word to another - all the while still thinking about the goat on that ledge.

It was almost certainly Coptic, and her heart nearly stopped when she saw the word "Origen" on the bottom of the page. My God, she thought, they'll kill me for this.

Rachel pulled the folded sack out of Sabik's backpack and laid it across the length of the urn. She looked up, panicked.

"It won't fit," Sabik warned.

"Try it anyway," Rachel replied, and sinfully folded the page in half, re-rolling it and, while Sabik struggled to fit the bottom part of the jar into the burlap, lifting one leg of her khakis and plastering the page against her calf beneath her sock. "Please, Sabik, go check the ledge."

"Yes, ma'am," he said sadly, pulling his arms from the jar. He looked behind them into the darkness and then back at Rachel.

"Go," she commanded, and the moment Sabik vanished she plunged her hand into the mouth of the jar, then the other hand to grip the edges of the pages, and slowly wrestled them out. By the thickness, it felt like at least twenty pages, and she knew what she would find in its content.

"Ma'am," came Sabik's voice, muffled and low-toned. "It is fine," he added, "no danger."

"Thank goodness," Rachel replied, not believing him yet unable to move away. She continued to pull the pages out, knowing somehow that this wasn't Sabik's natural voice.

"I'm blind from the dust, let's take a break, all right?" Her eyes scanned the walls of the cave and there was only one way out - through the opening. She had all of the pages in both hands now and didn't stop to examine them. She rolled them loosely and took the hair-tie from her ponytail to fasten them, quickly reaching for the grip of the duffel bag.

"That's right, young lady—"

She froze.

"No, no, don't let me slow you down. Please, the whole lot of them," a man said with a handgun pointed toward her head. "In the duffel bag, then carry it out with you."

Rachel's mind rapidly processed the truth of her predicament, and the lie she had mentally suppressed all these months.

"Now!"

The man's voice echoed on the insides of the cave walls over and over, NOW - now now now now. I'll no doubt hear that sound for the rest of my life, she thought, until a scarier thought occurred - how much longer would that be?

She rose with the duffel bag in hand, the sacred jar unearthed, emptied of most of its contents, and moved toward the doorway where she could almost make out the man's face, then her eyes slid down his form and saw a lush red cape, like velvet, covering a long white caftan and tall black boots. This strange dress combined with his stiff, European accent confused her.

"Uh!" she heard from the entryway now …

"Sabik!" she screamed, and then a boom clouded her ears and the air in the cave, followed by a heavy thud upon the dirt ground. Sabik's thin body slumped on the ground and as she took in this image of a dark fluid spilling from his right ear, the man tugged on her elbow. She scrutinized him only then, the shrewd, cold face, wrinkled gray skin, beady, dark lidless eyes and a large letter "I" embroidered on the left side of the cape.

Rachel thrust forward the duffel bag held out in her right hand. The man put it over his shoulder and dragged her to the cave entrance. She looked back at Sabik and reminded herself to breathe.

"Come with me."

One

BOSTON, MASSACHUSETTS, 2010

Approaching 70 Fargo Street, Alex Careski tried to forget what day it was. The building he had walked into for the past eleven years, a brick, nine-story monstrosity, carried both modern sterility and mid-century elegance.

The scent of low tide and the squawk of seagulls lured him out of his mental funk while he crossed from the parking lot to the shining double glass doors.

Ginger appeared as the elevator doors opened and kissed him on the cheek.

"What, do I have a sign on my forehead?"

Ginger's perfectly complexioned face scowled. "Be kind to your elders?"

"That's just cold," he said brushing past her.

Monihan's office was still dark. Good, Alex thought. He turned on his laptop, opened his Mega Crossword Puzzle Book #14 while it booted up, then slid into the kitchen and poured coffee into the largest mug in the cupboard. No cream, two sugars. A box of fresh donuts sat unopened on the counter, probably another of Ginger's birthday ploys.

Don Ramsey leaned into the doorway.

"Morning," Alex said.

"Monihan," Ramsey replied dryly.

"What?"

"Just walked in ...with Wollman."

"Shit." Alex quickly wiped his mouth. "What's that about?"

Ramsey shook his head. "Better check in with Classifieds before you leave."

"Very funny."

Ramsey stared. "Who's being funny?"

8:55 a.m. Heads started popping up over the tops of cubes.

"Alex," Corinna Buchman said as she passed his desk. She had on a dark pink pantsuit with a tight, black shirt underneath. Her trademark. "Isn't today some kind of special day for you or something? Your fiftieth birthday?"

"Aww, how could you say that," he whined, "you know I'm only ... thirty."

Back in his office sipping more coffee, he gazed out of the window and remembered yesterday's nagging crossword clue - a two-letter word for pastries. He scanned the list he'd compiled last night of today's tasks, which looked more than daunting. Interview three senators for the Ways and Means Committee corruption piece, staff meeting at three o'clock, that was if they all didn't get sacked before then. Monihan. Wollman. A cross between underworld enforcers and mafia hit men.

His email inbox showed forty-three new messages. LL Bean, a calendar invitation from Ginger for the mandatory staff meeting, and another from someone he didn't recognize. He hovered his cursor over the email address, squinted, reached for the spare pair of drugstore reading glasses and moved inches from the screen.

Several seconds clicked by before he remembered to breathe. The sender's email address displayed as **careskisor@attbi.com**.

Alex's mouth went dry.

His own last name and the first three letters of his father's first name … Soren? How could this be? He rose to close and lock his office door and saw Monihan and Wollman marching toward him like the Gestapo. The two men stopped at his door, peered in through the blinds and Monihan knocked slowly three times. Jesus.

Alex typed as fast and audibly as he could. "On a deadline, Jason, I'll talk to you later?" More frantic pretend-typing, reading notes off an imaginary notebook.

The men reluctantly moved away from the door, at least long enough for him to open the email message.

Loading …

Loading …

"I want everybody in here now," Wollman shouted. "We won't be more than fifteen minutes."

Monihan looked at him and pointed. "And I wanna talk to you about Rome."

Rome? "One minute," Alex raised his index finger.

For God's sake, please, he nagged at the email that would not load. Was their network down again? Plan B - he printed the attachment from the email rather than opening it first. The printer clicked on and slowly dragged a sheet of white paper from the tray. With one eye on Monihan and the other on the printer, Alex remembered the door next to his office leading down two flights of stairs to an alley behind Fargo Street. The alley faced the huge, brick apartment complex where he'd spied on Senator Michael Trudeau two years prior, an effort that helped the Boston PD nail him and three other high-level officials on drug trafficking charges - the only time he would have ever preferred death over journalism.

Monihan alternated his gaze between his office and the conference room. The message printed, Alex folded the single sheet of paper in half without looking at it, stuffed it in his jacket and slid out of the exit door to the back stairs.

The echo of his shoes against the steps sounded different, and his chest felt oddly tight as he ran two at a time to the bottom. Four hours' sleep had become, over the past decade, the norm. But even though he'd adjusted to this deficit long ago, exhaustion still caught up unexpectedly. He could have lain down on the concrete stairs right now and slept an entire day.

The cold September air slapped his cheeks and nose as he stepped out onto the landing overlooking the rear parking lot. The perfect vantage point of the city landscape. From the alley, he saw elementary school kids playing during recess, and the dumpsters behind Imperial Palace and Ku's Korean Garden, the Chinese and Korean restaurants illogically located side-by-side further down the block.

Alex ducked behind the building and through the back entrance to the underground parking garage, and unlocked his 1985 Camaro, wondering if he'd have a job tomorrow. Wollman, the owner of the newspaper, had proven over the years that his presence only foretold bad news. Glancing at the overcast sky, he thought about the printed email as he drove the car onto the parking garage exit ramp.

He reached back and pulled it from the inner pocket of his jacket, and heard a deafening clap directly behind him that shot his body against the steering wheel and his angled head against the car roof. "Jesus," Alex moaned as his forehead and nose hit the hard plastic. Blood gushed down his face faster than he could wipe it with the sleeve of his jacket. Blood? His blood? What the hell—?

In his rearview mirror, a car pressed against his bumper with a blond man in the front seat holding the nose of a pistol in view. The man screeched his car back a few feet from the Camaro, obviously preparing another assault. Without moving more than was absolutely necessary, Alex held one hand to his gushing nose and flicked open the door handle with the other one, trying to judge how close he was to the back door of Ku's, where he'd eaten lunch every day for the past decade.

Twelve feet and slightly more than twenty-five degrees to the left.

He saw that a huge steel support pillar would miraculously block the man's line of vision after Alex got out of the car. In a quick thrust, Alex shoved open the driver's side door with his knee and tore out of the car and behind the shield of the steel pillar with his hand over his nose. He gently opened the back door to Ku's, closed, locked it behind him, and ducked into the dark hallway outside the employee restrooms near the kitchen.

The erratic movements and yelling in the busy kitchen continued after a split second's notice of his presence. The head chef, Jae-Sun Lee, looked up from the piles of vegetables he'd chopped on a floured board, saw Alex, and squinted toward the back door. Jae-Sun moved to the dark corridor and dragged Alex into a vacant office.

The calm, impeccably dressed chef stood over him. "Why bleeding?"

Alex tried to speak but couldn't. "Lock," he exhaled, "I locked the back door. Call the police."

Jae-Sun stared into Alex's eyes for a quick moment, opened the office door and shouted something into the busy kitchen.

"Who follow you?" he asked.

"I don't know," Alex stammered. "Some guy rear-ended me in the parking garage, and when I was about to get out and confront him, he backed up and did it again.

"This man is stranger?"

"I guess."

"Do not think so," Jae-Sun replied thoughtfully.

Alex checked Jae-Sun's expression. "You know this man?"

"No act is purely random. Think now ... what did you do today?"

Alex rubbed his eyes and leaned against the wall in the cluttered office. "I got up, showered, went to work ..."

"That's it?"

Alex looked briefly at the floor as a realization crystallized. "I got an email."

"From whom?"

Alex paused before answering, knowing full well how it would sound if he said it, that it couldn't possibly be true. "From a dead man."

Two

BOSTON

"Alex?"

Simone's refined beauty could always lure Alex out of the murkiest funk. He watched the swing of her black hair and the angle of her delicate back as he thought about her question, about how to answer it. Or not answer.

"I don't know who it was," he moaned for the third time, pacing the floor of the kitchen, and pausing to pull the bloody cotton ball off his nose.

"Stop," she said. "How could you not know? You're telling me you were personally targeted by someone trying to harm you, and you have no idea who that could be? You're a journalist, you might have written a piece exposing corruption or something, and now someone wants a payback."

"You read too many crime novels, Simone. It was just some psycho in a parking garage. I jumped in the back door of Ku's till the car sped away finally."

"What did the man look like?"

"Blond hair, clean shaven, sort of a," he waved his hands in the air while looking for the word, realizing he felt light-headed, "crooked nose."

Simone bit her lip. "What do you think?" she asked.

He pulled the folded page from his pocket. "It does have a warning on the bottom. Almost like whoever sent this knew it would happen."

"Or made it happen themselves," she added. Simone took his hand and led him to the living room sofa. This was Simone's style and what he loved most about her. Passionate, intuitive, struggling to understand the human mind deeper than most people, and never afraid of the outcome, because relationships didn't scare her. He'd always envied that trait.

"How could you just be okay with not knowing what happened to him?" she begged. "All this time, after Soren died, when you wouldn't talk to me about it, I let you go on in silence because I didn't want to pull grief out of you. I knew, or I'd hoped it would come in time. But it never did. I never got to ask all the questions that you wouldn't." Simone paused and stood awkwardly in front of him. "Like where was the proof that he was dead? Who saw Soren's body, who autopsied it, where was it found? No one could substantiate that he'd been killed – no one substantiated anything. Yet you just blindly accepted this news and pretended to go on with your life. I never understood it." She lowered her head. "I still don't."

"Pretended?" he sighed. "I never understood it either, Soren's obsession with those old scrolls and scripts. I guess I always hated him for choosing his research over us. Maybe that's why I refused to deal with it."

"With what, specifically?"

"His vanishing act."

Simone shook her head and peered at him. "You never believed he was dead, did you?" she asked now, astonished.

"Well, they weren't a new thing for him, disappearances."

"When?"

"About fifteen years ago. I don't remember all the details, but mom was still alive then and she pretty much went crazy. That's how she met Jack. Then Soren came back and didn't seem to care that she'd remarried. He was never really," he sighed, "part of the human race. He had other pursuits, even more than his obsession with linguistics and relics."

"I thought you didn't know anything about it?" she joked.

"I knew enough from living with him for almost twenty years." Alex moved to the kitchen and refilled his teacup with hot water. "Soren was fascinated by language," he explained. "More than that though, by words and alphabets. So symbols, yes, but on a more universal level than just the symbols and characters native to one language." He paused to see if she'd get his meaning without saying it.

"I don't understand."

Alex smiled. "He believed all languages, like every single language spoken on the planet, originated from one mother tongue. He didn't arrive at this epiphany until later in his life. At first, his obsessions took the form of secret texts and scripts, like parts of the Kabbalah, the Gospel of St. Thomas, Celtic Ogham. He was all over the map. And that's how it all started, I think. In his mind, he saw commonalities between these world languages and wanted to not only prove that they originated from the same place but to find the single, original source."

Simone sat back on the sofa with her arms crossed, brows furrowed. "What was the proximity between his realization of this and when he disappeared?"

Alex answered with his eyes.

"Where was he before he disappeared?"

"Egypt, Naples, no telling. And he also did some work that year in the UK, though I'm not certain where."

"You have to go, Alex." Simone stared now. "It's time."

"Go?" He chuckled. "I can't go anywhere now. For one thing, I'm probably about to be fired. Wollman called a meeting with Monihan this morning. I just couldn't handle being there today, so I split after I printed the email and ended up in Ku's. I have three articles due Friday, one of them I haven't started yet. There's no way."

Simone slid her delicate hands into the pocket of her long sweater and pulled out two folded pages. "Your birthday present."

"What?"

She held out two sealed envelopes and smiled. One of them had an American Airlines logo in the upper left corner, and the other, as he tore it open, contained a newspaper clipping. "You're making me a scrapbook of all my columns?" he mumbled. It was an article from an Italian newspaper.

"What's this?"

"Turn it over. I translated it."

He saw a photograph of dead teenagers in a van.

"So a bunch of teenage rebels is found dead." He looked up. "That's awful, Simone, but what's it got to do with anything? With me?"

The arms were still folded. "You're a journalist."

"What – you want me to go to Italy to write a story on this? I work at the Herald, for God's sake, not CNN."

"I think this will be good for you and it's time you stopped running from your past. From your father."

He hated that know-it-all voice. Simone could somehow make herself sound like Mrs. Manning, his scary third-grade teacher. That voice could incite riots, or at the very least, cold terror. "I'm not running," he said softly. "Just walking the other way."

"Part of why you never did anything about Soren, never figured out what really happened to him, is because you didn't really have an excuse to leave." She pointed to the clipping. "Here's a reason, a bona fide story of something that's happening overseas, an atrocity and someone needs to write about it. If the Herald doesn't, then the Globe certainly will. You've said yourself that you've always been interested in writing world stories. Here's your chance. Besides," Simone looked at the floor, "Monihan's approved it."

Alex's head jerked up. "What? How?"

Pause.

"For God's sake, Simone, like my mother approving a goddamn school field trip? How could you?"

"I didn't, you did. You sent him an email about the story, you attached a link to the newspaper article in *la Repubblica*, and he wrote back and approved a short trip for you to do research and then write a piece about it. It'll be your first piece on world events."

Alex unfolded the email from his father and stared at the strange, ancient script. Monihan. Rome. Ah, he thought.

"Don't waste time being angry. All those boxes in the basement, all of Soren's research, his diaries, they need to be unpacked. He's your flesh and blood. Not knowing what happened to him is like refusing to look in the mirror."

Alex sulked on the couch with the email printout. He gazed around the large living room, the fireplace, the wall of windows facing the swimming pool and patio. "What language is that?" Simone asked sitting beside him.

He shook his head, staring. "Could be Greek, Hebrew. Maybe older."

"Find this text and you will then find the truth – others will be watching," she read off the bottom of the page. "And you believe this could be from Soren?"

"The email address," he pointed. "**Careskisor@attbi.com**. Unless someone's pretending to be him. I don't know what to think anymore. But I do know this. If what happened this morning has anything to do with this email or his research, I—" His voice cut off as one of the back windows facing the pool shattered inwards and crashed onto the tile floor.

"What was—" Alex grabbed Simone by the shoulders and pulled her to the floor, shielding her back with his body. Had he heard two or three shots? And had they come from the front or the back?

"What happened?" her muffled voice screamed from beneath him.

"Don't move, I don't know yet." Alex looked at the back window at the shattered glass. "Came from the back. Okay, on three," he whispered, "I'll lift you up and we'll move to the hallway. One, two, three," he said and pulled up her hundred-pound weight and shoved her up the three stairs into the hall. He followed without looking back and opened the hall closet door. "Stay in here."

"Alex?" she screamed. "Stay in here with me. Please!"

"Wait here. I'm going upstairs. And don't make a sound. We don't know if he's in the house."

"Who?"

"The man who hit my car. He must have followed me here."

Alex disappeared up the carpeted stairs and fumbled for the key to his locked file cabinet where he kept the one single artifact he had unpacked from Soren's research boxes. He dropped the key on the floor and as he leaned down, thought he saw a shadow moving on the other side of the second floor in the guest bedroom.

Jesus, Soren, he thought, what have you gotten me into now?

Behind a thick wall of manila folders sat a package wrapped in newspaper. He pushed his body against the file drawer, his arms extended inside it to muffle the noise of the paper. Layer by layer, snapping up old bits of tape that held it together, his fingers finally reached the cold steel of what he knew was Soren's Glock.9mm pistol, a pistol he'd always kept for safety but never actually used, felt its muzzle, the trigger, and a small box of ammo.

Thank God he included bullets, he thought to himself and then shuddered at the implication. Why had Soren sent him his gun and bullets? Had he disappeared, or gone into hiding, to protect him and Simone?

The shadow moved again, this time in the other direction toward the guest bathroom, one room closer to his study.

Three

BOSTON

But when he peered down the hall and looked closer, Alex saw that the shadow was actually moving down the stairs toward the hallway.

The closet was at the end of that hallway.

Simone's in that closet.

His legs refused to move in spite of the pounding in his chest until he heard the familiar creak on the bottom stair. A sheer of sunlight bleeding in through the dining room curtains lit up the man's fair hair. Alex heard cat-like steps move to the living room, like a well-informed panther toward potential prey.

Had he memorized where the floor squeaked in his upstairs office? And even if it did, would the man hear him below? Alex applied his weight evenly to the carpet and padded out into the hallway to peer over the banister, remembering how he'd learned to walk on the top layer of snow as a child. With his head pressed against the wall, Alex saw the other man's head and shoulders, then watched him draw his gun into position.

Now Alex did the same with Soren's gun, only he was confident he was considerably less familiar with this weapon than the intruder was with his. The thought of a demonic birthday prank occurred to him, but had luck ever been on his side when he needed it? He shook himself into focus and slowly aimed the gun at the back of the man's head. As long as neither of them moved more than an inch in either direction, he had a chance of making the shot.

Could I shoot someone in cold blood? Alex wondered, and then watched as the man reached to touch the knob on the closet door.

Carefully controlling his movements, he saw the man turn the knob. He felt Simone's terror vibrating in his palms. There was only one chance now. As the closet door pulled open a few inches, Alex leaned on the hallway wall for stability and yanked the trigger back. He flinched at the recoil and sudden pain in his right ear from the unexpected volume of the shot. He watched the man lose his balance and fall to the living room floor.

Did I hit him?

In a split second, Alex was down the stairs and peering at Simone's wide eyes, with one eye peeled toward the man.

Why was there no blood on the floor?

Grabbing Simone under the arms, he pulled her up and shielded her body with his own to peek around the corner into the living room at the downed assailant.

"Shit!" Where is he?

"What's the matter?" Simone stammered.

"Get the keys and go out to the car," he hissed.

Simone looked back with a blank expression.

"Go. Now! Lock the doors and crouch down in front of the passenger seat and wait for me."

"But where are you going? Come with me, Alex. Don't go after him!"

"I'll be there in a minute. Go," he said quietly.

Staring at the floor in front of her, Simone walked to the front door and picked up a bag from one of the coat hooks before exiting. Alex held the gun at his side while watching her make the twenty-step journey to the car, not taking his eyes off her. She opened the door and climbed in, slid down onto the floor and crouched with her hands over her head.

Moving into the house, Alex caught a glimpse of the blond man running out the back door. As he turned to the garage, Alex spotted something written on an index card on the end table – slanted handwriting, not his own, with one word in block letters – ROME. And on the back of the card was a large calligraphic "I" in the center, and written below it in smaller letters were the words "am the Inquisition."

Alex cut through the garage and went out of the side door just as the man was about to jump the fence into the neighbor's yard. He aimed Soren's gun at him, and before he even had a chance to take a breath, a bullet exited the man's gun and hit the side of the house just above Alex's head. Alex fired back, this time hitting the man in the leg; he heard a whimper and the man fell off the fence into a bed of soft weeds. Alex took one step closer and saw blood under the man's body, but not from his leg. Blood pooled under the man's prostrate body, spilling out under his arms.

Was he dead? Had he just killed a complete stranger in his own backyard?

A strange quiet hung in the air now. Alex ran back through the house, crunching on broken glass and coats that had fallen from the coat rack by the door. He headed to the basement.

The collection of Soren's file boxes by the water heater in the corner had sat untouched for eight years, maybe longer. His shaking hands fumbled to get the covers off and he dug blindly through the contents for the familiar feel of smooth leather covers. Ah, there's one, he thought, and pulled out a journal and tossed it on the floor. He stood back and looked at all six file boxes and knew, if he knew Soren at all, that each box must represent a year of Soren's work and, therefore, the diary he'd just found must be replicated in each year and was probably in the same place in each box.

He knelt on the dusty cellar floor and blinked, waiting for his pupils to dilate enough to see into the darkness. Should he call the police? Should he run upstairs and check on Simone? Too many thoughts, too much confusion.

Simone's safe in the front seat of the car for the moment, he thought, and kept digging. Or is she?

He yanked his cell phone out of his back pocket and texted, "I'll be right up – you ok for a minute?" and waited. Damn that broken light, he thought, remembering it was one of the projects Simone had assigned him last Christmas vacation.

The second and third boxes had similar diaries, small, leather-bound with every page filled up. The fourth box had a stack of manila folders, all sealed, with three spiral-bound notebooks on top. He reached below the folders, fumbled over a thick set of bound papers, and found the diary buried inside the paper stack. Odd how this diary had been concealed beneath a pile of papers. He crouched over the next box, remembering the dead man in his backyard and Simone waiting.

The fifth box had the same contents as the rest – bound stacks of papers, spiral notebooks and sealed manila envelopes. But no diary. He spotted Soren's violin case propped up against some file boxes, one of his paranoid precautions about carrying his research with him.

A familiar sound shocked him out of his scavenger hunt – a siren. Jesus, he thought, tearing through the sixth box. No diary in there either. He checked his phone and Simone hadn't replied. He tore up the stairs with the violin case in his hand and four diaries under his arm, peeked around the corner before he ran through the kitchen and out the front to the driveway. Without even glancing at the car, he scanned up and down the street for a police car or for a sign of any other intruders.

"Why didn't you answer my text?" he panted as he jumped into the driver's side seat. "Take these." He passed over the diaries. They fell in a pile on the empty front seat.

Simone was not in the car.

And the dead man was gone.

Four

LONDON

Oscillating waves of questions and answers, reverse psychology, truth and lies, filled the cramped conference room of the British Museum's second floor. Lily Frasier's mouth twitched at the nagging sound of the officer's voice.

"And what's your title here, Ms. Frasier?" the man asked standing over her, his judgment of her obviously already formed.

"Librarian."

"Director of Antiquities isn't it?" the officer replied, pointing at her desk nameplate.

"Hard for you to believe a woman could escalate beyond the secretarial pool?"

"Do you know why we're here right now?" the man asked.

"A book has disappeared from the Castleman Library."

The officer raised a brow, apparently wanting more.

"A rare book."

The officer took out a pen and small spiral notebook. "What kind of rare book? I mean, how rare exactly?"

Lily paused, breathed, and slowly slid a tuft of hair behind her ear. "If I tell you, will this information stay in this room? What I mean to say is—"

"No, certainly not. This is a police investigation. We will—"

"Look, whoever you are, I am not at liberty to—"

The officer cocked his head. "Let's put it this way, shall we? If you don't cooperate and answer our questions—"

"Yes, yes, I know, haul me off to jail, shackle me up with the tarts and pushers and feed me dirty water and porridge. But know that I have no intention of putting the integrity of this museum in jeopardy just because of a minor theft."

The policeman sat down. "You make it sound so routine, miss. Almost ... how shall I put it, planned?"

Lily bit her lip and glanced around the room. "Let me rephrase my request, officers." She looked at both of them now. "Would the police be so kind as to offer its most sincere discretion when dealing with the press on this matter? The museum would suffer a terrible loss if this incident got back to our most treasured donors and investors. We are, after all, The British Museum, not a pawn shop."

The officers smiled, glanced at each other and nodded hesitantly.

"There were two books, then," she admitted.

"Together in a collection?" one of them asked.

"No. Matter of fact, they've got absolutely nothing to do with each other, except for their value. One of them, called the *Auraicept Na N-eces,* is a first edition, 1917 English translation of the Ogham Tract from the *Book of Ballymote,* an ancient Celtic text. And the other is one of the Coptic texts from Nag Hammadi."

The stouter of the two policemen raised a brow.

"In 1945, a library of manuscripts was discovered in a tomb in Nag Hammadi, Egypt. They're extremely old and fragile, very rare—"

"What's so valuable about them? Just that they're old?" asked one of the officers.

"We believe, well, some of us believe that they include some of the lost Bible gospels including the Gospel of St. Thomas the Apostle, with text dating back to 250AD." Lily cleared her throat and couldn't help looking around the room. The walls, the door, floor, window. She felt vulnerable, suddenly, as if she'd just broken a code of silence. Probably because she had.

"Go on."

"There were thirteen books discovered in 1946," she continued, "in a tomb in the limestone cliffs near Luxor. They were divided into forty-four treatises, one of which was a forgotten gospel ... containing, supposedly, 114 actual sayings of Christ."

"Like the Dead Sea Scrolls," the same detective replied.

"Well, sort of, but the significance of this find was far greater, as it spoke of religious implications not previously known. Religious scholars, well, I should clarify that. Religious scholars, many of them quite renowned, believe wholeheartedly in the authenticity of the volumes, but the Vatican maintains that they're bunk - cheap imitations drawn up by greedy, itinerant merchants."

"Could someone sell them on the black market?"

"Sure," Lily shrugged, "for a modest sum. Certainly not for what they're worth."

"Why not?"

Now she smiled. "That's the beauty of them - they're old, beat up, dusty, unassuming volumes with text written in a language only a handful of people in the entire world even recognize, let alone able to translate. No one would think anything of them."

"No one but a member of that select handful."

Lily nodded. "That's right."

The lanky officer loomed over her and stared at the top of her head. "Do you recall anything strange happening lately, no matter how trivial it may have seemed at the time?"

"Like what?"

The officer doodled on his notepad. "A strange person, perhaps, showing up in an unauthorized place?"

"This is the British Museum, officer. We don't have unauthorized places here. Every inch of this structure contains the highest security of any museum on the planet."

The officer raised a brow, glanced out into the main room and smiled at the irony of her words. "Then what about odd pieces of mail or correspondence, phone calls, or have you heard about anything like this happening in some other part of the museum?"

For a split second, Lily remembered the light-haired man in an old convertible appearing in her rearview mirror last week, but not just once - she had noticed him three times throughout the day. The first time, she had only noticed his dark sunglasses, and after that, his crooked nose. "No," she quickly replied.

The officer scribbled something in a tiny notepad. "Who discovered the missing books?"

"My assistant, Adrian Marcali."

"Male or female?"

"Male."

The officer tapped his pen on the desktop. "Where is he now?"

"In Milan for a curator's conference. He left yesterday afternoon."

"Do you find that convenient at all?" asked the other officer.

Lily glared at both of them - the tall one assuming an attack posture, and the plump, red-faced cherub seething in the corner. "Adrian left yesterday afternoon. I drove him to the airport myself." To protect him, she thought. But from what, or whom?

"What happened before then?"

Lily sighed. "I called an emergency meeting of all the board members at lunchtime to inform everyone, but that only lasted an hour. Adrian left a few hours later."

A thin, light-haired man poked his head in the doorway of the conference room and glared at Lily.

One of the officers turned around sharply. "This is a private meeting. Whatever you need Ms. Frasier for, it'll have to wait."

The other officer took two steps forward. "In the event of a major theft and potential scandal, why would a board meeting only last an hour? What was decided?"

The man at the door remained. Lily, sensing his presence, turned around.

"What is it, Tal?" she said.

"There's a call for you on your office phone. The Torlonia."

Lily's face tightened. She felt her jaw clench as the dark, beady eyes of the shorter officer tried to interpret her reaction. "May I take this?" she asked calmly.

"It can wait."

"I'm afraid not. The Torlonia Museum is in Rome, and if I miss this call now, I can't speak to them until Monday morning because of the time difference. The admin offices are about to close." She paused for three seconds. "I beg your indulgence, officers. I won't be a minute."

The two officers exchanged glances and seemed tangled in an inner negotiation. "We'll take a ten-minute break," the taller one agreed.

Lily nodded, left the room accompanied by Tal Gardner, Assistant Curator, and charged up the stairs to her private office.

"What did Mona say?" she whispered to Tal, who trailed inches behind her.

"Something about a document she emailed you. She seemed, how should I say it, unnerved."

"That's how she always sounds. Is she holding the line?"

"I said you'd call her right back. The number's by the phone and she's waiting for you."

Lily picked up the index card with the number and fondled it with her fingers. She had long memorized Mona's phone number, although she sometimes called from some strange man's house after one of her "encounters." Once a British rock star, another time a National Geographic travel writer from Burma, her half-sister had tried any of them enough, for a short time, to escape from her boring, over-privileged life. Mona picked up after the first ring.

"Took you long enough."

Lily breathed deeply, preparing herself for what would inevitably follow. "Let me guess. You need money."

"That's not why I'm calling. Did you get it?"

"Get what?"

"The email! I forwarded one to you earlier this morning." Long sigh. "I thought you would have seen it hours ago. I've been sitting by the phone all day."

Doubt it, Lily thought, imagining a harem of men all over Mona's bed. Nothing would surprise her. "I was about to open it but Adrian called me away this morning to a meeting."

Silence. Then, "I thought Adrian was at a conference."

"Oh, that's right, I meant Tal." Pause. "How do you know Adrian's out of town?"

"I didn't hear from you this morning so I got worried and started making calls."

"To whom? The embassy, for God's sake?"

"I called Adrian's cell and spoke to him at about seven. His flight was delayed and he was waiting it out at Heathrow."

Lily felt a wave of blood rise in her body. "His cell phone? Where did you get that?"

"Look, we're wasting time. Did you see my email or not?"

"I saw it was from you but haven't had a chance to open it yet. Why? What's the urgency?"

Mona exhaled a lungful of air. "Someone sent it to me, and now, I don't know, weird things are happening."

"Since you got the email?"

"Yeah."

"Like what?"

Pause. "Someone's following me," Mona whispered. "I'm certain of it."

"You live in the mob capital of Europe, Mona, and you walk around half dressed and stay out all night with strangers. What do you expect?"

"I do not," she protested, "and I know a wise guy when I see one. This one isn't. He looks more like a college professor."

Lily stared at her laptop and pressed the "on" button to her printer, and then opened a browser. "I'll print it right now." She turned to see if Tal was behind her - she was alone. Gently, she nudged the door closed with the toe of her Amalfi black leather shoe. The email message opened, revealing an image inch by agonizing inch.

"It's a huge file. What is this an—" Lily started to say and then stopped when a familiar type of script unfolded on the digitized screen. She scanned bottom to top and right and left, looking for familiar words or characters. They all looked similar to what she had seen before but not an exact match either. "Where did you get this?" she whispered into the receiver. No answer came to her question. "Mona?"

"What? I'm here. What?"

"Where and when did you get this?" Lily repeated with deliberation.

"I'm not sure when it was *sent* but I got the email last—"

"Who sent it to you?" Emotion cracked through Lily's tough exterior, her hands instantly cold.

"I don't recognize the email address. I got it last night."

"Were you online when it came in?"

"No ... I was ... occupied. Didn't see it till this morning."

Lily paused and gritted her teeth.

"Are you there? I can barely hear you. This connection's staticky."

"Mona, listen to me very closely. You have to get out of there. Now, I mean it. Throw a few things in an overnight bag and go."

"Where?" Mona laughed.

"I don't have time to ..." Lily's mind raced through possibilities while she tried to calm the banging in her chest. Her palms were sweaty and her mouth had dried up. She gazed at the email on and off, and then hit the print button and poised her hands over the empty tray. "Rome. I'll meet you there."

"I don't ... Why should you have to go? Don't get involved in this."

"I *am* involved. That message was meant for me." She closed her eyes and held onto the desk. "There are only a few people who even know about this, and only one who would have sent it."

"Knew about what?"

"I'll tell you when I see you."

"Why didn't they send it to you directly?"

Lily glanced behind her, reached back to pull open her office door and then closed and locked it when she saw no one in the area. "I'm too obvious, too high profile. So they went through you instead, knowing you'd contact me when you got it. It's actually a rather brilliant plan."

"I don't get it, though. Why all the secrecy and what would be the harm in going to you direct?"

Lily swiveled her chair toward the window, wondering. Wondering if it was prudent to tell Mona about the organization, wondering if they even existed, really, or if it had all been a figment of her imagination. "There are people here," she whispered, "a group of people at the museum, well that's not exactly true, but people who are at the museum's disposal to help them prove or disprove the authenticity of ancient artifacts."

"So ... security people?"

Lily shook her head. "Not really, but in a way, yes. Security, if you want to call them that, to help the museum track down hoaxes and false leads, and mainly document forgeries. Whoever sent this email to you knew about these people. Knew enough to circumnavigate it by involving an outside source."

"Me," Mona said.

"That's right."

"So why are you worried about my safety, though? Why go all the way to Rome?"

"I can't tell you that now. This phone line may be—"

"Cut it out, Lily. If you want me to hop a plane right now, I want to know at least what I'm running from."

Lily sighed, and just then remembered the impatient policemen in the conference room downstairs. "All right. There was a theft here last night." She drew in a breath and secretly appreciated Mona allowing her to finish before her typical interruptions. "I think the text on that email came from one of the two ancient texts that were stolen. Now, is that enough of a reason? And besides all that, you just finished telling me you're being followed."

"It's probably just some prank or someone I met in a bar."

Lily tapped her long fingernails on the desktop and waited. "Do you really think that?"

No response.

"Mona?"

"Maybe not. Actually ... no."

A bright light from the street poked in through the heavy, canvas curtains - Lily hated those curtains, and the small, sinister windows they covered up.

"I'll wait for you on the top floor of the Angelica Library. Do you know where it is?"

"No, but I'll find it."

"Get there as soon as you can. Leave now, Mona. I mean it."

"What's this about?" Mona whined.

"The only man who could have sent this, the only person who knew about a) this text, b) the museum's security branch, and c) about you and how to contact you ... has been dead for eight years."

She said it in the older-sister voice she had cultivated, a voice capable of inciting both rage and change. She pictured Mona, who failed to verbally respond to the directive, stuffing jeans, light sweaters, socks and skimpy underwear into her faded, threadbare black duffel bag and wondering, all the while, about the cost of a ticket to Rome and whether this was reason enough to make a withdrawal from the family trust.

Lily sat back in her chair and took a minute to breathe as streaks of orange stained the darkening sky. The color reflected onto her computer monitor.

God, the email, she thought again.

Re-checking the lock on her office door, she printed two copies of the email, locked one in her drawer and put the other in her pocket. Then she pulled a jump drive from the assortment on her desk and copied the image onto it, and then saved it to her external hard drive. Now there were two hard copies of the ancient text and two digital copies of the image stored in a safe place. And she was the only person, out of the entire British Museum staff, who had a key to her desk. Though comforted by this thought, she couldn't help but look behind her every few seconds as she left the office.

Lily took an Uber home and asked the driver to wait while she packed a small bag. The posh, overpriced apartment in Russell Square, so convenient for the museum, had an eerie cast to it today. No texts, no Facebook notifications, no new emails showed on her MacBook and not a single decibel of the typically constant hum of street noise. She moved silently and with care, folding clothing into a small carry-on, dragging it into the bathroom to add makeup, a toothbrush, and shampoo and conditioner.

All right, that's it, she thought, deciding right then and there that it was too quiet in the apartment.

She called out into the empty atmosphere just to hear her own voice. "Is somebody there?" But the words returned just more static silence. She put her hand on the knob of the hall closet door, then remembered the coat she had on was fine for a quick trip to Rome. Her pounding heartbeat drummed in her ears and almost muffled the sound of her key locking the door. Lily thought of the closet again, oddly, and found herself unlocking the apartment's front door again. The Uber driver leaned on the horn, probably about to drive off.

Oh shut up, she thought and re-entered her apartment.

She eased through the dark to the closet and opened the door.

The closet was empty.

None of the winter coats that had been in there just this morning were there now. She felt her hands sweating. What the hell was going on here? Had the same person who stole the two most valuable volumes in the museum also stolen her Mackintosh and Barbour?

Fifty minutes later, worrying the whole ride, she arrived at Heathrow, thanked the driver for waiting for her, walked past the porters, and stood in a surprisingly short queue at the Virgin Atlantic counter. Even the ticket clerk peered at her suspiciously. My closet, she wondered, pulling a credit card out of her wallet. A wiry, bald man with smart glasses handed her a boarding pass and directed her to the gate for a flight that would board in fifty minutes. The carry-on bag strained her shoulder muscles by the time she got to B2. By B10 she had already switched arms twice.

Damn, I hate traveling, she thought.

And then a man approached from behind her and brushed the bag on her shoulder.

"What the hell are you—"

"Lily!" beamed a round-faced man. "I hardly ever get to see that pretty face anymore since those bastards moved me to the fourth floor." The man kissed her on the cheek. It was Geoffrey Voss from the International Museum Academy.

God help me, she thought. "What a surprise, Geoffrey," she said, trying to keep the whine out of her contralto.

"So where does an antiquities scholar slip away to at this time of night?"

Think quickly. Her mind raced back and forth, searching, searching ... "I'm going to Milan to join Adrian at a conference. Just for a few days though," she added as if this would somehow make the trip less suspicious. "Were you at work today?" she asked, changing the subject.

"Only this afternoon. I've had long, dreary meetings at the Academy all week. Matter of fact, someone was looking for you this afternoon just before I left. A copper, if I'm not mistaken. Not in uniform, but they showed me a badge and stopped me at the back entrance, asking if I'd seen you."

Lily drew her hand to her mouth. Oh my God, the police, meeting, conference room, how could I forget? Now they're looking for me. Good job.

"Are you all right?" Geoffrey moved his face strategically close to her cheek again.

"I forgot. Everything's, sort of," her voice quaked, "upside down all of a sudden."

"Why would the police want to talk to you?"

She waved her hand in dismissal. "I was meeting with them about the Castleman theft. I left to take a phone call and, sort of, forgot about them."

Geoffrey leaned back and stood tall. "Must've been some phone call."

"Not really. Just one of our benefactors. Some old coot who likes to pontificate about dinosaur bones, and gives us a half a million pounds every year, so I'm obliged to listen."

"Someone who likes to hear himself talk, no doubt."

Yeah, like you, she thought. "Geoffrey look, I'd better be going. They're boarding my flight in—" and the image of a crooked nose and stark, blond hair constricted the words from leaving her mouth. It was the blond man who had followed her yesterday afternoon.

Five

BOSTON

Officer Tom Kirby of the Boston Police Department waved Alex Careski in through the glass doors of the precinct.

"Thanks for coming in," he said and shook Alex's hand, then awkwardly embraced him. "You're shaking, man. You okay?"

"There's a dead man in my yard and my wife's missing. What do you think?" Alex repeated, having called him en route.

Kirby motioned ahead and stood in front of a closed door. "Follow me – we can talk in here."

Alex noticed that his former partner, Officer Tom Kirby, had put on more than just a few pounds. Twelve years ago he had been tall, thin, with a thick crop of light brown hair ornamented with sideburns and a mustache. Tom could have had any woman in the precinct back then, not that there were many worthy specimens. He was balding now, fifty pounds heavier with no facial hair and a hardened look to his gaze. Not just the face had changed, he noticed, it was more than that. Something else.

"What do I do, Tommy?" Alex pleaded. "Tell me what to do."

"Nothing, I'm afraid. You remember how it works."

"Like yesterday's breakfast." The table in front of them was new. Almost everything in the precinct looked new and updated compared with when he had lived, breathed, sweated and bled the PD. Back in the dark days before Simone. Another lifetime.

"Two officers have already been out there."

"And?"

Officer Kirby paused and swallowed.

"Nothing?"

"No."

Alex jerked to stand up. The chair fell back behind him. "Jesus, Tommy! What the fuck are you telling me? That I imagined shooting a man, that I imagined him shooting through my living room window and that Simone's really at work right now? Do you think I made the whole thing up?"

"Sit down, Alex."

Alex felt any residual composure drip out of him through his wrenching hands. He stood back from Kirby and watched for a moment, studied this new face attached to a new body that used to belong to someone he loved. He eased the chair back and sat.

"Let me recap everything for you, from the PD's point of view. And I'm not trying to unravel you but I want you to look at the facts from my perspective. Facts, Alex, that's what our jobs are based on."

"I know. It sounds crazy. But it happened. I have the bullet holes in my living room to prove it."

"I know. One of the officers confirmed this. The bullet holes I mean, and your shattered window." Pause. "That's pretty much all they can confirm though."

"You've got to do something, Tom. I gotta do something. You can't ask me to just sit around when Simone's missing. Especially not now."

"Meaning what?" Kirby asked.

"Meaning I've got a feeling this whole thing has more to do with Simone than me."

"Listen," Kirby leaned forward and grabbed Alex's arm. "You show up here frantic, like a raving lunatic, making accusations that can't be backed up, claiming to have shot and killed a man whose body is missing, claiming that your wife has been kidnapped and carrying an unregistered weapon."

Alex jerked his arm away. "I never said anything about that."

Kirby shook his head and smirked. "The weapon you used to supposedly kill the man who shot through your window … belonged to Soren. Didn't it? And if it did, we both know that gun wasn't registered to either you or him. I'm not saying this didn't happen, and we've got people looking for Simone right now as we speak, unofficially of course. But unless you can tell me something more about this man, there's not much we can do, but wait."

"He was driving an old Jaguar, late thirties early forties, blond hair and a broken nose, carrying what looked like a Beretta 9 mm." Alex knew, from his experience as Kirby's partner, that he kept a notebook in the breast pocket of his uniform and it should have been taken out by now; he should have been making notes in it.

Why wasn't he? Was anyone at all going to take him seriously? Would Simone have to die before they did?

"And what's the significance of this man?"

"The significance?" Alex repeated. "I don't follow you."

"You don't know him? You're saying a complete stranger shot through your living room window, chased you down and now your wife has vanished without a trace?"

Alex stood up again and walked around the small conference room. No, he wasn't telling Kirby everything because there was no point. Tom knew of Soren but had no idea about what kind of life he had led, the thrust of his research, and the kinds of risks he customarily took in the course of that research. So telling him about Soren's diaries would have no effect on Simone's whereabouts. Probably.

Kirby's head was bent down toward the conference table.

"Okay," Alex said with his hands up. "He hit me in the parking garage."

"Hit you? Where?"

"Rear-ended me in the Herald garage this morning. I had no idea who he was, I still don't. Out of nowhere he just drove into my rear bumper, then backed up and did it again."

"You're sure this is the same man who shot through y—"

"You don't just forget a face like that."

"Like what?"

"Of a man pointing a fucking gun at you. Why don't we drive out there together and I'll show you where—"

"There's nothing out there, Alex. The two officers dispatched to your house haven't even found any empty rounds. From what you've told me, it was like the OK Corral out there. Except that there's no trace of any blood on the ground near the fence where you saw him fall after you shot him. I know you're not seeing things, but I don't have any explanation either. I suggest you drive around the neighborhood, knock on doors and ask if anyone saw what direction the car took off in or maybe a license plate number. And another thing - leave that gun with me so we can have ballistics check it out."

"I don't think so." Alex stood up and gripped the door handle. "I can see now that if anyone's gonna find Simone, it'll be me."

Alex wanted more than anything to hole up somewhere safe to think - spend all night studying the strange email and the rescued diaries from the basement boxes. But with Simone missing, he had no time. He didn't even want to think about her condition, but worse yet - he had nowhere to go. Work, out of the question. And home was an even worse idea. So he drove along the outskirts of both neighborhoods, scanning for old European cars or for something that might pull it all together.

He took out his phone and punched in Corinna's number and left a message for her to meet him at Constitution Marina. He loved it there, even in the rain. He parked the Camaro in the most visible part of the parking lot and lost himself in a view of roiling waves and bobbing sailboats, which for a minute or two quelled the pounding in his chest. The seagulls squawking took him back to the Marconi Beach of his childhood on Cape Cod, where he could disappear in the sand for a day, or weeks on end.

He pulled his laptop out of the backseat, booted it up and logged online, there had to be Wi-Fi somewhere around here. He'd thought of little else except the email since this morning, when usually he checked it only once a day.

An hour later his stomach grumbled but he felt no inclination to actually eat. It was almost dark and Corinna hadn't called back. And then he saw her white Nissan tear around the corner and park two spaces over. He got out of the car and intercepted her.

Her face looked frozen. "What are you doing out here? There's insurrection at the paper right now."

He had figured as much. "Layoffs?"

"Yep."

"Not you?"

"Uh huh." He saw as she got closer that her eyes were red and puffy.

"Me?" he asked.

"They're deciding about senior staff tonight, but word is they're eliminating two jobs and one of them is yours."

"Jesus."

"That's all you have to say? How about telling me what the hell you're doing out here and why it was so important I didn't tell anyone I was coming to see you?" Her voice cracked and sobs escaped her lips. "I've got my own problems, Alex."

He grabbed her shoulders, then pulled his hands off abruptly. "You didn't, did you? Tell anyone you were coming?"

"I *can* follow directions." Corinna was a pretty woman, he had always thought so, even after he found out she and Simone were best friends. Laughing green eyes, light hair, tall, and plump without appearing heavy, which he'd always thought was a hard balance for a woman over thirty-five.

"It's drizzling again. Come and sit in the car."

"How about my car?" she said. "At least mine has heat that works."

He followed her, amazed to discover that checking out his surroundings had become second nature to him, for the second time in his life. Was he paranoid or, even worse, was he becoming a cop all over again? Or worse yet, like Soren?

One old man stooped over the lock on his driver's side door about ten feet away and a woman, early twenties in high heels and chewing gum, approached a brand new Prius and got in. So far, no blond men with guns, and no trace of a journalist's missing wife.

Corinna wiped her eyes.

"Simone's missing," he blurted.

Her face showed no reaction at first. "No, she's not. I just talked to her."

"What? When?"

"I don't know, this morning - sometime. Maybe it was—"

He took hold of her shoulders again. "It's important that you remember, Corinna. She was kidnapped this morning shortly after I left work. Did she contact you any time after about ten? Think!"

Corinna's mouth opened. "I," she paused, "maybe I ..." and her thought vanished. "I think it was right after you left work, actually. I told her what was going on and that you'd ducked out and she laughed, said it was your birthday and said she couldn't blame you. Then I called you a coward." Her face sagged. She wiped instant tears from her eye.

"You're probably right."

"I didn't mean it, Alex. Just girl talk. You know?"

"Look, I need to know if Simone said anything in the last couple of days, weeks, ever, about a blond man showing up and trying to make contact with her."

"Not that I remember. Did you see him? Do you know what happened?"

"Not that it makes any sense, but yeah. Some guy rear-ended me in the parking garage this morning, then he showed up at my house later on and shot a hole through my window. He kicked in the back door, shot at me and took off with Simone."

Corinna stared. "What else?"

"He's dead." Alex shook his head and shrugged. "I shot him in the leg and watched him go down. He was lying in my backyard near the fence. I saw his blood on the ground. Anyway, all of that's beside the point now. The blond man's gone, Simone's missing, and I have no idea where to even look for her."

"What are you gonna do?"

Alex fumbled with the folded papers in his jacket and held them out in front of him as if looking for the answer in an envelope of airline tickets. "I guess I'm going to Rome."

Corinna wiped away another round of tears and stared at him with narrowed eyes. "Italy?"

"I now have three reasons to go there. Simone bought me a ticket and teamed up with Monihan on a story he wants me to write."

"Now? How could you go now?" Corinna's voice was strained, incredulous. She drew in a deep breath to calm herself. "I'm sorry. You said three reasons."

"I found this on a table in my living room." Alex held out a white index card with the word 'ROME' printed in block letters.

"How do you know it's not Georgia?"

He barely knew this himself, let alone able to explain it. "It's not Georgia. Besides," he pulled out the folded email script from this morning, "I need to go to Rome to try to get this translated."

"What is it?" Simone lowered her head and studied the contents. "This looks like the weird stuff your fa—" she looked up, "*he* didn't—"

"I don't know. I only know that I got this email this morning from an email address labeled as **careskisor@ attbi.com**, and since the moment I printed it out, my life's gone straight to hell and back, and I have a feeling this ride hasn't even begun."

"How can you trust these people, Alex? This man shot through your window, trashed your car. What the hell is going on?"

The large green eyes filled with unfallen tears. He couldn't stand to see her cry. He put his arm around her and whispered softly, with an intimacy tolerated between a man and his wife's best friend. "I have to do something, Corinna. I got a text message saying that a driver will meet me at the airport with further instructions."

"You don't know what you're getting into." Corinna aimed her face up toward his. "How can you do this?"

"How can I not?" He wiped a tear from her right eye and remembered, in a split second, how they'd slept together once after an office party the year before he'd met Simone and how the guilt of their communal sin was strong enough to tarnish even the strongest physical urge. He backed away a few inches and wiped his face with his palms. "I'm taking the laptop with me and leaving now for the airport. So check your email. I'll stay in touch that way."

He kissed Corinna on her wet cheek and strode to the Camaro.

"She's the best friend I ever had. I can't live without her," she yelled at him, still sobbing.

Neither can I, he thought.

Six

NAPLES, ITALY

Mona Delfreggio exited the jam-packed ladies' room and noticed her bag was unzipped. She glanced around the Napoli Centrale train station before she bent down to look, well versed in the intricacies of urban dwelling. First, the glasses sliding down her nose disappeared into an outer pouch of the handbag slung across her body, then she inspected the half-zipped bag while still looking around. Two uniforms guarded the station's glass doors, armed with knives, a pistol and a rifle worn on a chest strap. For some reason, they both had their eyes on her.

Miguel returned with two large cokes from the snack bar.

"What's the matter?" he said, investigating her expression.

She shrugged. "Coming out of the bathroom, I noticed my bag was unzipped part way." She looked directly at him. "I didn't unzip it."

Miguel turned his back to the two guards and leaned forward. "Is it still there?"

"I was just about to check." Mona reached into the bag and, without unzipping it any further, reached with her fingertips to touch the pointed edge of the folded paper she'd printed out from her email message.

"Call Lily."

"What? I'm not calling her. Why should I?"

"What if someone tried to steal it? Maybe someone knows you're carrying it."

Mona studied the ceiling. "You're such a pessimist, Miguel. You'd find something wrong with a million dollars if it fell from the sky."

"If someone's following you already, I'm not letting you on that train." Miguel folded his arms and hovered over her, accentuating his six-foot-four stature. "It's a long ride to Rome, Mona."

"Two hours. Not even," she replied. "What are you so worried about, anyway? I'll be fine." She returned her attention to the bag, looked down, and then, "Ah. It's here. Zipper must've gotten stuck on someone's clothing or something." Mona sipped the coke through the straw and appraised Miguel's sullen look. "I know."

"I want to go with you."

"No," she snapped. "We've been through this ten times already and I only bought my ticket an hour ago. I need some time away from you, away from Naples, from the shelter, from all those needy, desperate souls. Counseling work bleeds all the life out of you. You told me that yourself."

"So you're leaving *them*? And not me?"

"Yes, I mean no, I - don't take everything so personally. I need to spend some time with my sister and make sure she's all right."

"Ironic, as she wants you to meet her so she can make sure you're all right."

Mona smirked and drank more of the soothing, cold liquid. "I know. One little email and she's off to the airport like a racehorse."

"Did she tell you anything about it?"

"Not much, but she was scared. I think she knows who sent it to me, though. She seemed to know as soon as she saw the image." Mona glanced at her watch and stood on her toes to kiss Miguel on the cheek. But he turned fast enough to receive it on the lips and held her there with his gentle hands on the back of her head.

"When's your return ticket?" said the hungry polar bear to the baby seal.

"A week from today."

"I love you, Mona."

"I know." She smiled at him and turned toward platform number three.

Is he right behind me, Lily wondered pushing through the wall of bodies in the exit line from the Boeing 737 at Da Vinci airport in Rome. She had eluded a confrontation with the blond man at the Boston gate by attacking Geoffrey Voss with an unexpected farewell kiss. From the sweat on his face, he'd either had a heart attack or wet his pants.

Poor Geoffrey, she thought and quickly returned her attention to the thudding in her chest.

She felt him behind her.

Rotating her head forty-five degrees, she caught sight of the dark-rimmed glasses and light hair … and ran. I have two extra copies, she reminded herself, and then thought about what good they would do her if no one knew about them. Tal! She could tell him to give the email to the police if she disappeared. But what then? What would the police do with a jpeg of some ancient, untranslatable language?

People yelled back and groaned as she shoved her way desperately through the crowd. One of the flight attendants spoke in Italian to her, but there was no time to break out her translation dictionary. *"Mi scusi,"* she repeated over and over, weaving through the field of bodies and luggage.

With no time to look back, she proceeded through the crowded gate, veered around an overfull luggage cart and sped across the tile floor. Her mind raced up, down, and sideways to process the suddenness of this new reality - chased by a strange gunman, a missing artifact at the museum library, and a strange email from a dead colleague. She looked back quickly and saw the yellow hair amid a sea of brunettes. Run, she thought. Faster. Her heart coming out of her chest, her pulse throbbed in her throat and limbs. Her forehead perspired.

Jesus, she thought, am I going to die of a heart attack before I'm even thirty?

He was twenty feet away now.

She'd slipped ahead and he'd fallen behind an old man burdened with two heavy bags. The bright red, bilingual baggage claim sign was visible up ahead. No, she reconsidered and peeled down a narrow corridor to the right.

He thinks I'm going to baggage claim because he assumes that I've checked in my cases. If he followed me from Heathrow, he thinks I'm going for a long stay.

Facing the wall with her neck craned around, she peered over her shoulder at the slim, dark blue pants and hip-length leather jacket walking past her now. Past her, further, further. Now the blond head looked for her ahead of him, rather than behind.

One chance.

She fled across the stream of people, colliding for the second time with bodies and luggage. A security guard posted near the escalators stared at her as she fumbled forward, scanning all the signs for the exit. As she approached him, his lips formed into a seething grin and his hand reached for the weapon on his belt.

"Exit? Can you tell me where the exit is? There's a man following me. Don't you understand?"

He looked her up and down, less from sexual interest and more to gauge her potential as a national security threat. Lily turned her head back for a split second and caught sight of a tall blond man walking toward the escalator, but ... wait ... false alarm. Wasn't him. But behind him was another blond man.

Him? The man from Naples was now in Rome? Chasing her? "Shit!" she heard herself say aloud, and shoved past the security guard and charged up the escalator. The man turned around, then blew a whistle in her direction and shouted, "*Arresto*!"

God, she thought. That's all I need is the police chasing me.

The straps on her carry-on and her purse dug deep grooves in her shoulders as she struggled to heave her weight forward. Her leg muscles strained, her lungs about to collapse. The whistle blew again and the security guard yelled to another guard at the top of the stairs. But she was already past and racing toward another set of stairs leading to the street level of Viale di Porto.

Two guards ran down the escalator to the lower level now as she took cover behind the awning of an espresso stand. One guard ran left, the other right, and she bolted out the door and hailed one of the cabs that always waited outside airport terminals. Naturally, today, there were none.

Alex had taken both of the airline tickets with him. Unsure of why the human mind resorted to the quirkiest of behaviors during times of duress, he felt himself fondling Simone's ticket as he gazed out of the window at a sea of twinkling lights. The sky over Rome looked like the sky over Boston. The only difference was that there were now two people in Rome who clearly shouldn't be there.

This very difference, the change in atmosphere, the upside-down feeling in his stomach, nagged at his brain as he disembarked from the plane. He walked with his briefcase down the long, crowded aisles toward a *Ritiro Bagagli* sign fifty yards ahead. Demonstrative Italian couples kissed and hugged in his periphery the whole way down the corridor - yet one more thing to remind him of Simone and the emptiness he felt, he always felt, without her.

Her hair was what he missed first. Long, jet black, smoother than silk. Half Japanese and a quarter each Hawaiian and Italian, he couldn't think of a more potent recipe for beauty. Simone could have had any man in the world, and she had most of them back then, most any man she wanted, even some she didn't. That's how it was for her as a twenty-year-old model. Swimming with sharks, traveling around the globe posing semi-nude in shiny clothes on sunny beaches. Yet she still managed to lead a normal life with a career, a house, and enough grit to take out the garbage.

If a man like him, ordinary on the inside and only slightly charismatic on the outside, could be lucky enough to marry a former runway model, he should surely count his blessings. Then again, she was missing, now, wasn't she? Screw the blessings on second thought, and the gratitude to go with it. He would chase her far into the next three lives if he had to.

Exiting baggage claim with the suitcase he swore he'd replace twenty years ago, Alex caught sight of something he clearly shouldn't have. The automatic doors leading from the lower level of the airport in baggage claim accessed a landing lined with yellow cabs. He assumed he'd take one and make a reservation at a hotel, which one he wasn't sure. He'd had plenty of time to think about it but, well, other things occupied his mind. He touched the back pocket of his jeans and felt the presence of Soren's message. He kept his hand on it as he walked toward the landing through the glass doors.

A small, older, well-kept man with an honest face held a white sign that read "Careski."

Here we go, he thought.

Seven

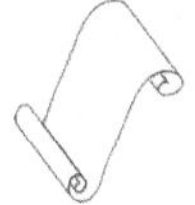

ITALY

The midday bells from the Gloriosa Clock Tower clanged twelve times, dragging its low-pitched pulse across the green hills of Padua and low buildings of Montagnana. The man rarely felt the push of age and pull of gravity on his bones despite his eighty years. And today, even a sigh felt like a burden. In five minutes Marta, his dutiful maid, would arrive with a white tray carrying a porcelain cup and saucer for his lunchtime cappuccino, complete with a chip of lemon rind that he never touched. The insistent bells ... six, seven, eight ... never varied in pitch or volume, piping their monotonous drone as a reminder of all things inescapable. Like age, death, and revenge. Today the man knew that even Marta's cappuccino would not revive his spirit, or thaw the glacial chill folding into his chest.

"Mi dispiace intromettermi, ciao," Marta announced setting the platter on the marble table before him with an unconvincing smile.

You know what day it is, he thought watching her, sipping the strong, hot brew. Marta would have already retrieved his folio from the upstairs closet, his woolen coat and scarf, knowing that it was Thursday and he would leave soon not to return till after dark.

"*C'e un brivido in aria,*" the woman mumbled from her tight-lipped red mouth. Ten years ago when she'd first arrived, he had thought about her, how she might feel in his arms, the scent of her perfume, how she'd look with her hair un-bunned and wild, in a white nightgown. A brunette Botticelli, he had thought of her soft steps and porcelain skin, almost seeming more Irish than Italian.

Had she feared him back then? Did she still?

Long ago, steeled from the guilt of such nihilistic thoughts, the idea ate at his insides today, everything did. The cold air, bitter coffee, and the deep eyes of his fantasy mistress. I am tired, he thought, rising toward the staircase, wondering if he had the strength to do this one more time.

Eight

WHERE?

It smelled of dead fish and glue.

Alex turned his head and experienced two things – a combination of dizziness and nausea that corresponded to a throbbing pain in the right side of his skull, and a marked lack of light.

Okay, time for my other senses to kick in now. Be a blind person. I can't see anything, so let me hear something, or smell, or sense through intuition.

Nothing came.

The large room had an ice-cold, dungeon-like concrete floor. Were there places like this left in the world? Ancient Roman catacombs? How long had he been unconscious? And was he still in Italy, or even in Europe?

His pupils had already widened, yet there was just no ambient light filtering in to pierce the cloak of black air. Even so, his perception reached a far wall and he sensed he could walk at least twelve paces in any direction. He stretched out his arms on each side. The air was cold and damp. His nostrils picked up something salty. Was he near the sea?

Fish and glue. A boathouse?

His assessment started with the concrete floor. No carpet, no particular smell, and hardly any echo when he scraped the sole of his shoe against it. He knocked on the floor and barely heard the sound of flesh and bone. Though he wore the same clothes as when he had deboarded the plane in Rome, something felt different about them. Cold. Were they worn? He fumbled around with his hands and found not tears but water. The back of his shirt was wet.

What is this place?

A scraping noise sounded just ahead of him.

"Who's there? Is someone out there? Please, just say something." He couldn't keep the panic from his voice.

Someone moaned. A woman. From the sound, she was in a far-off corner.

"Scusi," he said, fumbling through a leftover graveyard of childhood words. *"Mi scusi?"*

"Si." A woman's small voice answered, and he could tell absolutely nothing from the accent - age, attitude, degree of injury. She had surely been injured, her voice at least betrayed tightened vocal chords, and he'd heard her labored breathing even before she spoke.

"Parli Inglese?"

The woman cleared her throat and coughed. From this he knew several things - he knew how she felt, for one thing – she was young, or youngish, had been struck in the head, perhaps even the face, so her mouth didn't quite recall how to form words yet. He was confident she was not Italian. And he felt something else – she was only ten feet away.

"Where are we?" the woman asked. "And are we the only ones here?"

"I don't know but I have about a thousand questions. Like how we got here, for one thing. I don't recall being … taken. Don't mean to sound *X-Files*-ish, but I just have no memory of being brought here."

"Rohypnol."

"I'm sorry?" Alex slid a few inches closer to the voice.

"Rohypnol, you know, the date rape drug. That's what they use."

He felt his lids closing and the pain in the side of his head throbbed worse than ever. He was fading in and out – the oscillation was almost palpable, but not in and out of consciousness. More like in and out of the here and now, this reality. During the "out" parts, he slipped into a gray cloak of silent warmth, hushed yellow lighting, wooden tables with glasses on them and the clanking sound of bone china, men's voices concealed from prying eavesdroppers. And when he swung back "in," he returned to the dark cell, their cell, he and … Mona. Somehow, he knew the woman's name and knew some part of his brain was awake when they'd interrogated her. One of the guards must have said her name, or was Mona someone else? Now … suddenly …

a memory of his face pushed against the cold grates of a heating vent …

… "Ow!" A woman screamed. "Let me go, you bastard, I'll never tell yo—"

"Where is it? Tell us and we might let you live."

Then more screams, moans, a man approached her, touched her, she whined and rolled away from him on a platform with metal springs, the fumble of clothes and shoes and zippers and brute force penetrating something it shouldn't …

The woman's scream still in his ears. Maybe it always would be.

Was *this* the same woman?

A moment later, he shook himself awake and considered the woman's words. They, she had said. "They? Who's they?"

"Mm," the woman mumbled. It was hard for her to talk. "They have many names. The Chain. The Great Danes."

"I don't understand."

"Who are you?" the woman asked, and then shifted to pull herself up.

"Who are these Great Danes? Danes as in dogs or Denmark?"

"Tell me who you are," she said flatly.

Alex couldn't answer, feeling himself drift back to the other place momentarily.

"The fact that you and I are both here indicates that we are both part of something. The same something."

"What's that?"

A guttural laugh. "How should I know? What do you do?"

"Nothing. Or nothing that has anything to do with foreign intrigue or international scandals."

"Has anything happened in your life lately that was out of the ordinary?"

"My wife was kidnapped, yesterday," Alex replied.

"*Voilà*. That's something out of the ordinary. And I'm sorry to hear it. Do you live in Rome?"

"No. Do you?" he asked.

"No."

His eyes adjusted, finally, to some scant ambient light filtering in between the slats in the ceiling. He could barely see them now, slanted, wooden eaves, bent and contorted from bearing too much weight, the concrete floor, a large heater in the corner and, behind it, the form of the woman. He stood and took three steps toward her. "What's your name?" he asked, knowing his presence near her might be interpreted as an intrusion.

She looked up, seeing him now for the first time. The woman combed her hands through her hair and rubbed her face. "Mona."

"Alex. What do you do for a living, Mona?"

"Get into trouble, mostly. You?"

"Not enough. Or too much. Always one or the other."

That sarcastic laugh again.

He crouched and took two more steps toward her. "I think I heard them."

"The Danes?"

"They were hurting you. That was you, wasn't it?"

The woman lowered her head. "Better off playing dead, I should think. Go back to your side of the room, it's safer. If they'd known we both spoke English, they'd have never put us together."

Alex obliged but only took two steps back. "Who are these Danes and what do they want with us? Do they have Simone?"

"Simone?"

"My wife. Is she here? Have you seen or heard anything?"

She shook her head. "They took me, from what I can tell, a few hours before you, which is why most of the drug's worn off me by now. I've been here almost a day, you were only brought a few hours ago."

Alex chewed on this new information for a few silent moments. He tried to see the chronology of events – woke up, went to work, left early, rear-ended, home, got shot at, wife kidnapped, police, hopped plane to Rome, concrete cell.

"Do you know who took your wife?"

"Yes and no." Pause. "I'm pretty sure I know what they are. Just not who, exactly."

"Well, what are they?"

"Scientists, probably. Archaeologists. Cryptographers, epigraphers."

"What do they want with her?"

"Not her, with me. They've taken her, or this is just a theory I've formulated, to motivate me to do something. Or more likely to give them something that I probably don't even have."

"Have you got a lot of money?" Mona asked.

"Some. Enough. Not a lot, no. And that's not what they want."

She paused a moment as if to gather her thoughts. "If you could write a note and leave it for someone to find you, what would you write to sum up your life right now?"

Alex noticed the muscles in his face felt strange. "I'm a journalist. My wife has been kidnapped, my house has been ransacked, and my dead father's trying to contact me. My name is Alex Careski. Welcome to hell."

"Hey, that's pretty good. I can tell you're a writer."

"I never said that," he replied. "I'm a reporter. I see things and describe them. You could lock me in a room for a year and the most fiction I could possibly write is a page."

"More than I could write. Mine would say 'Mona Delfreggio, 28, D-cup, party-girl outside, piranha inside.'"

Alex allowed himself to chuckle and felt his eyes penetrate the darkness to see the front of her blouse. "That's some personal ad. Might meet yourself a nice mobster that way."

"Wouldn't be the first time. I live in Naples," she replied.

It was silent between them for a while. Alex, though he didn't move back to his original spot, felt himself revert to that other place, looking for what his mind couldn't remember, searching for the words and thoughts hidden behind a shell of pharmaceuticals. Blood trudged through his veins, dragging the yellowy liquid through every inch of his interior, painting the muscles and tendons and ligaments and organs with the "forget-me" drug. His movements sluggish, his eyes scanned the environment left to right, but in an exaggerated half-time.

Simone's here, he thought. I can feel her, almost smell the lilt of her French perfume in the damp air. I'll find you. If it kills me, if God forbid it kills us both, it is my last wish on earth.

"I've got to know what we're doing here. I don't have time to waste." If Simone's even still alive, he caught himself thinking.

Mona leaned back and stretched out her legs. "Well, you know a lot more than I do. All I know is that some dude followed me for the past two nights, I got this weird email that was really meant for my sister, apparently from a dead guy and when I told her about it, she demanded I fly to Rome to meet her in person."

Alex felt a contracting movement in his stomach.

Email?

Nine

LONDON

Lily Frasier had quit smoking over a year ago. Tal Gardner, in the hall outside her office, smiled as the memory of her edict resurfaced.

"What, cold turkey?" he had said to bait her. "That'll be the day."

"A little support would be quite civilized and, as I am your boss, could put you in my good graces."

"For how long? Till the next time I schedule a Friday afternoon appointment with one of our hundred-year-old patrons?"

Where are you, Tal thought, unable to ignore the nervous pangs in the pit of his stomach. The hall clock read 2:30 a.m. Most of the other museum personnel left promptly at five o'clock, the administrative staff for sure, some of them even earlier. Curators might stay till six but no later. Certainly not this time of night. Tal had worked on exhibit planning till nine o'clock, left to pick up a sandwich, came back and worked on inventorying, and then correspondence with conservators till midnight.

"Where are you?" he said aloud this time, alarmed by the empty trail of sound his voice left on the cold air. Empty voice, empty hallway - reminded him of an old European cathedral or a mausoleum. Was Lily in a tomb right now, like one of the Egyptian mummies on Level 3, suffocating in a web of stained muslin? Or was his imagination responding to the horror movies he had watched last night? She hadn't picked up her cell phone and he knew the phone was turned off because it went to straight to voicemail.

He'd been to her apartment already and The Princess Louise, where they all went for Friday cocktails. Oddly, no one saw Lily leave the museum, least of all the constables who'd been awaiting her return to the conference room after Mona's interruption. Mona. God, he'd nearly forgotten. Could Lily's disappearance have something to do with Mona? In that case, anything could have happened. Flown to Naples to bail her out of jail, rescue her from the grips of some underworld prostitution ring, provided the getaway car in a bank robbery.

Now, even the empty hallway was too quiet.

Had some ambient noise ceased? A motor, the hum of a light bulb or appliance, tapping of pens, rustling of papers? The kind of sound you only noticed when it stopped.

And if you're not here, he thought, staring at Lily's opened office door ahead of him, who's in your office in the middle of the night?

Tal tried to see through the door crack but only burned his retinas on the slide of the fluorescent overhead. He pushed it, slowly, slowl—

"Come in, Tal. Do sit down," a man's voice called, while someone else who had been standing behind the door grabbed him by the shirt collar and tossed him into a chair.

Tal scanned the ransacked mess first, then raked his eyes across Richard Wexler's beady snake eyes.

What was there to like about a man like Wexler? Tal hated him, Lily loathed the sight of him, even Adrian, who lacked any capacity for hatred, lowered his eyes in his presence. One of the admins on the first floor was rumored to have a rare form of Wexleritis and, from a distance, Tal could see how a young woman might find him attractive. But to his keen eyes and instinct, Richard Wexler had the look of a ghoul lurking beneath a sheath of refined British features.

"Pity, isn't it?" Wexler asked, his pointy voice like an icepick against warm skin.

"What?"

"That she's not here - missing *all* the fun." Then came the sinister, devious laugh of Moriarty mocking Holmes in a rare escape.

Tal braced himself. "Shouldn't you be off playing with the other vampires this time of night?"

Wexler raised a brow and half grinned.

"You're not allowed in here you know."

"I'm security," Wexler reminded him. "Or have you forgotten?"

"Mafia's a better word for it. Security protects what's yours. The mafia takes what's yours, assumes ownership of it, and then charges you money to have access to it. You're worse than that, come to think of it."

"Your mistrust devastates me."

"How much did you make in artifact kickbacks this week? Ten thousand quid? Twenty?"

"Watch it, little one. Your pretty Rottweiler isn't here to defend you."

Tal stood feebly. "You don't scare me. Come to think of it," chuckle, "you don't scare her, either."

"Well, it appears I might need a new tactic then. After all, fear, to some … is a form of food."

Tal lowered himself to the chair beside Lily's now untidy desk and rubbed his forehead. "What are you doing here, Wexler? Fumbling through classified materials while Lily's away? Par for the course, I suppose."

"Do shut up. We did have a fairly substantial theft, or didn't you know about it?"

Shaking his head. "'Course I knew about it, Adrian informed me. I was there when he told Lily."

The room fell silent and Tal's stomach did another somersault.

"Let it slip, now, did you? Don't worry, I already knew."

"What do you want?"

"I'm performing my contracted duty to investigate this theft any way I can, which includes examining files and records. What, may I ask, are you still doing here? Would've expected you to be asleep in her bed, sniffing her pillow … groping her silk pajamas."

"Fuck off. Least I'm capable of bonding with other humans."

Wexler sneered. "A bit effeminate, aren't you?"

"You, on the other hand, are a predator. A shark trawling for anything lunch-worthy."

"Sticks and stones, Tal. Really. Now let me get to the point. Where's the ubiquitous Mr. Marcali?"

"Adrian's in Milan. Lily dispatched him two days ago to that curator symposium the Louvre sponsors every year. What do you want with him?"

"Timing," he mumbled.

"What's that?"

He shook his head. "The timing is, let's just say, bothering me. And it's either bothering you as well or perhaps you just don't care."

"Say what you mean, for God's sake."

"Adrian flew out of here the very day the two ancient texts disappeared. Did he not?"

"For God's sake. Adrian discovered the theft on Tuesday morning, reported it to Lily immediately, and he left in the afternoon to attend a pre-scheduled event. You can't possibly think he—"

"No," Wexler mocked, "I couldn't possibly. Could I? Just a bit coincidental, don't you think?"

Tal scanned Lily's untidy office, watched Wexler wringing his hands, and decided then and there that he would stay up all night to restore it to proper order. "What if you stole them?"

Wexler gave a haughty laugh. "Wouldn't that be a proper scandal? How about we focus on one thing at a time." He rubbed his hands together. "Let's call him. Shall we?"

"It's two-thirty in the morning. We're not calling anyone." Tal looked back to the door to the office, responding to an amorphous sound in the hallway. The muzzle of Wexler's pistol pointed between his eyes when he looked back.

"Pick up the phone."

"Jesus." Tal picked it up and dialed Adrian Marcali's cell phone number.

"It's Tal," he said when someone picked up on the first ring, eyeing Wexler beside him. "Yeah, no, I'm at Lily's office and you'd better get over here. That's right. No, I mean right now, yes, right." Tal hung up and Wexler made a gathering gesture with his hands. "He took the red-eye out of Milan and is on his way back from Heathrow right now. He'll be five minutes."

"Fine, fine." Wexler lit a cigarette and resumed his search through the file cabinet. In the silence, Tal

Gardner wondered why he hadn't just stayed at Lily's apartment. The thought of Lily in silk pajamas shot instant heat through his veins.

God help me ...

A loud boom sounded from the far end of the hallway.

Tal froze.

Wexler positioned himself just outside the office door. "That sounded suspiciously like a gunshot, did it not?"

"Well, thank God security's here," Tal mocked.

Wexler shot Tal a loaded glare. "Don't move," he said and took off down the hallway.

Ten

LONDON

Two more shots sounded from the same direction as the first round. Tal picked up a strange, uncomfortable buzz vibrating on an invisible current throughout the lower level of the museum.

Shots fired, Lily missing, Wexler roaming the halls like a restless demon.

With Wexler and his goons in the hallway, Tal rose in a sort of haze, oddly apathetic about the gunfire and the hapless recipient. Police cars would be called, people would be screaming. Yet amongst this peril, here he was, aimlessly wandering.

The signpost for the Rosetta Stone in the Ancient Egypt room was only barely visible in the dark. He had passed it a thousand times since he'd first been hired and knew every step and curve of the hallway leading to the East Wing. With soft, almost silent footsteps, he moved down the hallway into the main exhibit space on the bottom floor and turned into a room with one of the traveling exhibits: "The Roman Catholic Inquisition."

He was thirty and had a long passion for history, some history. Medieval history, somehow, had always felt too remote, too random to have any relevance to the modern world. It just had never interested him that much. After four months of walking past this exhibit, he'd never actually come in here before. But something about it tonight, right now, yanked him in from the dark hallway and Wexler's interrogation. There's something here, he thought as he moved to the first section which focused on clothing and fabric remnants of former inquisitors. The next section had a series of paintings, mostly by Goya, whom he had always admired. And yet, this exhibit had held no interest for him. Scanning the room with his arms wrapped around his body, Tal's eyes landed on something impossible. Unthinkable.

One of the paintings was crooked.

Crooked?

He rubbed his eyes with his fists and reminded himself that most people, at this time of night, had been asleep for three to five hours. He inhaled the scent of musty air pumping through a hundred-year-old ventilation system and the unmistakable smell of age. Then he slowly returned his eyes to the picture on the wall.

Indeed. Crooked.

How could this be? We're the bloody British Museum. The pictures are double hung with two hooks and double-stranded braided wire holding each piece in place.

The installation centerpiece, a ceramic relief bust of Pope Theophilus of Alexandria, listed twenty degrees to port unless, of course, his vision had spontaneously deteriorated.

Standing perfectly still, Tal peered down the hall from behind the support wall in the main exhibit room, shielded by the shadows and quietude of what was now 3:00 a.m. Female footsteps clicked down the hallway, an ambulance siren, the mumble of Wexler's controlled voice, a body sprawled across a stretcher …

Only by the familiar Fossil watch on a wrist dangling off the trolley did he realize that the body belonged to Adrian Marcali, Senior Conservator, a fine mentor and not a bad drinking companion, who had, what, now been shot? Could this be? Even this failed to reach him completely.

Adrian's dead?

As the hallway noise grew from elevated voices, radio commands and the clank of metal equipment, Tal reverted deeper into his head and disappeared one level deeper into the Inquisition room. His mind drew him, tractor-beam-like, back to the centerpiece.

Shrieking in the corridor …

Tal's eyes gravitated to half-opened eyes, the chalky white face. He scanned the room for any other installation defects or anomalies, saw scene paintings of hangings, beheadings, medieval torturers; one whole section on torture paraphernalia.

... "Constable Blevins here, what's going on?"

"A man down, or I should hope you'd noticed."

"Mm, looks like two gunshot wounds, close range, possibly a thirty-eight—"

"Bloody Christ, he's still breathing! Get an ambulance, now!" ...

Paintings of heretics being burned alive, Goya's *Inquisition Trial*. Sculptures. Nothing awry. Nothing except the centerpiece. There had to be a reason, Tal knew, why he was seeing this only now for the first time.

... An EMT leaned over the stretcher performing CPR, another EMT stood ready a few feet back, Wexler coolly smoked at the end of the hall ...

Tal opened his eyes wide, really looked at the picture rather than just looking into it. And this time, he saw that he had been wrong.

The picture wasn't hung improperly on the wall - it was *mounted* crookedly, which was even less likely than the first scenario. Two steps closer and he saw that the entire image, frame and matte, was tilted by about twenty degrees.

How could this be, and how had no one reported this before now?

.... More footsteps, and the clanky sound of uneven metal wheels across linoleum ...

Myriad possibilities flooded his brain at once, so much so that he instinctively closed his eyes and reminded himself what to do. Damage on an artifact from an exhibit? Check the shipping manifest and the inventory logs to determine when the damage occurred. Had it happened before or after it got to them? But surely someone would have noticed? How had he not noticed himself if he had supervised the installation?

The file drawers in Lily's office were home to the master files of the exhibit inventory for Medieval Antiquities, Lily's personal domain. But, there was no telling where something like *The Inquisition* might be kept. He checked the file drawer anyway, but none matched the name of the exhibit or even the subtitle: *The Roman Catholic Inquisition: History's Stain*. After authenticating himself to the museum primary firewall, he searched through the three "Work" folders on Lily's computer but found nothing corresponding to either the exhibit title or the acronym, which she was known for using more often than not. Jane Lowry's computer was the next possibility.

Exhibit Secretary and a British Museum veteran of twelve years, Jane had a reputation for logging every conversation she'd ever had, including those that took place in the ladies' room. She must have something on this, he chanted the whole way up the stairs to her office. Logging on too easily, Jane's computer was apparently not password protected.

Impossible.

He clicked on each folder stored on her desktop, and then recalled that all computers were linked by a server, which meant he could have done this research on Lily's computer. Then again, Wexler was closer to Lily's office, so he was probably better off up here.

A folder called "RCI2008" contained twelve files on the exhibit, including correspondence from the curator, jpegs of all of the images as well as inventory sheets of the pieces with titles, artists, dimensions, and media. Assuming the centerpiece image would be titled "RCI-1," Tal opened the file and recognized the image, with the central position of the Ferris wheel on the photograph, perfectly straight and aligned.

But this tells me nothing, he mused, deciding that it had to be something that happened post-delivery and pre-installation. The installation logs showed a catalog of abbreviated titles, with columns at the top for dimensions, media, owner name, curator name, and a final column for comments. He scanned the entire list of twenty-eight pieces and saw that they each were identical with the exception of the titles, which read as RCI1, RCI2, et cetera. The last column in the RCI1 row had nothing typed. No comments, no stipulations, no details of the piece, no damage, nothing whatsoever to explain why that picture was mounted crooked.

Tal took the back staircase this time to return to the main exhibit room on the first floor. The wall-mounted security module accepted the code he had punched in for the past six years; it paused after the last number and changed the blinking red light to a solid green. Tal exhaled slowly and pulled the picture off the wall and carried it to the windowsill where ambient moonlight spilled across the floor. He found a small piece of writing paper stuck inside the bottom of the frame, pushing against the relief.

... Police radios played their medley of static and hissing, doors squeaked open and then closed ...

Tal pulled the sheet of paper away and slid it into his pocket. And, as methodically as he had been trained to preserve the artifacts within the walls of the museum, he returned the picture to its position on the wall and reset the security alarm from the wall module.

He returned to the window ... and unfolded the page.

Eleven

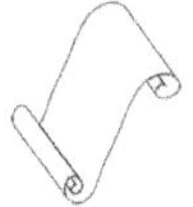

ROME

"Padre," a neatly dressed man announced as he propped open a set of heavy glass doors. "You are early today."

The man raised his eyes, blinked once, and kept walking. Polished black stick in his right hand; folio in his left. His steps, slow and deliberate, echoed off the Carrara marble floors of the building's foyer, one of four identical foyers in the Piazza del Campidoglio administration office. He lowered himself into a burgundy velvet chair, positioned diagonally between a marble fireplace and a wet bar with tall, crystal bottles.

The young man re-entered with a tray of croissants and a pot of something. Food, he'd always thought, should be eaten jovially, with music, wine, bright lights and warm companions, not in sterile white halls alone with anticipation.

"She's coming," the young man assured, quickly lowering his eyes before he retreated behind the glass doors.

Fondling the edge of a croissant, the man heard the hssh of the doors, this time a woman entered with her hands clasped loosely, in a pale yellow knee-length skirt and short jacket. She leaned down and kissed the man's right, then left cheek and sat on the edge of the fireplace before him, which looked a precarious perch, but the woman seemed completely at ease. He knew that smile.

"You look well today," she said, with a bigger smile.

"And you always look like a talk show host," the man commented but refused to smile.

"I have just three questions today," she said.

The man snickered. "And I doubt I have any answers for you."

"Should I bother, then?"

"I have come all this way today," he replied. "Why not?" The man sighed long and deep.

"You come here every week though, of your own accord, despite what your doctor says. So that argument won't work."

That smile again. He cringed inside. "Ask your question, Ariana. Then I'll be good enough to leave you to your legal battles and whoever it is you wage war against here."

She blinked, impassively. "Utility companies. Mostly."

"I don't care about the legal profession" the man confessed.

The woman paused and wrestled a tiny notebook and small pen from the folds in her skirt. She opened to a bookmarked page and breathed.

"Do you want it?" she asked.

"Yes."

"Do you need it?"

"Yes."

"What would you give for it?"

"What do you want?"

"All that you have."

Twelve

SOMEWHERE

He knows. I'm nearly certain of it. Not that I've made so much as a single sound in here, wherever "here" is, and not that I haven't tried to conceal my betrayal in constantly plotting my escape. I hear confidence in the heavy footsteps, an angst, perhaps arrogance, as if he saw the doorknob, felt and heard the jangling of metal to wood when he gripped it with his meaty hands. It reminds me of the movie *Misery* when James Caan realizes that Annie Wilkes is on to him, and the ugly truth of his impending doom.

He doesn't blame me for my attempted escape, my captor. From the beginning, whenever that was, I've sensed a sort of passive empathy in the way he glances at me and quickly averts his eyes, delivers my food tray, and the way his monstrous hands knock ever gently on the door to my cell. He pities me. But even more than pity, my captor is afraid. Not of me, certainly. He's afraid of himself around me. Of what he might do to me inadvertently, without knowing it, having so little control over his emotions and impulses. Though I've never seen him in full flesh, I know his overall size and sense the power of his bulky frame. Wide, leathery paws like oven mitts grabbed me from outside the car and whisked me into the dark van like a sack of cotton balls. I saw the back of his head as he left my room the first night. Hair grows haphazardly on his misshapen head – I can only surmise this is due to a birth defect, or else disease.

His name, from two phone conversations I overhead, is Buckle. Perhaps Buchel, spelled in Yiddish, or maybe an English name, Arbuckle. Maybe Buckle's a nickname. Maybe he's a spy. Either way, he takes orders from a man he's deathly afraid of. So maybe his size makes up for lack of brains. Then again, though, as I always seem to remind myself too late, things aren't always what they seem.

My captor, on the surface, is a savant – tall and blocky stature, clunky steps plodding across the wood floors, shaking the teacups in the corner hutch as he moves, barely speaking, moaning and crying in his sleep – a tortured, troubled soul. But is he? Perhaps he's the Professor of Linguistics at The Sorbonne, speaks twelve languages, does logarithms in his head and can spell every African capital.

I hear him downstairs now and chuckle at my overestimation of his abilities. More likely, he is neither smart nor dumb but somewhere in between, a social misfit, child abuse victim, who for fun draws chalk body outlines in the street and lays in them until onlookers approach and scream.

His boisterous approach to my room includes the stomping steps, labored breathing, coughing, clearing his throat, as though he's been asked to do the Olympic Triathlon at a moment's notice. The lock clicks and the door opens, first just a few inches, then swings wide.

He looks at my breasts; then his eyes drop down to my waist, then lower, down to my long legs and back up again. As he feels me glaring at him, he meets my gaze and jerks his head toward the living room.

"Come."

I follow him, slowly, still groggy from whatever I was forced to inhale in the back of the dark van. He moves close, his long nose touching my hair. The narrow hallway is dark, and the ceiling slopes down just over the man's head. It is awkward for a moment, this moment, while he seems to decide what to do with me next. Then, as abruptly as the door to my room opened, he pushes open another door directly behind me - a bathroom the size of a closet.

"Go. You. Now."

I nod and vanish behind the door. The light switch reveals a single unsheathed bulb with a long dangling chain. I hear him behind the door, listening to the sound of my piss in the toilet bowl. He's wondering about me - whether I am weak or strong, whether I will resist him and what my method of resistance will be, whether I can think fast or will make a compliant victim.

The bathroom window is boarded up with plywood, two layers thick. The sink has no water, the toilet doesn't flush. Just kill me now, I think, focusing my thoughts on Alex. But even this doesn't quell the anticipation buzzing inside my chest.

Sitting, wiping, then sitting some more, a new fear climbs through my body. My face, I feel the muscles, is blank and contracted, the pale skin even paler than a moment ago. I try to move my fingers, my arms, but the signal from my brain has disconnected from my flesh and limbs.

I hear the first knock, but even this sounds farther away than the other side of the door. "*Depechez-vous!*"

I know in less than thirty seconds the door will be pulled from its hinges and the large angry face and those giant hands will pull me off the toilet, in my indecent state, and God knows what will happen then. But I can't make myself move. I tighten the muscles in my face, my neck, to coax the rest of my muscles to respond in kind, but they're not listening. The unwelcome drug still flows through my veins. I feel my mouth open as I try to speak but nothing comes out. Not even a moan. I hate my captor right now, for not realizing his effect on my psychological state, and for not caring.

Alex, where are you?

Banging now. First three, more yelling, pause, then five more bangs. The wood splinters with his last punch and I now know the certainty of my fate. In my mind, I travel back through time to the back of the van, and inject my arm with twice as much of the magic yellow liquid that kept me sleeping for three days. For the beauty of this drug is that it absorbs fear.

His red, bulbous fist pushes through the door. The flimsy wood boards fly away from the frame. He kicks through the bottom portion and lifts me off the commode. The green eye, the hazy one, stares off somewhere else, idly waiting while the dark blue one, the smarter one, stares unblinking at the exposed flesh of my thighs and buttocks.

My fear, in this old house, in the arms of my giant savant, is like a tarantula. It lives, usually dormant, in the pit of my belly - sleeping, beautiful, gently coiled with its hair matted down neatly over its folded legs. But now, I feel the legs unfurl as the dark blue eye studies me, squinting, discerning, reading and assimilating all it can about me, a fragile victim.

Buckle carries me over his shoulder down the hall and up a short flight of stairs. Under the eaves again, a window bleeds moonlight into the room, illuminating a path from the doorway to a sad, little bed with no pillows. He flings me over his shoulder onto the mattress and stares hungrily at my waist, visible from the wrinkled sweater scrunched up around my bra. Still unable to move, I look away from him and count the lines in the paneled walls. One … two …five … six …

His hands clasp and wring, as I watch him losing a war between primal urge and reason. And with every inch of his impending approach, my tarantula unfolds, first its legs, then its large head raises, the legs bend and push up, its hair stands erect making a majesty out of its previous withered guise.

I can barely make my lungs take in air. Some part of me knows I'm about to die, and all I can do is blink my helpless eyes.

The spider is standing inside my stomach now, and begins walking up my sternum to the inside of my ribcage. A symbol of my fear, the tarantula puffs up as the man inches toward me, glancing every two seconds out the window as if his director might catch him in an untoward act. I want so desperately to pull up my underwear and pants, as I know the sight of female flesh is more than Savant can bear. After all, a human without brains or intellect is nothing but brute strength and primal urge.

In a parallel universe, I might have felt compassion.

His touch is a fine sandpaper burnishing my skin, moving slowly left and right. He bites his own lip to quell the fiery desire inside him and, when the lip bleeds, he knows what he is then. A bloody demon, a monster held six feet four inches in the air, looming over me, hungrily taking what I don't have the strength to withhold.

The tarantula is three times its normal size now, growing and expanding with every touch. Both of Savant's hands are around my slender waist and moving upward toward the breasts he can't take his eyes off. I breathe in, I breathe out, and suddenly feel the air balloon in my lungs. I rise up and shove against the man's forearms, but it is too late. The greeny eye lays in wait, fearing what the other eye will see, and the dark blue one glints back at me, the completed act of violation already formed in its memory.

And once again, I am forced into paralysis. I can't move, can't breathe. I lie still with my tarantula furling its long legs around the inside of my throat.

Alex …

Thirteen

LONDON

Tal held the piece of folded paper in his hands before opening it, noticing the sudden silence in the corridor.

3:20 a.m.

His vision, slightly blurred as he unfolded the white sheet of paper near the side window, focused on one phrase of text typed in the very center: "RCI4".

A catalog reference. Listening into the hallway still, he scanned the array of pictures - twenty-eight of them in total. RCI4 - the fourth installation in the series, or else fourth piece of art from the left, fourth from the right?

Had he stuck his penlight in his back pocket, as he usually did? He fumbled his hands around and drew it out, pressing the tiny button to illuminate a round spot on the tiled floor. And then he began - left to right.

But how would he know?

Scanning Jane's printout of the list of artwork in the exhibit, number four referred to an oil painting of Pope Theophilus of Alexandria. He scanned left to right from the centerpiece relief and found *Cyril of Alexandria* by J. Savage dated 1813. Were Cyril and Theophilus the same person and, if so, why him?

After checking for the ground floor security guard, Tal lifted picture number twenty-eight off of the wall. It came up too easily, or easily enough to trip Tal's panic response.

What have I forgotten? The alarm! Did I press the security code? Why can't I remember? And then a scarier thought hit him. If I didn't press the code, what's happened to the alarm?

But a jarring, familiar stab in the pit of his stomach redirected his thoughts away from the museum's security system.

Another piece of paper, folded the same way as the first, crumpled slightly with typed text, and strategically placed in the very center of the page:

154 Carnaby Street, 8B

Soho

020 412 3579

Carnaby, near Oxford Street and Regent Street. Tal slipped into the second-floor freight elevator, which led to the parking garage.

After a short drive, he found himself wandering around his own apartment, confused and disoriented, folding and unfolding the strange sheet of paper that randomly, inexplicably, had ended up in his hands. He hardly ever resorted to external stimulation to help himself relax, but a bottle of cognac left over from last year's New Year's Eve party seemed appropriate in the circumstances.

He poured three fingers into a tall glass on the counter and chucked it to the back of his throat at lightning speed, swallowed, and chased the throat burn with water. The remnants of a hasty life stared back at him, from the jacket tossed on the back of a living room chair, dishes in the sink, and a six-inch stack of unopened mail on the table by the door.

Too late to do anything about all that now, he thought, there's only one thing left to do. Picking up his mobile, his fingers trembled. From the alcohol, that had to be it. He punched in the number.

"Hello?" an old man answered on the fourth ring.

It was only then that Tal wondered what he might actually say. "Um, right. Hello. I got your number from a friend, and, um ..."

"What friend?" a Rottweiler voice barked. "Who is this?"

"My name... you see, I work at the British Museum. I'm one of the ... curators." Pause. This half-truth gave him a measure of credibility, but nothing more. "I was wondering," he went on, "what you might know about ... the Inquisition."

Click.

Damn it. He slammed down the phone and instinctively redialed, but then hung up before the line started ringing again.

On the way down the stairs, he tried to calculate the distance from his flat to the old man's Soho residence. This time of night, a five-minute drive.

154 Carnaby Street was one of those ancient, Victorian-era apartment buildings converted in the 1950s into art studios. Apartment 8B was at the end of the west hallway on the first floor. Tal smirked as he saw the first bit of daylight peek out over the horizon. Ignoring the doorbell, he knocked three times. Exactly sixty seconds later, he knocked again, this time louder and four times. The next time would be five times, and so on.

No answer.

But he heard footsteps approach the door. They paused and someone checked the peephole. He politely stepped two inches back to allow his boyish looks to disarm the man's fears of burglary.

"You the man on the phone? I've got nothing to say."

"I'm Tal. Tal Gardner."

The door opened a crack. "I thought your name was Adrian. There is a curator by that name at the museum. I checked."

"Checked how, exactly, seeing as it is four in the morning? Adrian Marcali's number is not listed individually on the website masthead, nor in the printed directory – only the department heads are listed. So you must know Adrian personally." Tal stepped away after he finished, to both size up the man and allow the stranger to do the same.

The door opened wider. The man appeared about sixty-five years old, tall, with a large, roundish head and a thin mat of dark gray hair.

"What do you want from me? I know nothing of ... what did you say on the phone ... the Spanish—"

"Yes, yes, the Inquisition. Or more precisely, the Roman Catholic Inquisition. And I beg to differ. I believe that you tacked your contact information to the back of one of the exhibit pieces, for what reason God only knows." Tal folded his arms.

The man hung his head and rubbed his eyes. "What did you say your name was? I think I might just call the museum and let them know that you're harassing elderly men at all hours of the morning. I'll call that man, Adrian-something was it?"

"So you don't know him?"

The man's face remained frozen.

"Your answer to that question is of great curiosity to me."

"And why is that?"

"Because Adrian Marcali's very likely dead."

The tall forehead furrowed. A pair of eyes, that clearly belonged to a man in his sixties but looked as if they had seen the span of three hundred years, widened into globes. "Why are you here?" the man said, opening his front door a bit wider.

"You summoned me, that's why. As a matter of fact, I have no idea why this means anything to me at all. I was sort of compelled, for inexplicable reasons, to look into the Inquisition exhibit at the museum tonight, and to try to determine why your address and telephone number were on the back of one of the paintings. I think," Tal shook his head, "that it has something to do with a painting of Pope Theophilus." Tal looked at the ground. "It's ridiculous, I know. I shouldn't have bothered you. You probably know less than I do about it."

In a way, he was waiting for the man to stop him as he lingered on the edge of the doorway. But that only happened in the movies.

Thirty minutes later Tal's head hit the pillow and his lids dropped like tiny guillotines. Lying on top of the bedspread, fully clothed, he dreamed the same thing as every other night - imagining lying next to Lily Frasier - and then the shadowy sound of a doorbell chiming. There it was again. Only louder.

Wait here, darling, I'll get that, he told Lily's imaginary image.

Ding dong.

It chimed again, followed by a fist pounding on the wood.

His eyes snapped open. Sitting up, he looked at the empty sheets beside him and considered the pounding on his front door.

5:40 a.m. No Lily. No dream.

Ding dong.

The peephole revealed nothing, as it was too dark to see and the hallway bulb had burned out three weeks ago.

He clicked the deadbolt and opened the door. The old man from Carnaby.

"Mr. Gardner," barked the gravelly voice.

"What?"The man stared blankly at him for several moments. "Well, you had the audacity to wake me up. Now I've done the same to you."

"Congratulations. Now—" he yawned.

"May I come in?"

They sat quietly, civilized, like two old-world gentlemen in the overly decorated living room of Tal's flat - the room Lily had insisted on decorating for him out of her love of interior design. She'd found frugal ways to incorporate a Persian rug, diaphanous draperies, new windows, a refinished credenza, mahogany end tables, and alarming abstract art. Tal poured his guest a cognac, assuming by his age and attire that he was accustomed to such things. If he smoked, he would have offered a Cuban cigar.

Someone in an upstairs apartment clicked across the wood floors in loud shoes. He wondered about the man, wondered what he had done after he left, wondered about the man's deliberation in deciding whether or not to come out into the evening cold and clarify matters, or muddle them, with additional information. And how had he known where he lived?

"Would you like another, sir?" Tal asked when the man drained his glass.

"Don't call me that."

"Well, seeing as you haven't yet told me your name and you're obviously at least ninety, I thought it an appropriate choice."

"Max," the man sniggered.

"Well then, may I ask, Max, the same question you asked of me two hours ago? What are you doing here?"

"To warn you," he answered quickly. The man moved to the edge of his chair.

"About what?"

"About asking questions."

"As I recall, I've only asked one. And I think my reasons for asking were fairly sound. Don't you? I mean, who else would purposely plant your contact information on the back of an exhibit painting? Had to be someone who knew the security code to dismantle the alarm prior to taking down the picture. And, while we're asking questions, why did they choose to put this information behind the only two pieces of art that depict Cyril of Alexandria? He's not exactly a household name."

"So you're an Inquisition scholar?"

Tal sighed. "Well, no. In fact, I've never been interested in it."

"You might not like what you hear, and once you hear it, there's no going back."

"Okay," Tal nodded. "Blue pill, red pill. I'll take the—"

"So I ask you to seriously consider whether you want to take on any new information, or if you'd prefer to go on living in ignorant bliss and live a happy, normal life as a productive young man, a museum curator, someone destined for a good life, marriage, a family, prosperity and longevity."

Tal rose and paced the floor in front of the bay window. "What the hell are you talking about? I don't know anything about what you know, or anything about you for that matter."

"To warn you," he answered quickly. The man moved to the edge of his chair.

"About what?"

"About asking questions."

"As I recall, I've only asked one. And I think my reasons for asking were fairly sound. Don't you? I mean, who else would purposely plant your contact information on the back of an exhibit painting? Had to be someone who knew the security code to dismantle the alarm prior to taking down the picture. And, while we're asking questions, why did they choose to put this information behind the only two pieces of art that depict Cyril of Alexandria? He's not exactly a household name."

"So you're an Inquisition scholar?"

Tal sighed. "Well, no. In fact, I've never been interested in it."

"You might not like what you hear, and once you hear it, there's no going back."

"Okay," Tal nodded. "Blue pill, red pill. I'll take the—"

"So I ask you to seriously consider whether you want to take on any new information, or if you'd prefer to go on living in ignorant bliss and live a happy, normal life as a productive young man, a museum curator, someone destined for a good life, marriage, a family, prosperity and longevity."

Tal rose and paced the floor in front of the bay window. "What the hell are you talking about? I don't know anything about what you know, or anything about you for that matter."

The old man shook his head.

"What, then? What? What do you have to tell me that will change my life?"

"Secrets."

Fourteen

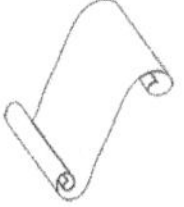

LONDON

"I don't know what secrets you feel you have to tell me, but I believe I only asked one question."

"What was that?"

"If you knew anything about Cyril of Alexandria."

Max stared at the floor.

"You know of this painting?" Tal lowered his voice. "You've seen it?"

The man blinked back at him and then stared.

Tal thought for a moment. Lily, Adrian, the book theft and the police. Since the two books disappeared from the second floor, Adrian Marcali had been shot and Lily had disappeared. Not only that, but the very day of the theft, Lily had an urgent phone call from her sister in Italy and no one's seen her since.

"Are you saying there's some connection between the recent museum theft and that particular exhibit painting?"

The old man thought for a moment. "I'm not saying anything, now, am I?"

"But that is what you think. It's your inclination."

Silence.

"Look," Tal sighed, "I know nothing about you and I presume you know even less about me. But—"

"Then you presume wrong."

Tal gave an exhausted sigh. "Let me just state the obvious, then. Seems it's all I'm good at lately. Here we are, two strange men, sitting together in the dark, drinking cognac at five-thirty in the morning. Logic would suggest that if we don't know each other in an obvious way, then something else has brought us together."

"Not an unreasonable assumption."

Tal moved to the window again and paced. The dove gray sliver on the horizon had thickened, lightening the edges of brick buildings. "Is it that painting that's brought us together? Is there, perhaps, something else we both know about it?"

"Move away from the window, Mr. Gardner."

Tal jerked his head up. The old man was still perched on the edge of the armchair. "Why?"

"It may not be safe."

"Are you going to ask me to tape an "X" on the glass?'

"If you're asking if I believe extra-terrestrials have been roaming the earth for decades, no. But if you're asking whether I believe in secret government plots and massive cover-ups, well, that's something else entirely."

"Getting back to my original question then, I will safely assume that yes, you do know something about the exhibit painting and, for argument's sake, let's assume that you planted that contact information on the back of the painting yourself."

The old man raised and lowered a brow.

"What about my other question? What about a connection between the painting and the theft of those two books?"

"Would you really call them books?" the old man asked.

"What would you call them?"

"Keys."

"To what?"

"That's something you'll have to answer for yourself."

"Are you saying that the museum exhibit on the Inquisition relates to two of the most significant books in literary history?"

The man blinked back. A silent affirmation.

"Or are you saying that ..." Tal paused to gather his thoughts and resumed his spot by the window. "...that perhaps the *content* of the painting has something to do with the missing books?"

"I'm not saying anything."

"Then why did you come here? Incidentally, you interrupted the most incredible dream any man could ask for."

"If it involves Ms. Frasier, I don't want to hear about it," the man said and his face twitched on one side.

Why not, Tal wondered. "Lily ... so you know her, too? What are you really doing here?"

"I told you - to warn you."

"About what? How many ways do I have to ask?"

"About your line of questioning. You're certainly smart enough to be asking the right questions, but the last person who asked such questions has been dead for eight years."

"Who was that?"

"My partner. He was ... how shall I put it ... quite possibly the greatest historian and most gifted researcher of this century. A man of science, a teacher, and one of the most enlightened minds I've ever encountered."

Tal leaned forward. "A writer?"

"No, an archaeologist and the most prominent linguist of our time."

"Who?"

The old man laughed lightly. "Soren Careski."

Fifteen

SOMEWHERE SOUTH OF ROME

"Email?"

"Keep your voice down! Are you mad? If they know we speak the same language they'll separate us." Mona Delfreggio stopped talking and listened to voices outside the door. In the dark, she pointed in their direction. Alex turned his head and crept back to his part of the cell.

"You have to tell me about that email," Alex pressed. "That's what all this is about."

"Why? Who cares? I get emails all the time."

"Not like that one, you don't."

She studied him with wide eyes, eyes that for the first time he actually saw from the shards of reflected moonlight. Full brown eyes, slightly elongated, like Cleopatra, high cheekbones and an alluringly downturned shape to her mouth that cast a sadness upon the smooth face.

"You got it too?"

Alex sighed. "I don't know ... what I got, really. I just know that since I downloaded and printed it, my life as I've known it has completely fallen apart."

"Describe it," Mona said, inching closer. She kept an eye on the door to the cell.

"An image of a page with a bunch of strange script that I didn't recognize."

"You didn't?" she asked, dubious.

"Well, I have my theories, but I know very little about ancient scripts."

"Who said it was ancient?"

"I just said—"

"You're right, it is ancient. Probably Coptic. Yes?"

How could she know this? "Could be anything," he shrugged.

"I got the same email, though it was intended for my sister. She works for the British Museum."

Alex worked the bits of new information through the grate in his head. "What does she do there?"

"Director of Medieval Antiquities."

He shook his head.

"She was on her way to meet me at the Angelica Library in Rome when I was taken. She could be here, for all I know."

"With my wife," Alex added and heard a clanking metal sound on the floor below them.

Mona stood and came to sit beside Alex. "Why did they take her?"

He shook his head. "If I hadn't gotten the email, I might have suspected it was some kind of revenge for a story I wrote, maybe some politician's goons, Mafia, whatever."

"But now?"

"In light of the email, I suspect someone's really looking for my father. I suppose I am too."

"Where is he?"

"Dead."

"So … you're looking in graveyards, or what?"

"He may not really be dead, but the rest of the academic world thinks so."

"Do you?"

Long pause, deep sigh, cold air, darkness. "I don't know."

"How can you be so unemotional about it?"

Another deep sigh, which led to another sigh, and something loosened inside Alex's chest. A tightness that had been growing, tighter and tighter, maybe over the past eight years. Eight years since Soren disappeared, and only a few months since he'd actually started thinking about him again. How was it possible to lose a father and block out an entire lifetime of experience and memories? This stranger was right – why *was* he so frozen about it? He felt a cinderblock on his chest start to give way, a warming in his chest as he thought of Simone, and Soren, and what his house would look like when he returned to Herald Square. He thought of Corinna, and the office and his legacy as a writer. It all cracked open in that moment, a cinderblock smashed into a thousand pieces. He felt hot tears on his cold cheeks. He didn't try to stop them.

Then he felt Mona's hand on his shoulder. "I'm sorry. I can be so callous sometimes. Forgive me."

He didn't move to wipe away evidence of his emotion, of his weakness. Around Simone, he would have done this, Corinna, any of his friends. But around this strange, young woman, his captive co-habitant, he felt no need to cover his vulnerability. God help me, he thought.

Simone had been the first woman he slept with after the divorce, and the first woman he ever in his life totally fell in love with. But in this dreary place, a prison cell with no lights or heat, he knew something could happen with this strange woman, with Mona Delfreggio. It hadn't yet, but it could. He was weak, she was strong, she was okay with his weakness, and that was a quality that instantly bonded a man with a woman, or at least until she made him sorry for trusting her.

Wasn't that the typical pattern? One person opens heart, other person consoles them, *first person* stomps on other person's heart, and the other heart closes. Mars, Venus, different planets were the least of it.

"Did you—" Alex turned toward the cell door.

"Yeah, I heard it too. Should we see if it's unlocked?"

Alex grabbed her arm and held her there. "Wait. Don't move yet. Get back to your place over there. It could be a trap." Mona moved five feet away toward the back wall and they waited there, in silence, in darkness, for thirty minutes without talking or moving. In those minutes, Alex counted the sounds. Water dripped from the ceiling into a shallow pool on the floor, crickets screeched, Mona's labored breathing, intermittent footsteps from a room at the end of a hallway, and the murmur of voices from an upper floor.

"Are we ever getting out of here?" Mona asked softly, breaking the silence.

"Do you believe in miracles?"

"No."

"Then probably not."

"Oh, you thought I wanted the truth. Apparently, I wasn't clear."

Pushing himself to a standing position, Alex felt the sticky flume of blood cake through his tired veins.

Rohypnol. That was what she called it, wasn't it?

He should know about it since he had written about the date rape drug once.

"I'm gonna see if the door's open and go scout around."

Mona jumped up. "Are you fucking crazy? Do you have a gun? Do you have any kind of weapon with which to defend yourself? You're still seventy-five percent under the influence, so to speak. Let me go on the suicide mission."

"No."

"What did you have with you when they took you?" she asked.

"A violin case."

She looked at his hands. "You don't look like a musician."

"Never said I was."

He turned the door handle an inch to the left, then another inch. He felt Mona breathing just behind him. "It's unlocked. I'll come back and get you shortly."

"Don't say what you don't mean."

He turned back to look at her. She was leaning down with her hands on her knees. "I wouldn't leave you here."

"Why not? You don't even know me."

He leaned close to her face. Her eyes widened. "Because we're being held captive in the pit of some creepy old dungeon, and there are, no doubt, fifty kinds of monsters down here."

"Thanks."

He smirked. "Anytime."

Sixteen

LONDON

The moon, fixed like an anchor to the vast ocean-sky, stared. Not mocking tonight, not laughing its devious, hideous laugh, it seemed almost sympathetic now. Tal tried to connect with it, to the moon over London, the city of his world. Instead, he just felt alone and scared.

Another hour. More darkness, and a denser, thicker cold that showered in through his wool coat and sweater to the thin cotton of his Oxford shirt and the untouched white of his own flesh. This is a fragment of a life, he thought. Hardly living, hardly breathing, Lily off God knows where, the department splitting apart at the seams.

He looked at his watch again, this time under the flickering streetlight, uncaring now of things like concealment and the integrity of surveillance. 6:30 a.m. It would be light soon, and that would mean that Max Dearden hasn't left his home in exactly twenty-four hours.

Max Dearden, this stranger whom the universe presented on a silver platter, a stranger who came to him in a daydream within the main exhibit room of the museum, a stranger with whom he had no previous connection but now, what, was supposed to be a shaman? Or his guardian angel? Was he an opportunity for spiritual growth or a catalyst for research? Was he a connection to the past? If so, whose?

The question continued its slithering path through the passive parts of his brain while he contemplated the logic of their chance meeting. Still, though, it persisted. Why has Max Dearden not left his apartment in twenty-four hours? The man was old, perhaps ailing. Or tired. Or just plain lazy. But the evil Sea Hag in his head, the voice of an old fear, the oldest of fears, suggested a fourth possibility.

The door was unlocked. Typical, in a way, yet atypical in another. This part of Soho, stained with a past of sex shops, now housed cardiac surgeons and barristers, a few members of parliament and the rest of that vast, mystery-caste representing everything between East London and Buckingham Palace. So Max Dearden left his door unlocked. So what? Even so, Tal proceeded cautiously through the dark space. Eyes still adjusting, he made out a fairly large hallway that led to the kitchen. Small, maybe too small for a regular kitchen, yet these homes did not customarily contain servant's or guest's quarters. All right, he thought, hall, very small kitchen.

Maybe he doesn't eat much. He drew slow breaths as he walked the length of the entire apartment.

You're scared, said the Sea Hag voice. Scared to turn on the lights. Admit it! Tal shook his head and switched on a table lamp. Nothing but a living room, a very normal, ordinary living room. But the Sea Hag's voice moaned now, almost laughed at the sight of his fists clenched in steady oscillation. Max Dearden's dead, she kept saying.

"What's wrong with me?" Tal said into the cold quiet of the strange flat.

True, ever since he'd first seen the Inquisition painting, nothing had felt quite normal. Max Dearden knew something about this, and more than just a casual, conversational amount. He wasn't certain if Max actually put his own contact information on the photograph, but if he didn't, someone wanted the museum to know that he was connected, in some way, to the museum theft. The house was empty, he surmised, after walking through every room. Flipping off the lamp, he thought he sensed a slow movement near the door, almost as if he remembered hearing it before and it was being played back to him now.

Was that possible?

Fists clenched again, Tal moved down the dark hallway and into the small kitchen, still far too small for a regular kitchen, he thought again.

He heard the sound of bone on bone even before he felt the impact of a fist upon his right eye. "Oh," he groaned and fell back, collapsing in a heap on the hardwood floor. His eyes did a lightning scan of the room for his assailant, but only saw the foggy shape of a long coat. With one hand on his eye, the shape came toward him again, in languorous steps, almost suspended from the ground. Closer, closer, a hand stretched out of the dark cloak and pulled him to a standing position by the collar of his coat, and another hand bored into his stomach, collapsing him, once again, into a dark corner of Max Dearden's kitchen. He coughed up blood. He couldn't see it, but he had a metallic taste in his mouth, different from saliva.

Breathe, the Sea Hag's voice told him, taking care of him now just as she had one other time in his life. The voice warned him about this place, mistaking Max Dearden for dead.

Well, obviously NOT dead, Tal thought in response.

Then again, this assailant could hardly be the old man he had spoken to two nights ago. This assailant was younger, more agile, yet moving slowly. Someone strong and confident, but … perhaps … injured. Then he remembered the hand. It had slipped out of a long, charcoal-gray wool and cashmere overcoat from Harrods. He knew that coat. He had helped to select it … with Adrian.

Adrian Marcali? Here?

The first hand came out of the coat again and hoisted Tal's entire weight off the ground, and the second hand formed into a fist and cracked against his jaw. He fell against the wall and blacked out for a split second.

Adrian. Here. In Max Dearden's house. What in God's name was ...

"Stay away from here."

"Adrian? Is that you? I know it's you. Stop this. Stop it!" Bleeding and dizzy, Tal pulled his body weight up and crawled toward a floor lamp. The coat fell to the floor in front of him and Adrian stood there, his blond hair dirty and greased back, darkly circled eyes and a large bandage wrapped around his bare stomach. "Wh- are you - you were shot. Shot! Weren't you? The other night. I was there."

"You were there that night?" Adrian sat on the floor, knees bent with his head leaning on them like he hadn't slept in a fortnight. "Why didn't you stop him?"

"Who?"

Adrian Marcali shook his head in long back and forth motions. "Wexler. You cannot be here, Tal. Go home, I mean it. Stop asking the questions you're asking. Max is not here, I tell you. I've ... they've ... asked me to stop you." He looked at Tal, but his eyes darted left and right. "Don't you see? They wanted to do it themselves, they might've killed you. So I asked to do it. Go home, take a shower, and show up for work tomorrow morning like nothing's happened. Please, Tal, do as I tell you. Go and don't look back."

Tal stood over Adrian. "Like nothing's happened? In the past three days, the two most valuable books have been stolen, stolen, from the museum - you do know we're talking about the British Museum don't you? - stolen, I can still hardly believe the word as it comes out of my mouth, but yes, well, and now Lily's fled a police interrogation and hasn't been heard from again. You've been shot, Lily's office has been ransacked ... and you want me to, what, act naturally? Are you mad? Well yes, I assume as much seeing that you were shot—"

"By our security agent, no less," Adrian added.

"Wexler? No ..."

"Of course it was him,' Adrian said. "He was there."

"There?" Tal questioned. "He was with me in Lily's office, removing her confidential files and setting the whole place aflame. He's the one who made me call you at the airport. He had a pistol aimed at my forehead."

Tal replayed the scene as best he could, but now his mouth was bleeding and his right eye had swelled shut. "I was with him when we heard the first shots. So—"

Adrian stood and balanced himself with both hands on each side of the narrow doorway. He looked out of the back door, then back at Tal, and did this a few more times. "Whatever Wexler told you, he's lying."

He made eye contact now and fixed his eyes on Tal, unblinking. "Remember what I said. If you want to stay alive, go to work tomorrow."

The quietude of early morning shocked him. He heard his own footsteps on the concrete, the squawk of pigeons fighting over a scrap of bread beside an apartment building on the corner. With his left eye on the Thames, his right eye saw a blurry fog of blood, tears and wind. But he remembered an all-night bar somewhere nearby. Go left, the voice said to him. The Sea Hag's voice. He could listen to her, or do the exact opposite. Either way was as much a risk as the other.

He turned left. The lights from the bar's sign startled him. He stepped back two paces and peered, and barely saw the form of a man, a man he knew. Max. Thank you, voice, he thought and quickly approached the door.

"Looks like you need more than a drink if you don't mind my saying so." Max Deardon leaned on a bar stool and nodded at the bartender, who poured Absolute vodka, orange juice, tomato juice, a squeeze of lime, and coffee into a shaker. "Sit down."

"Just nothing with raw eggs," Tal said still standing.

"If I promise it'll heal what ails you, will you drink it?"

Tal watched unblinking as the bartender poured a dark pink mixture into a clear glass. Tal grabbed it and sucked it down like a shot, the quicker the better.

"Works best with a Guinness chaser," the bartender said and poured a glass from the tap. "Drink up."

Regaining his ability to breathe, rubbing his nearly broken jaw and wiping his constantly tearing right eye, Tal looked around the main room of the bar and walked to the end of the hallway, which led to a darkened back room, no windows, and four booths along the back. He heard Max's steps behind him.

"Ready to talk to me now, Mr. Dearden?" he asked him.

The man scanned Tal's face and swollen eye and jaw. "What the hell happened to you?"

"We'll get to that," Tal shot back.

"And I don't recall telling you my surname," Max added.

"You're all over the goddamned internet, aren't you? You *and* your dead partner both. I know how to read and I know how to research."

"I should think so. And so tell me, what have you learned in the course of your research?"

"That you and your partner are extinct. Like the bloody T-Rex. You don't exist, people like you. You're like microbes and strands of DNA, doing your secret, invisible work without anyone knowing and hoping no one sees, hoping no one person will take the time to actually grasp the gravity of your discoveries and the potency of your crimes."

"Crimes? My partner was one of the greatest contributors to the study of linguistics the world has ever seen."

"Your crimes, Mr. Dearden, were that you raped history. And your punishment, well, has already come to fruition I expect. Your partner, I assume, was killed? In his sleep perhaps, or drove off a mountain cliff? Usually how it happens."

"He disappeared."

"No body found, no confirmation of his death? My God, that must just kill a man like you."

Max stared into his empty beer glass. "Yes, it does."

"Why would he be a target?" Tal asked.

"Why not? He shook up common definitions of America's prehistory. Target, young man? You have no idea. In twenty-six years, Soren and I personally excavated hundreds of antiquities, carbon dated and authenticated even more, traveled to every continent on the planet, spoke at conferences, wrote controversial papers, hid from the press and in all that time, Soren was formulating a theory that the scientific and intellectual world wasn't ready for."

"What was that?"

"You seem to know all about me - you tell me."

Seventeen

LONDON

Tal only now noticed a grandfather clock in the corner of the room. Across from him, Max Dearden started in on his second coughing fit.

Two more tall ales arrived at their table, and Max grabbed his hungrily and downed half of it at once. "You never did tell me," he said gesturing to Tal's jaw and eye. "About that. Have a run-in with a wall or something?"

"A man using my face as a punching bag." Pause for emphasis. "In your flat, no less."

Max's eyes widened, then narrowed. "I don't think so."

"Oh, you don't? How the hell would you know, as you've obviously been camped out here for the past twenty-four hours." Tal downed the entire beer, and then belched with the volume of twenty drunken sailors. "It was a warning. I've been getting a lot of those lately."

Two more glasses arrived. Tal grabbed the one closest to him and chugged on it, slower this time, stopping once to breathe.

"What's your hurry?"

Tal regarded him slowly. "Drinking to forget."

"Forget what? Or who?"

Tal wriggled out of his jacket, watching it slip onto the wooden bench. "Why should I tell you?"

"I'm curious. You looked a bit haunted when you mentioned warnings."

"It's a who, all right, but not the woman I work with," Tal said.

"What does she warn you about?"

"You, for example."

"And she's a woman?"

Tal slid lower on the bench and stretched his legs out in front of him. "She's a companion."

"A lover?"

"Not that kind of companion."

"A golden retriever?"

"Fuck off."

Max, visibly curious, scooted out to the end of the booth. "Okay, so, you're saying ..."

"I'm not saying anything." Tal smiled inside, and a moment later felt the entire contents of his stomach threaten to rise up to his lips.

"Is she young or old?" Max asked him.

"Hard to tell. Quite old, I suspect."

"Alive or dead?"

Tal shrugged at the irony of not knowing. "Dead, most likely."

"Have you seen her face?"

"If you want to call it that."

"What does she tell you?"

"Usually nothing, and only in ways that your average normal person in possession of an average amount of sanity would never acknowledge." Tal sighed.

Max turned his empty glass on the table top. "I wonder what you'd tell me about her if you hadn't just drunk enough to drown a busload of grown men."

"I saw her underwater once when I was twelve. I was drowning, at least I thought I was, and she appeared next to me as if she'd been there the whole time, sort of materialized out of the cold molecules of salt water. Her presence calmed me, but when I looked at her, her visage, like some demonic sea angel, terrified me. Her legs were a mottled mix of sub-dermal fluid combined with a tapestry of twisted vines imprinted onto the skin. It was a hideous sight, and yet even at twelve, I sensed that she was going to take care of me all my life. Like some sort of spirit guide."

"A mermaid then?"

"I call her Sea Hag, with the face of Medusa, the vision of an old shaman, and the heart of a warrior."

"And what did Sea Hag tell you about me?"

Tal looked up at Max Dearden now and made himself study the clear blue eyes, the unkempt gray hair and naked forehead, eyes framed with bushy gray-black brows, and decided. "That I'd find you here."

Max held out his empty glass in a toast. "Here's to the tangled lies we tell - the ones we don't, send us to hell."

Eighteen

SOMEWHERE SOUTH OF ROME

Through the thin fabric of her jeans, the icy fever penetrated deep inside her skin. Mona had begun to shake over an hour ago. Now her teeth chattered, her hands shook. Pupils fully dilated, she sensed a dim light behind the heavy door and the implication of moonlight beyond the hard concrete wall.

Tears are just not an option right now, she told herself, her right eye momentarily wet. There was no time for such indulgences. Staying alive was the predominant focus. Breathe in, breathe out, try not to think about anything else.

A thump sounded from behind the cell's door. She looked up, squinting. A light surrounded the sound, promising change. The door opened two inches and she immediately retreated toward the back wall's thick shadows.

"It's me, don't be afraid."

Alex. This stranger named Alex Careski. Had he really come back for her? Done what he said he would and not left her there to rot or worse? My God, she thought, do men like this really exist?

"I would've bet everything that you'd never come back to get me."

"You're not why I came back. Hell, look around, the feng shui in here's fantastic."

"Idiot," she mumbled.

"Thought you didn't believe in miracles."

"You call this a miracle?" Mona replied.

"There are two guards at the end of this hallway and—"

"What did you see out there?"

Alex sighed. "I'm trying to tell you ... two guards, and there are cells just like this all along the bottom floor. The rest are empty."

"So what's your big idea? You got a lasso?"

"No."

"How about a gun?"

Mona watched him try to conceal a wry smile. "I'll bet you order everything on the side when you eat in restaurants," he said.

"Whatever."

"Okay, listen. Both guards are sleeping right now, but the staircase is right across from them so we'll be in stealth mode." He grabbed her shoulders. "Can you do that?"

"Better than you can."

Alex nodded, half smiling. "We'll see."

Single file, they hugged the wall along the concrete corridor. The guards, each mangy and middle-aged, dozed in hard chairs on each side of the hallway's entrance. Passing them, Alex led the way to the staircase, turned quickly to motion upward, and heard the click of a bullet pushed into the chamber of a revolver.

"Shit," he whispered, freezing mid-step.

"*Fermati dove sei*!"

The other guard, shaken to alertness, stood confused, saw the other guard and the two escapees and started yelling. He drew a gun from his holster.

Alex turned to look at Mona. "How are you at improvisation?"

Mona turned toward Alex, eyed the guards and started frantically brushing her chest and screaming with a terrified look planted on her face. She brushed and fanned her blouse in and out, jumping up and down and screaming.

Fear glazed across Alex's cheeks and eyes as he watched the display, impressed that she had stolen the guards' attention away from himself so quickly.

"A spider, there's a s-s-spider down my shirt! Get it off, get it out, get it out get it out!!!" More jumping, slapping her shirt, now twirling around, which resulted in her falling down the stairs toward the first guard. Alex tried to explain the situation to the other guard while the first one grabbed her arm. "Get it off, get it off!!! Oh, shit, I think it stung me. Alex, Alex!!" Now the fake tears. "What do I do?"

Alex lunged at her, unsure whether she was serious, and pulled up the back of her thin white blouse. Eyeing the guards and seeing that their attention was solely focused upon Mona's flesh rather than detaining them at gunpoint, he realized he was watching a pro.

"Take it off," he said in a commanding voice. "Your shirt, take it off, quickly. I see a red spot back here - you may have been stung." He turned to one of the guards. "*Ospedale? Ospedale*!"

Mona obliged, lifting the fabric effortlessly over her head. Six eyes were glued to her voluptuous breasts and now was not the time for modesty. While she frantically brushed her fingers against her skin, Alex stepped back three paces toward the guards' two empty chairs. Mona continued jumping around and actually simulated tears, as the guards tried to remember how to do their jobs.

With their attention rapt, Alex retreated momentarily to retrieve an iron pipe his hands had discovered in the cell. He returned with the pipe to find Mona completely topless, sobbing and screaming at the guards. "It bit me, here ... here, look!!"

Poor bastards, Alex thought.

Begging his eyes away from Mona's bare chest, Alex hit the first guard in the back of the knees with the pipe and sent him toppling forward in a loud "Ooh!" The second guard turned toward him. The pipe collided with his forehead, made a loud *clunk,* and the man fell back.

In two seconds the bra and blouse were returned to their original position, face dried of any semblance of weeping, and Mona had already taken one of the revolvers and stuck it in the back of her pants. Alex walked up to her, slowly, studying her face. "What are you doing?"

"What?"

"Put the revolver back."

"No way. If you want to be unarmed, that's your business. You and I were kidnapped and until I find out why and by whom, I intend to protect myself."

"And who do you think you are, Meryl Streep?" Alex reached around her waist and yanked the revolver from her waistband and tossed it on the floor by the toppled guards, then grabbed his violin case.

Mona raised a brow as he backed away from her. "What was that? You're welcome."

The stairs led to another set of hallways. Alex led them down the one heading left, which took them to a locked gate.

"Nice job. Where's your compass?"

Speeding down the same hallway, he didn't even turn.

Alex stopped moving and crossed his arms. He looked at her and raised a brow. "That was brilliant, you know."

"So I answered your question?"

"What question?"

"If I can improvise."

The other hallway led to a tall foyer and, behind it, an entrance to the outside. They both stood in the great driveway, dwarfed by the age and height of the ancient building. Alex scanned the exterior, thinking there should have been a moat with a drawbridge and tall spires jutting up into the night sky.

Following her up the hill, Alex felt a familiar cramp in the back of his left knee. "But your methods, from what I've seen so far, are a bit unconventional."

"That's what tactical training's all about. Acting on impulse rather than practicality. I've lived most of my life that way, by the seat of my pants."

Alex smirked.

"Don't say it."

Up on the road now, Mona looked at the lightening sky and breathed in the air. "I'd guess there's no cell phone service out here. My battery's dead anyway. How much time do we have?"

"Not long. I didn't hit them all that hard, and you never know how a body will react to something like that."

"No food, no water, just a violin case full of secrets. We're like that Fellini movie, *La Strada*."

The veil of darkness began to slide off a postcard landscape. A vista of segmented, rolling hills and estates with tile roofs reminded Alex of Simone and him on their honeymoon. Florence, Pisa, Verona. The sting of Simone's absence caused another tightening in his chest. Had he checked every room in the villa for her? Would they have brought her there, and brought him and Mona to the same place? Probably not. It had been, to his best estimation, three days and he was no closer to finding her.

And again, this stranger named Mona seemed to read his thoughts.

"She's not dead, you know."

Alex stopped walking. "And how would you know that?"

"I just know. I can't say where she is or why she was taken, but I have a feeling she's okay. Do you think she's in Rome?"

"Probably," Alex said, remembering the white index card left on his living room table. And if she had been in Rome, was she still?

An hour later as the sky lightened, they approached a small square with cafes on each side.

"Must be Tivoli, I saw a sign back there," Mona said.

Alex nodded. It was morning and he detected the faint scent of eggs and toast. The day felt almost normal for a minute.

"Give me your case," Mona said as they sat at an indoor table.

Alex looked down at it, wondering how many times Soren had actually played the violin before he started using the case as his secret container while traveling abroad. It was a brilliant idea, but even he couldn't admit that at the time. He laid it on the table between their plates.

Mona opened the lid and pulled out the four leather volumes and replaced the case under the table. "What are these? Yours?"

"My father's diaries," Alex whispered. "I took them before I left for the airport. After Simone was taken." He sipped espresso and squeezed his cheeks against the bitterness. "I don't know what took me down there—"

"Where?"

"My basement. I hadn't gone down there since Soren, my *father* disappeared. He'd kept boxes stacked floor to ceiling in the back room with the water heater. I never went in there. Simone did a few times, not to pry but just to sort of check on them. Then that day when everything happened," he swallowed, "I felt I needed to keep these with me."

"To protect them," Mona suggested.

"No, more like I might find answers in them. These are his professional journals that chronicled his entire career, supposedly, over about twenty-five years."

"What did he do?"

Alex tipped his head back and looked at the stained ceiling tiles. "So many things. He was mainly a linguist." He looked into Mona's dark, liquid eyes. "Do you know what that is?"

"Do you think I'm an idiot?"

He laughed. "Okay, well, linguist. We'll start there. But also an archaeologist, anthropologist, and epigrapher."

"And before you ask me, an epigrapher, what, studies ancient scripts? On rocks and things?"

"Very good. So he traveled the world, tracing the antecedents of these ancient scripts, and got himself into a heap of international trouble. That's the long and short of it I guess."

"That's the short of it. Give me the rest. It's not like I have to be someplace." Mona reached up and twisted her hair into a messy bun, thinking through the details. "Okay, you need to find your wife, and I need to get back to Rome and find my sister. The sooner we establish why we were taken and find the connection, the sooner we can restore some normality to our lives."

Alex flipped through the first journal. "He was one of the world's renowned scholars who established the authenticity of ancient documents. One of only two, maybe three in the world."

"Like the Dead Sea Scrolls or something?"

Alex stopped chewing. "Interesting that you say that. One of the documents he authenticated came from a region very close to where the scrolls were found."

"Israel, right?"

"Actually closer to the Egyptian border. They're these large formations," he said lowering his voice, "of caves in Nag Hammadi in the desert in upper Egypt where these monks found some papyrus books."

"When was this?" Mona asked.

"Forties. Mid-forties."

An old woman returned to the table, brought another basket of rolls, and looked disapprovingly at Mona. Alex asked her in Italian about a bus or train.

She answered something in Italian and fanned her arms pointing toward the village square.

Alex raised a brow. "*Si. Grazie.*"

"What was the text?" Mona pressed.

"He was always so damned secretive, we never knew what he was working on, my mother and I. Half the time, he was only given a segment of a text to authenticate and forbidden to have any contact with the owners of the other parts. It was this whole Catholic Church paranoia, and this fear that bad things would happen in the world if all three parts of the text were ever brought back together again. To this day, I don't think anyone really knows where they are, not all of them anyway."

Mona blinked her large, dark eyes at him. "I think you know where and what they are."

"Whatever you think I know, I don't. Soren was, well," he cleared his throat, "secretive's not a strong enough word. This one text, in particular, was something from the Bible or related to a Biblical text, or that's what Soren thought, anyway. Maybe a duplicate of it, or a different version? All I know is that after Soren determined its authenticity, people started showing up and asking to have meetings with him all hours of the night. That was around the time he started disappearing for weeks at a time. This went on steadily until he finally disappeared eight years ago."

Mona leaned back against her chair and glanced out the window. "And these diaries are a full chronology of your father's discoveries? They're not just of the Egyptian texts, are they?"

"Oh, no. They go back many years, I think. Matter of fact, I'd be surprised if any of these even make a reference to the Gospel of St. Thomas."

"Gospel of St. Thomas?"

"What?" Alex said.

"Well, you know how I told you my sister works for the British Museum? Well, on the day I got the strange email, she said that two ancient texts had been stolen from the British Museum. I think one of them contained that gospel. I'm almost sure of it. They were found where the Dead Sea Scrolls were found."

Alex glanced around the interior of the tiny café, surveying the line of people walking past the door and the fossilized cooks mumbling to each other in the kitchen. "And the email, the same one that I got on the same day, was supposedly sent by Soren. The originator's email address was **careskisor@attbi.com**."

"Does that mean your father's alive?"

"Or someone wants me to think so."

"Why, though? What would someone have to gain by you thinking he's alive?"

He shook his head. "If I knew the answer to that, we wouldn't be here."

"Have you had any other emails since the one we both received? I mean, have you checked your email since then?"

Alex lowered his head. "I've been a bit busy."

"Sorry. If we make it back to Rome, we'll find a library or something that has public computers and check remotely. I can check mine, too. Have you got it with you?"

"What, the email?" Alex reached into his back pocket and pulled out the folded sheet and sneered at it. He tossed it on the table.

"And you think this is Coptic?" she asked.

"Why do you say that? I never suggested as much."

"It could be many things. Hebrew, Greek, many of them overlapped depending on where you were at the time." Mona picked up the sheet and absently paged through the back of one of the journals on the table. "Just out of curiosity, what language was the gospel your father authenticated?"

"Coptic, actually. Don't know how I remember that, but I do. It's an ancient form of Egyptian that's based on Greek, from what I remember."

Mona picked up the email page again. "Could this be Coptic?"

Alex paused to penetrate her thoughts. "You're thinking …"

"Yeah."

"Possible. No way to tell, though, as we don't have the gospel text with us."

Mona tapped her long fingernail on the table. "Don't we, though?" Mona patted the journal with her right hand. "Tell me, if you were Soren and you were asked, or commissioned, to authenticate one of the most significant Christian relics, if it was that, for instance, would you be so stupid as to simply hand it back after you'd reached your conclusions, or would you take every available risk to conceal and even duplicate it somehow?"

He raised a brow. "Interesting theory. So you're suggesting that they're in here somewhere?"

"Not necessarily, but somewhere. Maybe that's why he disappeared."

"Or maybe he wanted to disappear," Alex sighed. "He had a long history of unexplained absences, explained away by flimsy excuses and imaginary governments paying him to fly to Dublin and look at ancient Ogham stones, or urgent visits to castles and palaces to view the contents of last wills and testaments, or heads of state who asked him to authenticate a fossil. I remember that whole archaeopteryx debacle. That one lasted a good ten years before he finally—"

"Alex?"

"What?"

Mona stood and smiled. "I just remembered something," and she pulled her cell phone out of her boot. "I charged it at the airport for a few minutes and stuck it in there just before the van pulled up." It powered on and showed three bars' worth of battery.

She hit Lily's speed dial and waited, tapping her long nails on the table.

"Lily, it's me," she said into the phone. One of the old women in the kitchen looked up and started yelling in Italian. "I'm just outside Rome and don't even ask me how I got here. I'm okay, call me if you get this message. And I'll try calling you again once I find a hotel and charge my phone. Don't worry Miguel for the time being - I'll deal with him later." Mona disconnected the call and played with her coffee cup.

"Miguel?"

Mona's cheeks reddened. "Boyfriend, I suppose."

"Lover?"

"Yes."

"Companion?"

"Hardly." She bit into the bread.

"Soulmate?"

"Why do you care? You're happily married. I'm sorry. I'm so bad at discretion. Some people have it down to a science, like my sister. Guess that's why she's the director of a major European museum and I'm, well, a ..."

"A work in progress," Alex said kindly.

Mona reached up and grabbed his hand. "I can't say I've known too many men like you in my life."

"Maybe now that's gonna change."

Nineteen

LONDON

Even from the side entrance, Tal Gardner could see a twenty-foot queue of people at the front entrance to the museum. And it was barely ten o'clock. What sort of urgency could occur to bring this many people here at this time of day, he wondered, grateful that Bethany Godwin, the Antiquities Department Administrator and official Mother Hen, had arrived early and made coffee.

"Mister Gardner," she said in her singing voice, "you look absolutely awful."

"I'll give you a million pounds if you bring me a cup of that."

"I'm not your secretary. Besides, I'm stepping out in a minute, I got Lily's winter coats cleaned last week and I'm picking them up this morning."

She returned in two minutes with a cup of coffee and a blueberry muffin. "A million pounds, really?"

"You do Lily's dry cleaning for her?"

"She's busy!" she argued. "I only work part-time and besides, you know me, I like to help people."

"Any word?" Tal gently asked.

"Well, her sister Mona's got the police out looking everywhere, but Wexler's trying to keep it quiet. Feels that enough adverse attention has resulted from the missing texts and, from what I've heard, he blames her for their disappearance."

"They're not missing, they were stolen! Why am I the only one who thinks this?"

Bethany backed two feet away from his desk. "I might as well tell you that the latest hypothesis by the police is that she might be involved."

Tal shook his head, trying to distinguish confusion from exhaustion. "What about Adrian? I thought he was a suspect?"

Bethany's face paled and her hand reached out for the file cabinet behind her. "Adrian? Wh-what do you mean, suspect? Adrian's, well, he's dead, Tal. Adrian's dead."

Twenty

LONDON

Too distracted to work, Tal knew of another dreary tavern within walking distance. And he recalled an odd sort of antiques store in the front. Dappled with half-torn gold wallpaper and a collection of hideous Victorian loveseats, he retreated toward the door to reappraise the entrance.

"Tavern's in the back," hacked a crotchety voice from behind the glass counter. Tal peeked over it and a gnome-like creature emerged straight from the set of *Lord of the Rings*.

"Gollum?" Tal asked meekly.

"Gloria." The small woman pointed an arthritic finger to the back of the building. "Bar's back there."

Wooden booths, scuffed floors, Celtic music and cigar smoke. Ah, Tal thought. Now this is where I'd be if I were Max Dearden. He stood at the bar for a moment to get his bearings. And then heard a voice directly across from him.

"I could get you a room upstairs if you'd like," the voice offered.

Tal turned toward it, bewildered.

"To sleep, for God's sake. You're obviously homeless, as you've done nothing but hound after me for the past two days."

Tal lowered himself onto the bench seat of the middle booth. His pupils struggled to dilate amid the darkness. "Homeless, you should talk."

"I can't go home." Max Dearden sipped the last of a tall beer on the table. There were two empty glasses beside it.

"Why not?"

"There's a dead man in my living room."

"Be quiet!" Tal jerked left and right. "Do you want someone to—"

"Dead man, dead man, dead man!" Max sneered and fell forward onto the table. Tal grabbed him by the coat collar and dragged Max, protesting, outside through the alley door. He released him against a brick wall.

"Now will you be quiet?"

"Don't need to, no one's around out here. No one but the fairies—"

"For God's sake, shut up." Tal sighed, peered down the alley and leaned close. "What dead man?"

"How do I know who he is?" Cackling convulsively again, "I just know he ain't breathing—"

"How much have you had to drink?"

Max's eyes opened wide. "You mean my whole life? Lemme see—"

"Listen to me." Tal leaned in close just as a set of headlights illuminated the slick bed of filth along the alley floor. "That body you found—"

"The dead man. Say it. Dead. Man."

Looking at the oncoming car, Tal dragged Max back inside through the alley door and plopped him back into the booth. "Yes, the dead man, that's right," he whispered and released a long sigh. "Max, I've got a problem."

"You killed him?"

"No, but I may have been the last one to see him alive. I've got to get out of here. Seriously, like right now."

Max stiffened. "You're staying right here." Clearing his throat, "I can't think of a safer place. Look, did you see the troll up front? Gloria? Well everyone thinks this bar closed down when she bought the place." Short pause. "Get it?"

"Get what?" Tal asked.

"No sane copper would be caught dead hanging out in a *brocante* shop, let alone looking for murder suspects." Before Tal could answer, Max slapped the table twice. An old bartender arrived. "Two coffees, bread and cheese, and a pitcher of water with lemon. In the back, Emile."

Back, Tal thought. How many backs can a building have?

Max motioned for Tal to follow, led him down a hall, up four stairs and unlocked a door. "Here," he said. "Sit."

A dusty couch with no cushioning. He sat on the edge of it wondering if he should be at the museum waiting for a call from Lily. Adrian is dead, he kept thinking. Dead.

Max picked up a wall phone and pushed a single button. "Send Andre to the parlor please, Emile. Yes, well, all right." He hung up and stood stiffly by the window. "It'll be a while. Might as well make ourselves comfortable. Emile and I have known each other for forty years, and no one makes a better pot of coffee."

Tal leaned deeper into the sofa and rested his head on the arm, lids heavy.

Twenty-One

SOMEWHERE

"Get *away*, get away!!"

A wrap of hungry hands spread over her hot skin, rolling her left and right on the hard bed, pulling the blankets out from between her legs and around her waist. But this new hand, a third hand, didn't feel like a hand at all, but more like a snake. It was long like the sash on a bathrobe.

Twine? Rope? Whatever the instrument, she was certain it had been custom made precisely for her demise. Jerking in the direction opposite to what touched her, she realized, almost at once, that moving with the hands instead of against them might bring her closer to possible escape. It had already happened once, followed by an injection in the side of her neck. Carotid artery? Whatever it was, it allowed the yellowy liquid to move lightning speed through her veins and directly to her brain for proper processing.

The room smelled even more musty than she remembered, as though it was flooded with three inches of water. Was there even a way outside if she could sneak away from her captor?

The hands, she thought. Move with them, not against. First, she slowed her movements. She felt a cold palm on the back of her knee and slowly, almost sensuously, she moved her leg and up and down, and bent the knee up slightly. The hand stopped and then slowly moved up the back of her leg to her thigh.

What am I doing, she wondered, terrified to move but even more scared to stop moving. She'd started something now, a change in pattern, hope. Blinking against the watery residue of barbiturates, she rolled her hips forward, toward the hand, and felt an arm around her waist, smelled the breath of her captor, felt the grit of stubble on his chin. And then the horrifying realization jarred her consciousness.

Why can't I see?

"Buchel!" A gruff voice called up the hollow stairs. *"Viens maintenant, Depeche-toi!"*

For a moment, there was stillness on the bed, their bodies frozen, his planned attack and her impending plan of knee-to-groin subterfuge stunted, soundlessly, like a waterfall's halted flow. The man rose, finally, and clomped down the stairs in the same heavy shoes she had heard earlier that day. Or was it the day before? He had closed and locked the door behind him. But even from the bed, or maybe through the heat vents on the floor, she heard their conversation. Buchel, her slow-witted captor, spoke English to the other man, undoubtedly the operation's *jefe*.

"What are you doing up there for so long? She has been injected with the serum, no?"

"Yes, twice in the past two hours. I was checking on her a moment ago, making certain she was still breathing."

There was a long pause, then the jefe's chair scraped the floor and she heard five footsteps. Then, in a low voice, "Was she?"

Buchel didn't answer. She heard the five steps back to the scraping chair, and then the sound of water poured into a glass from a pitcher. "Well, my friend, tell me about this woman, now that you are so well acquainted with her after the past two hours."

"American. What else is there to know?"

"Doesn't look American. Looks Asian if you ask me."

"Japanese-Italian."

"Her name?"

"Simone. Wife of a, how do you say, *journaliste*."

Another pause, and the sound of a heavy glass scraping across and lifting from the table beneath it. "How do you know her?"

"Not her. Him. I only saw him once, never met him."

"That's how you got this assignment?"

"Yes," Buchel answered, as if he'd been asked by a police officer to remove the candy bar from his jacket pocket. "How did you end up here, Pietro?"

"Our mutual friend, the Dane. Well, not he himself – one of his, you know, whatever they're called. ACES. Who knows who's even alive anymore. I heard three of them disappeared in a matter of six months. All I know is that I've been paid a great deal of money to monitor the woman's progress. Don't know why they don't just have us kill her. Would be easier, certainly, than subjecting ourselves to the whims of a woman. Even with the drugs she's a bit of trouble. Though I must say you've done a splendid job of keeping her quiet. You must be, ah, more charming than I imagined." Laugh. "Well, not to me of course, but, as they say, love is blind." Scraping chair again.

Upstairs, Simone held her ear to the vent in the floorboards now, one hand on the bed to help her up in case someone charged up the stairs.

"Come to think of it," Pietro said, "love is dumb too. The Dane used to say that. Of all my prisoners, he was by far the most entertaining. And he died miserably, like a coward. Pity."

"Did you ever know his name?" Buchel asked in a timid voice.

Listening through the vents, Simone could almost taste his fear, anticipate how his hands would feel on her leg as a result of this fear, rubbing her skin bare and squeezing the delicate bones of her ankle, wrestling with the notions of goodness and rational behavior, all the while the proverbial white-and-black-angel's sword fighting on both shoulders.

"Coleski. Something like that. His first name was Soren, I remember that much."

"His death couldn't have been all that cowardly, Pietro," Buchel said in a much clearer voice, as if he had made a decision, or a secret made the decision for him.

Pietro moved suddenly and a chair thunked against the floor. "Why on earth would you say that? You weren't there."

"Because he's not dead. Soren Careski is alive."

Pietro clapped his hands in mock approval. "Very nice performance. Though I can't imagine for whom you are performing. I watched the man die myself. I saw his body lowered into the ground."

"No," Buchel mumbled. "You saw a casket. Soren Careski is most certainly not dead. The world just thinks he is."

Chair scraping, boots pacing the floors. "You have seen this man Soren? I mean yourself, with the eyes in your head?"

"No."

"You are in, what, telepathic contact with him then? Or is he, perhaps, a ghost contacting you from the other side? Perhaps you, Buchel, are administering the drugs to yourself instead of the woman."

"I do not mean to prove you wrong, Pietro. You saved my life once and you have earned my lifetime of respect. But I have seen emails from him."

"From Soren?"

"From Soren, yes. Emails with directions, with descriptions of where he is staying, with—"

"You saw this man, Soren, send you the actual emails?"

"What do yo—"

"Answer me! You saw him actually type the emails and submit them to your email address? Ah! No, then. Maybe you did not actually get an email *from* Soren directly. Is it possible you are getting communiques from someone impersonating Soren Careski or someone simply using his email address?"

"Who else would be doing this?" Buchel asked, "and for what reason?"

"Your friend Soren was connected to people in both high and low places, a very good place for a man to be. You snap two fingers and someone is mysteriously nominated for a Pulitzer, and those same two fingers snap and that very person dies in a car crash. The power of it all."

"You envy that power?" Her captor's voice, once again, became meek.

"I have that power. You, on the other hand, will never have that power, Buchel, as you are by trade, by profession, and by nature, weak. You do as you're told, take whatever money is given you and then quietly go home to plan your affairs. Let me ask you, have you ever uttered a single word that was not properly rehearsed? Done something spontaneous, out of the ordinary, broken a rule, maybe even broken the law?"

Buchel laughed quietly, like a mouse nibbling cheese in the corner of a pantry. Then the laugh grew in volume and shape until it was as boisterous, as ugly and false as had emerged from Pietro's own mouth not ten minutes before.

"Broken the law?" he shouted. "We have kidnapped an American woman, administered unauthorized narcotics to her against her will, held her captive and taken advantage of her incapacitation. What do you call that? A misdemeanor? I'll venture my Interpol file's longer than yours."

"You talk too much, Buchel. You know that?"

"Maybe not enough."

"Why would you say that?"

"Because the American woman is Soren Careski's daughter-in-law."

Twenty-Two

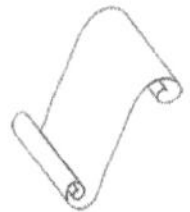

NORTHERN ITALY

"*Ciao, Padre.*"

Cyril Zander pulled back two steps. "I don't take to being summoned."

"It could not be avoided."

Zander followed the young man down a long hallway, his robe polishing the marble floor with each step. Then one turn down a short hallway and into a room with no lights.

"Please wait here a moment," the young man said, his gaze averted.

Zander stood, vulnerable and waiting. Single, tiny recessed lights turned on overhead one by one.

"Brother Matthew, what is this?" he called out.

The man rushed to the doorway from the hall. "Apologies, Your Eminence, I needed to ensure privacy, so I turned off the monitor that auto-starts with the overhead lights."

"Privacy?" Zander instinctively lowered his head to listen.

"We've found it," the man called Matthew whispered, barely moving his lips.

Twenty-Three

LONDON

"It'll be a while," Max said, lifting his chin. "Might as well sleep if you can."

Tal observed the man, appraising a surprising level of lucidity in spite of his inebriation. "I couldn't sleep now. Too much has happened in the last twenty-four hours."

A quiet knock sounded. Max moved quickly and pressed his mouth into the door jamb. "Marco?" he said, thinking of the bartender.

Pause. "It's Emile. Open the door."

Max paused and glanced at Tal. He drew the lever back on the deadbolt and ushered in the old-world butler. "Come in, old chap. We've got a … situation."

Emile, a neat, contracted man with disciplined movements, stood awkwardly in the center of the floor after setting a tray on the coffee table.

"Speaking of which, did you—"

Emile motioned to the door. "Andre's on his way. Let's just hope there aren't too many stops along his path."

Max pulled a folded twenty-quid note from his tattered wallet and leaned toward Emile. "That been much of an issue lately? With Andre?"

"Afraid so, yes. Then again, you are the reason for his impending visit today and I believe the rules are different for you."

Max nodded. "Yes. Quite." Max watched Tal bite ravenously into a slab of crusty bread. "Try some of Emile's legendary coffee, Tal. Best in England."

"And seeing as we're primarily known for tea – never mind ..." he let his voice trail.

Tal observed the intimacy between the two men, telling, to him, not only their years of knowing but the degree and depth of it as well. It was the kind of body language, hushed voices and direct eye contact necessary for the collection, maintenance, and dissemination of grave secrets. He didn't want to be here right now, with these strange, old criminals, with the knowledge that Adrian Marcali had been murdered and the certainty, somehow, that his own accidental contact with Max Dearden had something to do with it.

"I've got to get out of here," he said and rose.

Max and Emile moved toward the door. "I'm afraid that's a bad idea," Max replied quickly.

Emile poured coffee into one of the tiny cups. He held it out to Tal.

"I don't drink the stuff, actually."

"Better start," Max replied. "You've got a rough night ahead of you."

Emile disappeared quietly behind the heavy door.

Forty minutes later another knock, this time only one. Max, dozing, jerked his head up. He sat on the edge of the chair facing Tal and leaned close. "You must do everything Andre says."

"Provided it doesn't include large spiders or puppets, fine."

Twenty-Four

ITALY

From the back seat of an old station wagon, Mona Delfreggio saw the sculpted sideburns of the driver, no more than seventeen or eighteen years old. Alex, at attention in the front seat, smoked one of his chic brown cigarettes and tapped a finger on his knee to a song on the radio.

Mona touched his shoulder. "How long to wherever we're going?"

"Depends on where we're going," Alex replied.

"Wow, oldies," she commented.

"*Jagged Little Pill,*" Alex said and turned. "Alanis Morissette is oldies to you?

"Um, she was popular twenty years ago. So, yes."

"I'm surprised you know about anyone other than Drake and Kendrick Lamar."

"You might be surprised."

"Okay, we'll start with an easy one," Alex smiled. "Lead singer of Nirvana. What's his name and what's noteworthy about him?"

"Come on, give me a hard one."

"Who was he married to?"

"That blonde, Jennifer Love or something."

"Courtney. Close enough."

"Now give me one."

Mona leaned forward. "Okay, here's one – I'm going to help you find your wife."

Twenty-Five

LONDON

"Andre Doyle." The slim, gray-haired man presented an outstretched hand with finely manicured fingernails.

"Do you have insurance on those things?" Tal asked, shaking the man's hand and holding it up to the light.

Max closed his eyes and shook his head. Doyle, though, lifted his chin and half grinned at the comment. "I take great pride in presentation, Mr. Gardner. And by the looks of you," he pulled his hand away, lowered his eyes and scanned Tal from toe to head, "you could use someone like me in your life."

"He's had a rough few days," Max said and motioned toward the sofas. "Andre's going to help get you out of here—"

"So I can escape before the police find me?" Tal blinked at Andre. "Is that what you do? Encourage people to go on the lam, running away from demons they've created themselves?"

Max handed Tal another cup of coffee.

"Maybe he's had enough of that," Andre said to Max.

"Look, Popeye or whatever superhero you think you are, why don't I just save all of us some trouble and explain what's happened to the police," Tal said. "I'm sure they'll understand."

Andre and Max locked eyes and Andre motioned for the cordless phone on the end table. Max handed it to him.

"Hello, yes, thank you. I've got a friend with me who appears to have witnessed a homicide, and—"

"Christ, what is he doing?" Tal bellowed. Max tried to restrain him when he lunged at Andre.

"I wonder if you could come over here and talk with him," Andre went on. "I think he might have some useful information about a man found in—"

Lunging again, Tal snatched the phone from Andre's hand and threw it across the room. "Are you bloody mad?" He stared, pleadingly, at Max.

Andre shrugged and replaced the receiver. "You indicated a desire to involve the police. I was just saving you the trouble. You might consider—"

Tal sat on the edge of the couch with his face in his palms. "Okay, you made your point." He looked at both men. "What would you have me do, move to Buenos Aires for the next five years? And have I mentioned that I did not, in fact, kill that man?"

"What man?" Andre asked.

"Adrian Marcali," Max whispered to Andre. "Head Conservator at the Brit." Max leaned two inches closer to Andre. "Antiquities," he whispered.

"Mm, right. Anything to do with the disappearance of Ms. Frasier?" Andre mumbled to Max.

Tal jumped up again. "What do you know about her, for God's sake? If you've—"

Max put his hand up. "Tal, please."

"Mr. Gardner, I make it a point to know things, not to merely know *about* them," Andre said closing his eyes.

Tal stood by the couch, clenching and unclenching his fists.

"For instance," Andre continued in a lowered voice, "I know that you haven't been home in two days and that dreadful Painted Japanese fern by your sliding glass doors leading to your balcony is ninety-five percent dead."

Tal's eyes widened.

"All right, ninety-eight percent."

Tal listened.

"What's that? More? Oh, well, let's see, then there's that spot of spilled milk on the driver's side floor mat in your silver Audi that makes your car smell like a dairy farm on hot days. Shall I go on?"

"Who the fuck are you? Undercover police? MI6? Have you got a fingerprint file on me? And what's my mother's maiden name?"

"McCutcheon."

"Christ!"

Max put a hand on Tal's shoulder. "Calm down. Andre's just trying to—"

"What about Lily? Do you know where she is? And let me tell you something before you answer. If you so much as look at her—"

Andre looked on, calmly. "Look at her? How could you not look, Mr. Gardner? But then ... you love her, so of course you know that. You've loved her for, what, five, six years now? Loved her since that first staff meeting you stumbled into on your second day of work, falling right into her with your head landing on her chest. Bit of a rough start, had you? She took to you, though, didn't she? As I recall, she's written you three letters late at night that she's never mailed. Oh, you didn't know? Pity."

Tal paced in front of the couch like a caged lion, alternating his eyes between Max and Andre, Andre to Max, Max to the door of the squalid dark room. Then back to Andre's hideous Cheshire cat grin.

Then he opened the door ... and ran.

Twenty-Six

LONDON

First, out the door and down the dark, five-stair jump to the main floor of Emile's bar and through the antique shop. Then, thinking better of it, back through to the bar entrance and out the back alley door.

Ah, no lights, he thought, surprised that his mind would be even capable of such forethought right now.

I didn't kill Adrian, he chanted to the drumming of his fancy loafers, oddly juxtaposed against the puddled grit of the dreary cul-de-sac. And in the midst of chanting, another thought rattled his brain. Where am I going?

Tal loved this part of Westminster. Lovely, manicured lawns and gentrified old buildings from the front view; the back, though, revealed a squalid underbelly of neglected real estate dotted with overflowing dumpsters and cardboard box shelters. Tal shuddered, standing still for one second, inhaling fumes from the rotting garbage, the surprising quiet, and then took off again when he heard the creak of the back door.

"Faster, faster!" he screamed aloud, as if inspiring his feet to pound deeper into the damp pavement. He didn't dare turn around but knew at least one of them was following - more likely Max and Andre, with the ancient Emile guarding the back entrance. Why were they chasing him? Wasn't it his prerogative to run from the police if he wanted to?

"Tal!" One of them yelled above the cacophony of car horns and screeching tires. "Turn around, please!" It was Max's voice. He turned, only slightly, and saw a dark object extending from Andre's left hand - the manicured fingers gripped tightly around something black, suspiciously resembling the shape of a pistol. Almost to the end of the alley, he strained to see around the next corner. There were streetlights and traffic was at a steady stream.

Must be the High Str— something interrupted his thoughts. A set of headlights coming straight at him down the other end of the alley.

Jesus, he thought and spun into one of the skip bins on the right-hand side of the narrow passage.

But the car followed.

It crashed its right headlight into the corner of the skip and caught his pant leg, tearing the fabric at the knee. Bending sideways, he vaulted away from the bin and dodged left and right, to try to disorient the driver. At the other end of the alley, Emile, a single ancient sentry, stood guard over his sad, little, lost tavern. The car spun ahead of him, faster, screeching left and right. One shopkeeper from a shop two doors down stepped outside the alley door, looked out, then quickly retreated. Distracted by the onlooker, the demon car braked immediately left, it shuddered to a stop and a back door automatically flipped open.

"Get in," said a low voice. A tall, white-faced man with a crew cut stepped out in a suit three sizes too big for his frame. With a gun in one hand, he held the door open with the other and motioned to Tal. "I will not say it again," he said. The man had a strange accent. Not English.

"Do I have any choice in the matter? And I guess, since you're obviously not the police, you don't really care if I killed Arian Marcali or not."

Crew Cut Man didn't move a muscle, let alone look in his direction. Tal instinctively knew that any further conversation would apply a quick and painless end to his life. He climbed in the back seat crammed beside one other man. Then with Crew Cut Man beside him now, two more thugs lined the front seat. The large, black car twisted right, then left again to head out the other side of the alley. Even through darkened windows, Tal saw something, or someone, blocking its exit onto the street.

A man stood in the street at the alley's entrance holding a pistol pointed at the driver's head. He yelled something inaudible and, when the car failed to reduce speed, he aimed low and fired two shots. The car skidded and bucked, throwing Tal from the backseat into the open cavern of the front, the top of his head scraping the windshield. And then, in perfect synchronicity with the passengers' disorientation, the front and rear doors yanked open followed by two men with outstretched arms and guns.

"Gentlemen," Andre said with a grin and raised brow.

"Tal, out," Max directed.

"Get in, get out, make up your mind."

Crew Cut Man wriggled in his seat to reach into his jacket and a bullet discharged from Andre's pistol.

Tal felt drops of another man's blood splatter on his face. "You shot him in the … throat."

Andre glared back at him. "Yes."

"I was just wondering if that's what you were aiming for."

"Shut up," Andre said absently. Tal climbed out past Andre, and another shot sounded as he stepped onto the pavement.

Tal flinched. Max moved to the front of the car and addressed the driver and passenger. "You and you," he said. "Drive off now or die. Which is it?"

The car lurched forward to the street and thundered around the corner.

Max disappeared, and Tal followed Andre back through the tavern to the main street, where Emile gunned the engine on an old, well-preserved Rolls Royce. Red.

Emile drove with Andre, Tal in the back. "Just out of curiosity, then, you use a cherry red Rolls as your getaway car? Does that work for you, generally?"

Andre turned his head three inches to the left, then back to center. "You know, Mr. Gardner, aside from the fact that I just saved your life, you seem desperate to irritate me. I wouldn't advise any further actions down that path."

"Well, I don't want to get my throat shot out, that's for sure."

Emile swerved the car left and right, dodging from lane to lane, at breakneck speed.

"Where's Max?" Tal asked, as if the man's absence had only suddenly occurred to him.

"He knows where to go, Mr. Gardner," Emile said leaning his head back.

"How about telling me?"

Andre took out his phone and crossed his legs.

Tal tapped his fingers on his knee. "All right, how about telling me why it was necessary to kill two men back there."

Andre whipped around like a rabid dog. "Would you have preferred to go joyriding with those four thugs? If you'd like, I can find the remaining two and return you to them. Emile—"

"Look, since you think I'm sheltered anyway, I haven't been around a great deal of graphic death in my life. I don't think an explanation is out of order."

"In time, Mr. Gardner."

Tal blinked at the city landscape blur, realizing that he was running from the police with a manicured killer and his butler. And where had Max, his unlikely ally, gone to? Who were these people and how did they know so much about him?

Three things happened all at once.

Emile screeched the car up onto the curb and parked. Andre smiled and said, "Ah, home sweet home." And Max Dearden stood over them on the sidewalk, peering into the car.

Something's all wrong, he thought, looking at the front of a building he'd memorized over the past six years. Tal got out of the car.

"This is where Lily lives. What the fuck is going on?"

"We're here," Andre said simply, smiling at Max and polishing his fingernails on his gabardine jacket.

"Where is here, for God's sake? And why did you say Max knew where to go? Max knew to come to this house? I don't understand."

Andre nodded at Emile, and both men closed and locked the car doors and collected on the sidewalk near Max. "This is where the history of everything begins."

Twenty-Seven

LONDON

He didn't really walk, he slithered. Tal watched the man's thin body move like fluid up the old, twisted staircase in Lily's foyer. It was a beautiful apartment block, with cathedral ceilings, clerestory windows, stone hearth fireplace. As if a woman of her type could live anywhere else. And walking through her doorway now was a man who shot other men in the throat. On purpose.

"Close the door," Max commanded and sat like a puppy on the sofa beside Andre.

Tal stood at the fireplace and checked the interior of the house in a random sweep. Kitchen, living room, bedroom, hallway. Everything looked as it should. Everything except that Lily was missing and two thugs were making camp in her parlor.

Andre nodded slightly. "How much money does Ms. Frasier earn at the museum, Tal?"

He half-smiled and peered at them. "What *are* you two, exactly?"

"Answer the question." Max this time.

Tal was still peering. It started out as curiosity, but now it felt more like a game.

"Perhaps he's asleep," Andre mumbled in Max's ear. "You haven't given him anything, have you?"

"Not yet."

Tal stared grimly back at the odd pair.

"Ah yes, now, where were we? Money. You were about to tells us Ms. Frasier's salary."

"I venture to say that if you know about the wilted fern near my back door, you damn well know how much money she makes."

Andre winced. "Quite. The point, though, is not what *we* know but what *you* know. Do you know of her earnings?"

"Where is she?" he demanded. "Where's Lily? I mean right now? Is she in London even? Italy? Cyprus? Siberia?"

"With her ailments, I can't imagine her lasting more than a day anywhere north of Manchester. Expensive taste, well-put-together, pampered British academic, and a delicate constitution? No chance."

"Sixty thousand pounds per annum. That about right?"

Andre looked at Max and then nodded at Tal. "After taxes, that's, what, about eight hundred quid a week, then? Sixteen hundred a fortnight? Look around, Tal. What do you see?"

Tal swallowed hard. Right now he saw two jackals lounging in an empty chicken coop, licking their chops.

Andre, the designated speaker, cleared his throat. "I'm thinking of opulence. Doesn't this home remind you of it? A bit over the top? In other words, do you think Ms. Frasier could afford the monthly mortgage on a place like this?"

"She owns this home," Tal replied. "Outright, I thought. She's got a, what is it, rich uncle or grandfather or something. I thought she said they helped her pay for it. Bought the damn title deeds from the bank, come to think of it." Andre raised a brow at him. "Apparently not?"

"Your boss, Mr. Gardner," Andre began, "fluffy, red-headed Lily Frasier, has been involved in something rather serious, and for quite some time."

"What does that mean? She's what … a Russian spy?

"And this goes far beyond the Inquisition, Tal."

Tal shook his head now, utterly confused. "I'm sorry, but what's one thing got to do with the other?"

"Everything," Andre and Max said together.

His mind raced, gluing together a puzzle of disparate facts. "You're saying Adrian's death wa—"

"Adrian's murder. Might as well call it like it is," Andre said.

"All right, Adrian's murder … help me here now. The night Adrian was shot, I was," he paused to steady his thoughts, to remember, "inexplicably drawn to a painting in the Inquisition exhibit, and I found a note you left," he said to Max, "… apparently for me? Right so far?"

Silence. Max cleared his throat. "Not really, no."

"So ... you're saying you ... didn't put the note there on the back of the picture? It had your contact information on it. Who else would do such a thing?"

"She did."

"Lily?"

This time Max answered by unzipping his outer jacket.

"How do you know this?"

"How do we know?" Max said and laughed. "She's not exactly what you'd call low profile."

For the first time, Tal noticed the light in the living room - it was strange lighting, all wrong for the time of day, for his body time. An odd brightness reflected in from the dark, gloomy sky. Either the sun had peeked out from the cloud cover, or a UFO had landed in Russell Square. Lily, the Inquisition, Max Dearden - it was all too much.

As a distraction, he repositioned items on the fireplace mantel. Baby photographs, a set of Russian dolls, and a framed photograph of two smiling middle-aged men each standing on one side of one of the Rapa Nui monuments. On the bottom of the picture was what he immediately recognized as Lily's handwriting - "Max and Soren, 1975."

In slow motion, Tal picked up the photograph and brought it closer to his face. He held it out in front of him now, toward Max, and compared the younger face with the older one.

"This is you?" Two steps toward Max. "You and your partner, Soren Careski?" He took two steps back, the reality strangle-holding his brain. "Why are you … um …" his eyes scanned left to right, "why are you on Lily's mantel?" he asked softly. "Someone tell me what the hell's going on here. Please."

Max Dearden blinked, silently, for a long moment. "She's my daughter."

Twenty-Eight

ITALY

The four o'clock sun slipped down toward the Sabine hills while Alex watched Mona's hands flip through the second of Soren's diaries. A contradiction in every way, her hands and her long legs spoke of a journalist's aggressive pursuit of knowledge, yet her eyes, narrowed when they spied him over the tops of her chic Milano glasses, betrayed a sort of careful caution, conciliatory almost, apologizing for her brazenness, sorry for treading too hard on thin ice.

Little did she know that beneath the thin ice were the folds of a wounded heart. To look at her now meant to remember, only, his first glimpses of Simone.

Where was she now, was she being treated kindly, given food and water, held in a room with fresh flowers and sunlight? Alex kept his mind strategically fixed on this pleasant image, no matter how unlikely it was.

In Tivoli, just twenty kilometers east of Rome, in the café-of-the-hour, the orangey glow of dusk hung like gauze over the shiny red curtains, and Alex understood something new about Mona. Trust: illogical, yet instinctual. A girl he factually knew nothing about but, by instinct knew he was meant to protect her. Mona pinched her lips, obviously annoyed by his reticence. She had asked him about Simone three times in the past hour.

"Tell me about the Danes," Alex said finally. "You know, you mentioned them in the cell." He purposely used his casual voice to catch her off guard. And now she had a mouthful of bread stalling her answer. She raised her large brown eyes toward the ceiling as she tried to chew faster, wiping her mouth with her napkin every few seconds.

"I never saw them." She shrugged. "I don't know who they are or anything. Just what they do."

Alex remembered what she had said about her sister. "Your sister works for the British Museum. Do they have something to do with that?"

She globbed on another pat of butter and chomped hungrily into the bread. "They're some kind of museum mafia."

"What would they have to do with us, though?"

"If they think we're a threat to their latest cover-up, it would be natural for them to want to cover *us* up. The question is," Mona paused and took another bite of bread, "what would a group like that want with your wife?"

Alex rested his forehead in his opened palms and drew in a long breath. But nothing calmed his jittery nerves nor the itchy feeling that they were about to walk into a trap. Every step, lately, seemed to take him, take them, farther away from where he needed to go. Simone. Kidnapped. Because of him.

"What makes you so sure Simone's a part of this?" Alex asked finally.

"Is she involved with any of the museums in Boston?" Mona asked and set her butter knife down on the table.

He shook his head.

"What does she do for a living? Or are you so wealthy that your wife doesn't work?" Mona winked again.

"Get real, I'm a journalist. Simone's, well, she wasn't working for much of this year. We're trying to have a baby and there were complications. Her career though - she's an interpreter."

Mona wrinkled her brows.

"For the Japanese embassy."

Mona laughed slightly. "She speaks Japanese?"

"She is Japanese. Part, anyway."

"And does she speak any other languages?"

Alex nodded. "Oh yeah, several."

Mona slapped down the cover of Soren's diary. "Let me get this straight, your wife's a fucking translator and you, what, forgot to bring this up?"

"What should that matter?"

Mona leaned in. "Your father, for one thing," she whispered, "was this century's foremost linguist, from what you've told me. He vanished eight years ago and now he may have turned up again. And out of the blue, you tell me your wife's an interpreter for the Japanese government? You don't see the connection?"

"Mona," Alex grabbed her elbow across the table. "No. Soren, my father, studied ancient languages. Hebrew, Greek, Aramaic. And Simone speaks … a strange combination of modern languages - English, Italian, Romanian, and Japanese. Her parents moved her all over the world as a child. But more than that, Simone's an interpreter of *spoken* languages. An art and science in observing spoken words, in combination with inflection, gestures, facial expressions, body language, not to mention context." Alex stared momentarily out the small window. "She never had any interest or patience for old texts."

Mona pulled back her hand and nervously spread more globs of butter on another piece of crusty bread and returned her attention to the opened diary.

The dirty window, streaked with a combination of what resembled oily grime and Windex, had a hand crank that opened outward. Alex turned the crank three times and felt a warm breeze on the side of his cheek and nose.

"What's this?" she wondered and turned the diary upside down. "Some kind of code or something?"

Alex, pretending to look, just shrugged.

"Or an analysis of something? Do you recognize it? Any of these characters?"

"Gibberish. Most of his writings, his entire career, were the mumblings of a madman."

The sky seemed suddenly dark. Not dusky from the tranquil spill of afternoon, but dark.

Jesus, he thought, Soren's code. That's all Soren had ever been good for in this life, wasn't it? - a grand paradox. And now, ironically, here he was, searching for his missing wife in a strange country, stranded with a strange young woman who possessed an uncanny vision about the disconnected threads in his life. Soren and his damn codes. They'd get them absolutely nowhere, possibly even farther away from wherever Simone had been taken.

"What's the matter? Are you familiar with this?" she pressed, sliding the diary to him.

He saw that her long hair was in a messy ponytail now and remembered the spontaneous way Simone used to do that same thing, though her hair was always too silky and fine to stay up for very long. Soren used to call her the most beautiful woman on earth, more beautiful than the gods ever bargained for when they sold their souls to the devil for eternal life.

The café was silent now. Not a single sound came from the kitchen, no mumbling from the old ladies on the other side of the wall, no music from oncoming cars. No cars at all now, no traffic. Dark out, dark inside the café, and Mona's hypnotic brown eyes stared intently at his movements, at the folding of his hands, at his face, the collar of his shirt. He knew what she was searching for, what all people her age search for - meaning. And his search must bring him to Simone.

Alex stepped out to ask the old ladies to use their bathroom, and when he came back, Mona had pulled his violin case up to the table and leaned over it staring at something.

"What are you looking at?"

"These markings," she muttered, pointing at what looked like tiny claw marks across the bottom of the case.

Not again, he thought.

"Look," she demanded when he failed to inspect them.

"I don't know what they are," he lied and pulled out his wallet.

Mona glared across the table, then nodded as if making a tacit decision. She pulled out one of the diaries, flipped the pages back to front and landed on a page of tiny, patterned lines. "These," she began, still pointing, "match this style of Ogham, *hinge Ogham*. You know what this is, don't you?"

Alex waved a hand in disregard. "Sure, we used to write secret messages to each other in that language when I was little, treasure hunt type of thing. It's nothing, a childhood prank."

Mona took off her glasses. "These markings weren't here before."

"Sure they were, I saw them," he lied again.

"They're fresh," she argued.

"I'm tired, Mona, it's time to go find a hotel."

Twenty-Nine

ITALY?

Do you know the size of Orion?, Alex wrote in the partially filled Simone-journal he'd started on his frantic plane trip to Rome four days earlier. *I don't just mean across his belt but the entire constellation, east to west and floor to ceiling. Seventy times the size of Jupiter? Ha, you would say, pretending to be outraged by my ineptitude, scorning, snickering a ring of feigned insults, all the while admiring my uncanny knack for escapism. You know I'm right, don't you? All my hobbies, astronomy, Italian cooking, are lumped together in your mind as escapes. I can hear your thoughts now. I can't see where you are right now, but I can see you just the same, tapping your fingers on the window sill, arms boldly outstretched and legs and back bent, like a resting ballerina. In the womb of the sleeping muse, you would say, lies the only thing worth having in this world – imagination.*

The hotel room, decorated with a rack of gaudy, velvet curtains, hung haphazardly on a too-thin rod, stirred with a quiet energy. He watched Mona sleep, understood the sin of this activity and potential for disaster, but watched all the same, watched her dozing, he watched her sleeping, watched her white face wince in even intervals, her shoulders clench. In her slumber, she was running, or being chased.

Voices rose from the street, laughing, female, drunken voices poised in sharp, sarcastic tones, warding off the grip of men's hands and poised for battle. He could still remember times when he and Simone had gone to the corner bar, Carr's, and drank ale and played cards till all hours, and then swaggered home through the spaghetti-fumes of Boston's North End. He loved the North End, and right now Boston was a dull ache throbbing in the center of his heart. He didn't love who he was there, or what he did or even who he did it with. But once, long ago, he thought, I was a plain old newspaper man. Where is that man now?

The voices from the street turned from lilting feminine tones to dead silence, interrupted by an occasional car horn or screeching tires. This was the Rome he knew, the Rome he remembered from childhood, from three trips he had taken with Soren during his first year of junior high school. Not till thirty years later did he realize that Soren's motive for taking him wasn't exposure to worldly cultures, but to paint a picture of himself as an obsessive, discombobulated research scholar, instead of the conniving cutthroat he actually was. At 1:00 a.m. Mona rolled over in her sleep onto her back, breathing heavily. She sat up suddenly and swung her legs onto the floor, struggling to force her pupils to open in the darkness.

"Where are we?"

Lying on his side on the other bed, Alex shrugged. "Why are you up? You were having such a beautiful sleep."

"Was I?" she yawned. "What exactly is a beautiful sleep?"

"The kind of sleep that good, upright people earn."

Mona studied him. "You don't sleep like that? You're a writer, for God's sake. How much mischief can journalists get into?"

He gasped. "Ever hear of Woodward and Bernstein? And what about—"

She waved him off. "I'm too groggy to argue right now." She moved to sit on his bed and took the water glass from the bedside table, taking two sips.

"You were dreaming," Alex explained.

"You were watching me?"

"You were making noises like you were having a nightmare, I couldn't help but notice," he said sitting upright.

"Well, I'll tell you why I woke up. I thought of something. What's ACES?"

Alex shook his head. "Forget about them," he said, louder than he expected.

"I think maybe you don't want to find your wife at all. Maybe you're the one who did something to her." She sat up straight now.

Alex rubbed his face with his open palms, and kept it covered for a moment. He stood in front of the underwear-clad Mona Delfreggio and paced back and forth, then smiled.

"What?" she asked, annoyed.

"Simone does this. Baits me like this." He stopped the pacing when he was directly in front of her again and leaned down with his palms on his knees. Their foreheads were nearly touching. "Do you think I killed my own wife?" He felt her nervousness around him as the words slipped out of his mouth. He leaned closer. "Do you?"

"I think you're a man with a lot of secrets," she whispered.

She moved to the other side of the bed and slipped on her overshirt. "So ... ACES?"

"What do you want to know?"

"What does it stand for?" Mona asked.

He sighed, closed his eyes as a token of some internal decision, and nodded. "American Council of Epigraphy Scholars."

"Soren was a member?" she asked, picking up one of the journals from the corner table and carrying it back to the bed. She recorded something on a blank notebook page.

"Founding member. There's a difference."

"Did Simone know about this?"

Alex looked out the window and scanned the sky left to right. "I always thought so, but she never would tell me."

"Something about Soren?"

He shook his head. "Simone's a translator. And Soren's an epigrapher. I never really ... put the two together until tonight." He looked into Mona's eyes and searched for an explanation. "How would you know enough to ask?"

She shrugged. "I don't know. Ignorance, I guess. I just look at what's on the surface, like right in front of us. Two ancient texts were stolen from a museum where my sister works, and she's missing. Your wife's a translator - also missing. Your father, a linguist - missing. How could there *not* be a connection?" Mona shifted and went to the table to grab a different journal now. "How many members of ACES are there now, and where can we find them?"

"You can't."

She looked up. "Why not?"

"They're all dead."

Thirty

LONDON

The clang of steel grates jarred Tal out of the stupor of semi-consciousness, as if to inform him of the nature of his peril. Where am I, he thought, realizing that he was no longer in Lily's flat…but had no memory of leaving. I'm losing my mind.

He could barely recall a day lately without panic, when he hadn't feared for his life or the life of Lily Frasier, the woman he loved, not to mention the fate of Adrian Marcali, a friend and colleague, who now decorated a metal slab at the mortuary.

Nagging question number one: how had he escaped from Max Dearden and Andre Doyle?

So much of his waking energy was spent in a numb womb of unfeeling lately, probably due to prolonged lack of sleep, malnourishment and a constant state of unrest. Tal knew three unwavering truths about his life – he had to be the one to find Lily, he would very likely be accused of Adrian's murder if the police found him, and even more likely was the fact that he was out of a job. Then again, with people like Max, Andre and Richard Wexler working together, his job had never been more than a grand illusion. A good salary for a man his age, with moderate autonomy, and of course, the resumé cachet. It looked and smelled like a good job, like a good life, but as he was now learning, things are rarely as they seem.

Question number two: Where did Lily get her money?

And even more frightening was the question of her whereabouts. If she was a woman with not only secrets but means …

It was 4:00 a.m. now, and the Sea Hag's gentle whisper told him that they would be coming. Yet he walked slowly, sauntering almost, passing a cluster of working girls huddled under a cold streetlight on the corner of Dean and Bateman Streets.

"Need a date, love? Looking a tad lonely for this time of night," a tall, husky woman shouted as he crossed the street.

"Yeah, looky there," another one cackled. "He's too cute to be walking alone."

Ignoring their advances, Tal walked quietly back to Lily's neighborhood and her flat. Uncaring of who he might find inside, he jammed his key in the lock and peered into the darkness. Empty.

Lights, television, a nice strong pot of Earl Grey drunk out of Lily's finest Royal Albert bone china. Now, he decided, I can think. Tal untied his uncomfortable shoes, lay down flat on the white, leather sofa he'd helped Lily choose, and his eyes alighted on something on the narrow wall across from him. Without moving, he squinted to read the calligraphy script. A gilded etching in the center, set in red and gold, around which read the phrase, "Split a piece of wood and I'll be there. Lift a stone and you will find me."

It sounded Biblical, but Lily was specifically and purposefully unreligious. Or so she had said. Then again, all he thought he knew about her all this time had been proved false. Lily Frasier, though indisputably the love of his life so far, was a complete stranger.

"My God!" he said, snapping himself upright. Had he even thought to try her cell phone? Then he remembered she'd just got a new one with a different number. "Damn, where's that number," he said aloud, fumbling through the folded papers in his wallet. Library card, coffee loyalty card, where was Lily's old, stained business card that he'd taken from her desk at his job interview, the one he had fondled numerous times in an endless battle of whether to call her or not? Wait, he thought, here it - no, that's not it, this is a—

It was a crisp, new version of Lily's card. What's this doing here, he wondered, holding it close to his face. He rose to stand near the window for better light and flipped the card over.

Someone had handwritten the phrase, "Check Adrian's autopsy report."This card wasn't in his wallet the last time he looked, and it wasn't Lily's handwriting.

Thirty-One

BOSTON

"Ms. Buchman, you're not helping matters. Can we get back to my original question?"

Corinna glanced out the window of her second-story office in the Boston Herald building and wiped her eyes with a crumpled tissue. "In the past week," she said avoiding eye contact with Officer Tom Kirby, "nearly everyone in my department's been fired, and my best friend and her husband have disappeared. Sorry for my jangled nerves."

Kirby looked up from his clipboard, where he had taken notes. "Do you have a reason to suspect foul play as regards the disappearance of Simone Careski?"

Corinna just sighed. "Are you forgetting your visit with Alex? He told me what happened." She faced him now. "He came to see you immediately after she was kidnapped. He was hysterical, to say the least."

"That was on what date again?"

Another sigh. "September 10th. His birthday," she added softly. "And why hasn't any investigation been initiated on Simone's disappearance? I filed the missing person's report four days ago." Wiping more tears from her face, she moved to stand by the door.

Get a grip, Corinna, she thought.

"Ms. Careski has no other kin in Boston and you refused to give us contact information for her kin in Japan. The most obvious place to check is with her husband, who's also supposedly missing. We've posted notices about her disappearance in all of our usual places. Other than that, I'm afraid, we wait. Unless, of course, you'd like to cooperate with our investigation and—"

"And alarm her eighty-year-old Japanese mother who barely speaks a word of English? Forget it. Simone's not in Japan anyway. Alex told me she was being taken to Rome." Simone played the tape back in her head. "Did you say supposedly, officer?"

"Hmm?" he mumbled with his eyes on his clipboard.

"Alex," Corinna insisted.

Now Tom Kirby looked up, seeming to edit his thoughts before speaking. "Alex was, how should I say it, under a lot of stress, you know, God knows he's a workaholic if I ever—"

Corinna widened her gaze on the officer and folded her arms across her chest. "I can't believe what I'm hearing. What a - and you of all people, Tom, who was his partner for a goddamned decade. Alex is a … suspect? How can you live with yourself?"

Officer Kirby's palms went up. "No one's saying—"

"And you're asking for my cooperation? You think Alex kidnapped his own wife." She shook her head, and a strand of hair fell across her face. "Unbelievable."

"We have a digital image of the man who hit Alex in the parking garage, the blond man he mentioned as holding a gun up in his rearview mirror and, according to Alex, the same man who barged into his house and started shooting."

Tacitly impressed that they'd made *any* progress whatsoever, Corinna stayed to listen.

"We used facial recognition software to match the man's photograph," flipping a page, "a Michael Barbados, who was last seen in Ecuador ..." Corinna opened her mouth to speak, but the officer continued. "... as well as Miguel Sodabra, who was last seen in San Juan, Puerto Rico —"

"And what d—"

"One more - you'll like this one. M. David Brazos. Interpol investigator."

"What does that mean?" Corinna pressed.

Officer Kirby leaned on the desk, while Corinna remained awkwardly at the door. "It means, to me, a lot of things. That Michael Barbados is not this man's real name, nor are any of the others, that his pseudonyms are concealing the name of an individual with a long criminal history. He's smart, has an agenda, can vanish without a trace, but—"

"Access," Corinna interrupted.

"Exactly. Someone who knows a lot of people, knows how to network, how to collect and transfer information and probably gets paid a lot of money for it."

"Why do you say that? If he's on the run all the time—"

"We traced a British Airways ticket back to a Michael Barbados, purchased two months ago, to London. First class."

Corinna listened.

"Let me ask you something, Ms. Buchman. What do Alex and Simone have in common? I mean something ... noteworthy."

"Words."

"Meaning?"

"Alex is a journalist. One of the better-known journalists on the East Coast. Simone's an international translator."

"So languages then," said Officer Kirby, thinking.

"It all goes back to Soren," Corinna realized. "And I sort of think this is more about him than anyone else."

"You might be right."

After Kirby left, Corinna slid her office key into Alex's office door, entered the office and closed and locked the door behind her. "Come on, Alex, give me something here." She turned on his computer and reminded herself to breathe while waiting for it to boot up. Nothing in Alex's inbox looked promising and she opened a browser window and checked her own email from his computer. Twenty-seven new emails.

One from a **careski@bostonherald.com**.

I'll be damned, she thought, smiling for the first time in over a week. The email opened and had three lines of text on it, with a subject line that read "Earth to Alex, come in Alex."

I'm fine, can't tell you anything, don't worry. Go to my basement, pick up rest of boxes containing Soren's diaries. Keep at your house for now. My mind tells me to panic, but my heart says Simone's alive.

Love and hope.

Tal Gardner knew that the man he had been for the past thirty years had no business in this crazy life of running from strangers and hiding from the law. Where was that mild-mannered, bookish, shy lad from Lyme Regis, an only child of aging parents crazy about antiques? Long gone, he thought, standing in the alley between the two vine-covered halves of the Castleman Library.

He walked now in the safety of darkness, thrilled to be free from captivity or the illusion of such, out of the light of the streetlamps and slinked along curbsides in the shadows of sycamores, Siberian elms, and the occasional distempered junky. It was an alien life now, though he had no real memory of the transition between Assistant Curator and fringe dweller.

Do I even belong to England anymore, he asked himself, still walking. I'm lost in a city that no longer feels like my own, with scarcely any contact from other humans, eating crusty bread for breakfast, served coffee by strange, gun-throbbing Frenchmen. I remember my father's zoo-philosophy - never show fear. Eat, or be consumed by others. Am I a vampire, or a cockroach?

Walking toward the Westminster Public Mortuary, Tal reminded himself that his old persona would simply not do in this situation. Today, right now, if he was going to follow directions, he had to be someone else. Shotgun Tal, Gangster Tal, Homeboy Tal. "You gotta problem with that?" he mocked in his Godfather voice.

"Good morning," he bellowed into the air, leaning on the front counter of HM Coroner's Court in the Westminster Public Mortuary He made sure to groan, mess up his hair, and rub his eyes red prior to being seen.

"I'm Thomas Marcali," he lied to a pale-faced girl standing opposite him. He waited for his name to register. He sighed. Pulled a face in mock distress. "I called an hour ago and arranged to pick up my brother's autopsy report," he said as a question

The roundish, light blue eyes stared back in utter confusion. "Who, I'm sorry?" she stammered.

"I'm on my way to the," pause, "funeral now, miss. I'm Adrian Marcali's brother, my mum, heaven knows why, requested the autopsy repo—"

"Are you quite certain there is such a report? I mean, it's not customary, unless—"

"An autopsy is not customary with a fatal gunshot wound to the chest?" Tal replied, then paused, sighed and wiped his eyes. "Please, I implore you, could you hurry?"

The woman shook herself to attention suddenly. "Yes, of course. And who did you speak to about this?"

"I don't know, it was actually my wife who called and put in the family request." When had lying become so easy suddenly?

Five minutes later, he walked out with a file folder under his arm and checked the alleyway under the growing light of sunrise before exiting. The sky was changing. The world was changing.

And in the file folder were five empty sheets of paper, stapled together.

Thirty-Two

ITALY

Alex awoke to the sound of rustling paper.

"Is it Italian air that I smell?"

Mona rose from the other bed and placed a tall, Styrofoam cup on the bedside table, which already displayed a plate of rolls and butter. "Cappuccino. It's early," she continued. "Why don't you sleep?"

He felt her eyes on him. "How early?" he asked, opening one eye.

Mona peered at him now from the desk in the corner of the room. A dim lamp glowed, and her hand was between pages in one of Soren's diaries.

Alex spun to the edge of the bed. "Please don't tell me you've been up all night." He saw dark circles under Mona's eyes. "You'll go blind trying to read that garbage."

"Something you said in the café, something we said … I don't know … came back to me last night. We said that if Soren *had* discovered something about his mother language or whatever he was looking for, he wouldn't have recorded it in a diary that somebody could steal."

"Right ..." Alex replied and waited.

"But I don't think he would have written it anywhere else."

"So you think it's there, but it's not there?"

"Exactly." She half-smiled.

"Encoded." Of course, he thought.

"You know about this?" she asked.

"It's, no. It's gibberish," he blurted.

"Liar." Mona clapped the diary closed and crossed her arms. "You must know."

Alex pulled on the same pair of wrinkled khaki pants he'd worn for the past five days and stood awkwardly by the bed. "Look, as smart as you obviously are, people have been, I mean not regular people like us, but career scholars, cryptographers, trying to crack Soren's code for the past, what, twenty years? And you think you could do it in one night?"

"I did," she said quietly. Mona looked past Alex to the light bleeding in through the crack in the curtains, then returned her eyes to the diaries.

Alex picked his glasses off the bedside table, and walked, hands in pockets, from the window sill to the desk and knelt on the floor. "Okay, what am I looking at?"

"Code."

He sighed.

Mona flipped back one page, chewed the end of her pen and tapped it on the desk. "He's braided it."

"Define braided."

"From what I can tell, he braided four languages together to make an encryption system. Some of the languages are isolated - here," she flipped to the beginning pages of the diary, "this whole section's in what I believe is Aramaic, another part's all in, I don't know. I can only guess he's done that to conceal his findings from people who wanted to take credit for his discoveries."

Alex nodded. "Or debunk them, and there were many. All through childhood, I remember shouting matches and contentious meetings late at night where my mother had to mediate, threaten to call the police."

"I think, in this one particular part of the diary, he's concealed his findings by braiding four distinct languages." She looked up and smiled. "And what's so brilliant about this … is that they all look so similar that to an untrained eye, it's almost impossible to tell them apart."

"How did you, then?"

"Well, in the back of each diary," she flipped and pointed, "there's a legend, showing ten characters from one specific language. Here's Arkadian from 2400 BC," she flipped to another journal, "Phoenician, Tifinagh and Ogham."

Alex shook his head. "How do you know how to identify these?"

"Because he defined them. He's got another code here—"

"Jesus."

"Listen, numbers that correspond to letters in the English alphabet. I spelled them out, and though I'd never heard of Arkadian, it's said to be the oldest written Semitic language."

Alex gasped when he saw the paper. "You dog-eared pages in my father's diary?"

"Do you want to find your wife?" Mona asked, emotionless. "Shut up, then." She pointed halfway down the page. "Here – what do you think?"

"I see a bunch of lines," Alex moved closer.

"That's right. Arkadian has predominantly vertical lines, Hinge Ogham has diagonal lines, I've been comparing these all night."

"And this code," Alex said, "what's the overall message he's hidden?"

"Still working on it." She went to the bedside table, bit into one of the rolls and sipped the cappuccino. "Braids. What does that tell you?" she sat on the bed and stretched out.

"Braids." Alex shook his head. "You take three strands of hair, or cable, or protein strands or whatever and weave them together in a pattern to make a braid. How is he braiding languages?"

"I've isolated the common symbols identifying the individual languages, and when you unbraid them,

I believe they each spell something different in their individual language. A phrase or a sentence."

"Like a mnemonic?"

"For instance," she said and took another sip, "I took that entire section, eight pages in the middle of the diary that are encoded this way, and I isolated all the Ogham letters. They spell something." Another sip.

"Like an address?"

"It spelled '*Book of Ballymote.*' It didn't sound right, but it—"

Alex nodded. "I've heard of it. Have you heard of the *Book of Kells?*"

"No," she admitted.

"It's an ancient Celtic text with gospels from the *Bible* written in Latin. Then there's a *Book of Ballymote*, and several others like it. As far as I recall, they date back to the seventh century." Alex stopped to let the silence punctuate his words. Mona's expression mirrored the weight of what he'd said.

"One of the texts stolen from the Castleman Library was an excerpt from the *Book of Ballymote.*"

Alex wrinkled his brow. "How would you know that?"

Mona looked askance. "The news ... Twitter ... ever heard of it?"

Alex's mind wandered back to Boston, to the man in the parking garage, to what Simone had said about the article on Rome he was supposed to be writing, and now this. Soren Careski's secret language codes involving ancient texts, two ancient texts stolen from the British Museum in the same week, his wife - an international translator - kidnapped. There had to be a connection. And now Mona was tossing things into a backpack.

"Where do you think you're going?"

"Angelica Library. It's where my sister said we would meet, so there's at least a chance she's there."

Five hard knocks at the door.

Alex widened his eyes, darting them between Mona and the door. Her hand squeezed his forearm.

"Dude, you look like a deer in headlights. It's probably room service."

"More likely the police," Alex said and quickly slid into a shirt.

Mona, instantly in character, slipped into the bathroom, wrapped her hair in a towel, flicked water on her face, removed her pants and unbuttoned her blouse. "*Bon giorno,*" she said, out of breath and smiling.

Two middle-aged, male police officers stood at attention, their eyes immediately scanning her bare legs. They said nothing.

"*Si*?" she added, feigning annoyance.

"What is your name, miss? Are you on travel in Rome?"

Mona blinked her large eyes very slowly, tacitly informing them of her non-compliance. "Why?"

"Answer the question," barked the shorter of two men.

"To my knowledge, Italy is not a communist country. I can go wherever I please."

The officer moved two inches toward her.

"I live in Naples. Does that answer your question?"

The shorter officer smiled; the taller one shook his head.

"Mona DelFreggio, age 28, Sofia Loren wannabe," she replied wafting out the tails of her unbuttoned shirt.

"We need to speak with Alexander Careski. He filed a re—"

Alex appeared in the doorway. "Yes? I'm Alex." He looked at Mona and tapped the back of her head. "It's all right, sweetheart."

The officers glanced between the two of them.

"She's a bit protective of me, officers."

"For man looking for his wife, she is interesting distraction," one officer said with his eyes on Mona.

Alex rolled his eyes and set his jaw tight. "She's my daughter, for God's sake. Do you have information about Sim—"

"My stepmother?" Mona piped in. "Where is she?" Tears magically formed in the corners of her eyes. "Where is she?" She grabbed the front of the shorter officer's uniform.

"You need to come with us," one of them said to Alex. "Alone," he added.

Alex whispered imaginary words in Mona's ear and gently pushed her back into the room. "Get dressed, sweetheart." Then, to the officers, "Do you have information about Simone or not?"

Simultaneously, one said yes and the other said no.

"Shall I … flip a coin or do you want to arm wrestle?"

"We ask," said the taller, calmer officer, "that you ride with us to precinct so we can give information about your wife's disappearance."

"All right," he said, buttoning his shirt. As he turned, Mona tore through the doorway.

"Don't go!" Turning to Alex, she said, "Don't go with them. It's a trick." She took two steps closer and leaned up to his ear. "Please," she whispered.

"Yes, go to the convent, see Sister Angelica like you'd planned," he said and winked. "I'll meet you there in an hour. I'll have the officers give me a ride after I talk with them." He wrapped his arms paternally around her. "Don't worry, we'll find her."

Mona produced more fake tears and dragged her white sleeve across her eyes to blot them. "Not if they don't want you to find her."

"What's that supposed to mean?"

The officers sighed at the door. And Alex felt even more admiration for this young, strange woman who, at the drop of a hat, assumed the role of his daughter. He kissed her cheek. "See you later." From the door, he looked back at her and lip-synched the words, "Meryl Streep."

Thirty-Three

ITALY

"You visiting, *signorina*?"

Mona ignored the cab driver while scrutinizing the same page of text in Soren's diary. The young man, adorned with too-long sideburns, kept peeking in his rearview mirror, reminding her of Miguel.

Alex, he knows things. He feels things. He doesn't need to talk every second to take up space in the silence.

She shook Miguel's image out of her head. There had to be a way. Soren's code was more than just a challenge now, especially since scholars had unsuccessfully tried to unbraid it for two decades.

"Stop!" she announced, spotting a sign for an internet café. "Here," she pointed, closed the diary, and moistened her lips in lieu of lipstick. She leaned forward and half-smiled. "I need you to wait here."

"You pay. 'Ow long?"

Slow blink of her long lashes. "Five minutes."

Five small round tables and a coffee bar, a sign that read 'Wireless' she ordered a cappuccino and appraised the situation. The universe, manifestly in her favor today, seemed especially fond of her plan, as the last table was located just inside the back door of the café. A laptop waited, set up and blinking, its user obviously in the restroom.

"Two euros," said the young girl at the cash register, barely looking up from a book. Mona eyed the restroom and pulled a bill from her pocket, and picked up the cup. She remembered, then, what Miguel had taught her when she'd first moved to Naples. No fear. Moving deliberately to the last table, she set down her cup, closed up the unplugged laptop, tossed it into the bag beside it, and walked out the back door of the café.

She winked at the cabbie as she opened the rear door.

Without taking time to breathe, she closed and locked the cab door. "Angelica Library, *fretta*!"

Thirty-Four

LONDON

His lids had barely closed and four hours went by. The cup of Earl Grey on his bedside table was cold and the bright afternoon had turned to a foggy, dismal dusk. Tal Gardner stumbled into his kitchen to boil more water, hungry for the first time in weeks.

He stood at the stove in bare feet and pajama pants and wondered about painting the walls. Or rearranging furniture - something physical and concrete to commemorate every other change. Then he heard a sound in the foyer. His front door opened.

Putting down the tin of loose tea leaves, he tiptoed to the foyer and reached to pick up a hard-soled shoe off the floor. He held it sole-up over his head.

"Who's there?"

As the door thrust open, Tal saw only the swish of black fabric as flesh contacted his own flesh, bone to bone, knuckle to jaw. "Jesus Christ, wh—"

On his back now, someone stood over him with one leg on each side of his head. "Jesus isn't here just now, Mr. Gardner. How about you talk to me instead?"

Blinking, Tal saw Max Dearden move to his kitchen to remove the squealing kettle from the stove. Tal stood, pushed Andre in the chest with both hands, and steadied himself.

"Earl Grey? Yes, that'd be lovely," Max said reaching into a cupboard for a cup.

"Shall I bake some scones for us?" Tal moved to the bedroom to find a clean shirt.

"You were warned, Mr. Gardner," Andre bellowed from the living room.

Tal emerged from the bedroom tucking a pressed Oxford into a pair of jeans. "About what exactly?"

"What do you want with Adrian's autopsy report?" Andre asked, pulling open the slide on his semi-automatic pistol.

"I was hoping to read it, actually. Seems there might have been a problem with adequate ink in the printer?"

"Funny." Andre took a steaming cup of tea from Max. "Look, I think it's time to—"

Tal glanced at Max. "If Lily's your daughter," he interrupted, "where is she now? Have you hidden her somewhere to keep her from being arrested for the Castleman Library theft that you no doubt forced her to commit?"

Andre cleared his throat. "She's got nothing to do with that."

Again, Tal addressed his question to Max. "What about your partner, Max? He's still alive, obviously, so where is he?"

Andre took three steps and stood nose to nose with Tal. "You've got—"

"You want to kill me? Make my nose bleed, bruise my face?" Tal faced him unblinking, then took a step back and covered his throat with his hands.

"I'm trying to save your pathetic life," Andre whispered.

Tal backed off and sat on the edge of his sofa. "I want some answers." Long sigh. "And more tea, please."

"I'll get it," Max replied.

"First of all, what's Lily got to do with Soren Careski?"

Silence answered his question at first. Max passed him a cup, and Andre observed the ceiling tiles.

"All right, how about I answer my own question then? I think there was something hidden in one of the Castleman books. Lily, as Medieval Antiquities Director, had access to everything in the entire museum. So whoever removed her from the museum, or if she wasn't removed then whoever's looking for her, must believe that she saw or at least had access to whatever was hidden. And naturally, Lily might have informed Adrian of her discovery, and now he's dead. So at least *that* part's wrapped up nice and neat. And, well, Lily's your daughter, Max, so her knowledge of whatever it is you're trying to hide is a bit more difficult then, I suppose. Don't you agree?"

Max looked as if he might either cry or curl up in a ball on the sofa. "You're correct and incorrect."

"And what, you're putting me in danger by telling me anything?"

"There's nothing to tell," Andre answered this time.

"So you don't know anything, or you're waiting? Is that it?"

"Mr. Gardner, it's really up to you now," Andre said, slipping the gun into his jacket pocket and rising.

Thirty-Five

ROME

All exactly the same. Bodies everywhere. Bald heads static and unmoved, limbs frozen, even the walls. A tomb, Mona thought. It's a giant tomb in here, and they're all dead.

"Mausoleum," came an unexpected voice beside her.

"*Scusi*?" she said, turning to observe a dapper, middle-aged man in a heavy suit two sizes too big for his frame.

"You said the word tomb just now. The correct term is mausoleum."

Like a jackal skilled at overtaking prey, Mona stared across at the man, gauging what exactly she might need from him and the quickest method of obtaining it.

"Are you lost, miss?"

The combination of the man's East Indian accent, Tibetan bone structure and calming energy was not what she expected. He was not an academic. She liked him instantly. He must be a staff member.

"*Si, grazi.*" Then came her signature sparkling-white smile and the extension of her hand. "Mona Delfreggio."

As they shook hands, she noticed that the man's eyes hadn't left hers. This man was a thinker; not a user or even a predator like herself. Instantly readjusting her role from bimbo to passionate scholar, she set down the bag with the laptop and pulled out the diary she'd been reading. "This book," she said clutching it tight into her chest, "belonged to my father," she lied, leaning in close to the stranger, whose eyes scrutinized her every movement. "I need to find a translator," she whispered.

"We have plenty." The man looked up and behind him to the balconies over their heads and pointed. "On the Angelica Library staff are five translators who are fluent in—"

Mona looked at the man's nametag, now - Vajrini Khan. She touched his elbow lightly to interrupt him. "Arkadian? Or Tifinagh?"

Vaj stopped talking and glared at her. "Your father's diaries are written in ancient script?" He laughed quietly and shook his head. "What makes you think this? Don't you think it's more likely Hebrew?"

"No."

The man paused, scanned the main floor of the library and pointed to the end of the main hallway. "Follow me, please. There is an empty room where we can talk for a moment."

Mona pulled out the page from Lily's email and unfolded it. Vaj glanced at it and shook his head. "This is what you think is Arkadian?"

Mona said nothing.

"You are a linguistics student?"

"Yes," she lied. "My father was an epigrapher. He came across an old book just before he died, and this is a scan of one of the pages. Can you translate this, Vajrini?"

Knowing that addressing a stranger, especially an Old-World stranger, by their first name was a risk. But there was no time for protocol now. Lily had been missing for nearly two weeks, she had been kidnapped, and Alex's wife was likely dead - all because of one page from a manuscript.

"Come with me," the man said.

Outside the small conference room was a carpeted corridor with offices on each side. She noted that every door was closed, looked alike, and the hallway was devoid of sound. At the last door, they turned left and took an elevator up three floors.

"Does God live up here?" she half-joked, curious for his response.

Vaj's brow wrinkled as they exited the elevator. He led her down a long hallway with huge marble floor tiles. "There are plenty of churches and cathedrals in Rome, Miss, not to mention Vatican City. This is a library, plain and simple."

Vaj did not speak again until they'd passed through a set of heavy, glass doors at the end of the hallway. It was a long, cavernous room with six tables arranged in pairs down the center. "Rocco? Terese? Prego."

A young man peeked his head out of a dark corner of the room and motioned to Vaj. "Yeah, here - grandma's making lunch." He rose from a computer station and walked out into the artificial glow of fluorescent lights. Hair completely shaved on the sides and pink and blue on the crown, silver stud piercings in his nose, bottom lip and both ears, the man had on the most expensive wool suit jacket Mona had ever seen. Armani with ripped jeans and combat boots. Nice.

"You didn't tell me God was a punk rocker," she said aloud to Vaj.

The young man's eyes scanned Mona from bow to stern and grinned. "Usually takes three dates before a woman calls me God."

"Be nice to him," Vaj counseled. "Rocco's much smarter than he looks."

She turned toward Vaj and slid the folded email instinctively into her back pocket. "You're telling me *he's* going to translate my father's manuscript page? You've got to be kidding."

Rocco crossed his arms. "I'm being tutored by my grandmother, Terese D'Ambrosio." He paused to punctuate the name.

Mona stared, waiting.

"You don't know her? She's a famous linguist."

"More so than Soren Careski?" she blurted.

The ensuing silence made her instantly wish she could retrieve her words, hanging heavily on the air. Rocco and Vaj exchanged glances. The vibration of wooden chairs dragged against marble floors resonated from the ground floor as an old woman shuffled in with a notebook in her wrinkled hands.

"Grandma, this is … I'm sorry, we never did actually—"

Mona shook the woman's hand, warm and clammy to the touch.

By the grooves in her complexion, Mona guessed her to be at least ninety. The woman's head came up to Mona's chest and held a thick knot of coarse, grizzled hair. She turned her face up and stared thoughtfully. "Mo-na, Mona, such a pretty face …" she touched Mona's chin, "and such devious eyes. I don't trust you." Slight smile. "But I'll try."

"Could we talk privately for a moment?" Mona asked, glancing at Rocco. Vaj disappeared toward the elevators and Rocco stood before them with his fists stuffed in his pockets.

"Come," she said and shuffled into another room.

They sat in two heavy, wooden chairs beside an open window with a deep sill. The old woman picked up a plastic bag, gathered a handful of breadcrumbs and held her open palm out the window. Three doves instantly flew to the sill and ate quietly out of her hand. "You are afraid of something," she said without looking up.

Mona sighed, wondering how to begin. "I live in Naples. Isn't everyone?

"Only of ourselves, young lady. Are you married?"

"Terese, I don't mean to be rude, but I have a great urgency to get a sheet of manuscript translated. A woman's life is at stake."

Terese jerked her head toward Mona. "Whose? Yours?" she demanded.

"No. The wife of a friend."

"And what are you doing with the 'friend' while the wife is ... wherever she is?"

Mona smirked. "You remind me of my grandmother."

"Maybe I *am*."

"She died when I was six."

The old relic released a cackling laugh and pulled her hand from the feeding birds. Mona had no way of knowing this woman's credentials, if she was even still able to decipher ancient languages or if her eyes even worked anymore. But she had nowhere else to go. She laid Soren's diary open to one of the center pages.

"I'm trying to identify this page," she said pointing to a series of lines in Soren's diary. "If it even is a language."

The woman gave the page only a passing glance. "It's an alphabet, not a language, not really. You should go to the Royal Academy in Dublin. Speak with a woman named Bernadette."

Great, Mona thought, more referrals. She reluctantly pulled the folded sheet of paper from her back pocket. "Do you know Soren Careski?"

The wrinkled eyelids widened, the dark eyes stared. "You know I do," Terese answered quickly. "He's been gone a long time now. Yes?"

She unfolded the page and, without letting go of the corner, held it out in front of Terese.

The old woman breathed deeply, then her mouth tightened into a tiny dot. "I don't have my glasses. I left them on my intern's desk."

"Of course you did," Mona replied.

Something registered instantly on the woman's face. Was it pity? Or maybe fear? "This is very, very old."

"Coptic?" Mona pressed.

"Where did you get this?"

Feeling like she was sent to the principal's office, Mona worked quickly to negotiate her response. "Someone sent it to me, via email."

"Email?" asked the old woman, incredulous. "Somebody emailed you this page of text?"

Mona held the woman's spindly forearm. "You've got to translate it for me, there's no more time. Please!"

The old woman glanced nervously around the room, then pulled her chair nearer to Mona. She leaned into the page. "Yes."

"Yes what? You know what it is?"

"It's a religious text. That I can tell you," she whispered now.

Mona's brain spun the information around. "It's from the Bible? But it doesn't look like Aramaic to me."

Terese puckered her lips and shook her head. "No. Not really."

"What does that mean, not really? Either it is, or it isn't."

"Young lady, you know some things, indeed, but there are many things you don't. Life is not so cut and dried, I'm afraid. Especially when it comes to old languages and secret manuscripts. The Holy Bible has had hundreds, thousands of translations, editions, publishers, and the contents are not so locked down. What was included in the text two hundred, one hundred, even fifty years ago isn't necessarily what was included before that."

"Terese, please," Mona begged. "Tell me where I can go to get this page translated. I need to know what it says, what it is, not just for my curiosity, but to decipher a code. There must be someone or something."

Again, Terese's small head whipped left and right to scan the room. "A book. It comes from a text that was discovered in Egypt."

"This book, could it be in the British Museum?"

"It is in the British Museum, in their library of antiquities. A book was published in 1950 citing the findings from the Egypt discoveries in 1945."

"I'm afraid it *was* in the British Museum, Terese. That book was stolen from the Castleman Library the same day this email arrived on my computer."

The woman held up a finger as if to say wait here, and disappeared around the corner. Mona slid out of her shoes and, staying ten steps behind her, followed her. The old woman took the stairs, not the elevator, down one floor and scurried around a dark corner to a small, lit room. She closed the door to the room behind her. Inside the office, Mona heard another door close. Then another door opened and closed. Terese didn't come out of the office the same way she went in. She heard two female voices on the opposite side of the floor. Stopping in her tracks, one of the voices belonged to Terese. The other, she wasn't sure. A younger voice.

No time for formality and manners, Mona entered the small office and smelled a familiar scent - orange. She looked for a fruit basket on the desk in the reception area - none. She quickly got into the adjacent private office, and a small light illuminated the desk blotter. On it was a stack of envelopes, a pair of modern glasses, a nameplate that read Dr. L. Dearden, and a leather handbag. I know that handbag, she thought. Dooney & Bourke, dark red with a long shoulder strap. It was the same kind of handbag her half-sister carried.

My God, she thought. Lily.

Thirty-Six

ROME

Patience. It was her most poorly-evolved trait. The ladies' room on the main floor of the library seemed the most discreet, yet still an easily accessible meeting place. Thirty-eight acoustic ceiling tiles, and one hundred ninety-one squares of ceramic tile on the floors.

The ladies' room door creaked open.

Mona picked her feet up from the floor, balanced her body weight on the toilet seat and peeked in between the stall doors. She saw unmistakable strawberry blonde hair.

"Jesus, Lily, what took you so long? I thought you were dea—"

An older woman in a dark green suit stared as Mona opened the stall door.

"*Mi scusi,* I thought you were someone else," Mona said.

"Like me?"

Mona turned to the voice, staggered back two steps and then thrust her arms around her only sister.

"Oh my God, I'm glad to see you."

"Is that true?" Lily said, pulling away.

Ignoring the question, Mona wiped a single tear from her eye. "I thought something had happened to you. I've been waiting over an hour."

Lily raised a brow. "How long?"

"I left a note on your desk. An hour and ten minutes, to be exact."

"I've been waiting two weeks for you, Mona."

Lily's icy voice shook Mona out of whatever shock she'd felt in seeing her. "I left voicemails on your cell phone."

A long sigh, releasing what felt like the entire weight of decades' worth of sibling baggage. Mona leaned wearily against the clean, white sink. "You don't seem to have strained yourself looking for me."

Lily shook her head. "I've been in touch with the police in Naples *and* Rome, as I had no confirmation that you ever got here."

"And?"

"Oh, come on. Young woman in her twenties with long dark hair. At least half of Italy meets that description. The police informed me that I'd be arrested if I kept bothering them."

Mona turned away and stalled for time by splashing cold water on her face as the suited woman exited. "I don't know where they took me." She could almost see Lily rolling her eyes.

"Who?"

"I don't know who they were. There was a man there with me, too. We were both held in the same cell, and then we broke out and have been traveling together." Mona watched her older sister lean casually against the wall. Not one single flaw in her complexion, not a hair out of place, perfect body, impeccable speech, stellar career. Disgusting. For so many years, she'd wanted to be like her, or just *be* her, period. And now, a simple business transaction. Would there ever be anything more between them?

Mona held out the folded sheet. "Terese, the old woman, left the room in a hurry when I showed her this. Can you translate it?"

"This is what you emailed me?"

"That's right."

Lily blinked back, studying her. "What's your interest in this? Do you realize what it is?"

Lily's voice sounded strange. Mona instinctively backed two steps away from her and wondered if any of the stalls were occupied. "I know what it represents," she replied ducking to peek under each stall. "A language that hasn't been spoken in thousands of years. And if this text is written in that language, and if the manuscript related to this email was discovered in Nag Hammadi, it could be very threatening to a lot of people, including the Vatican."

"Not a language," Lily clarified.

"What do you mean?"

Lily kept her eyes on the floor. "You've been doing your homework," she said. "How exactly could you know all this?"

"I've got to get back to my hotel," she said. "I'm meeting a—"

Lily turned on her and grabbed both her shoulders. "Mona, listen to me - what you just told me is *very* dangerous information, and it's something you know very little about."

"You might be surprised."

Lily blinked twice.

"It took me this long to get here because I was abducted at the airport. I was held captive in the cellar of a large estate with a man named Alex."

"Alex?" Lily asked shakily.

"Yeah. Alex Careski."

Silence.

"I think you know that name."

Lily closed her eyes.

Thirty-Seven

LONDON

Max Dearden stood in front of his stove and said, "Earl Grey, hot." Nothing happened. "Engage," he commanded, trying again. "Engage!"

But his old, copper kettle was not a simulator on the Starship Enterprise and, sadly, no twenty-fourth-century transporter could return to him his lifelong academic partner … and best friend. Perhaps the ruse he'd perpetuated was actually true and Soren really was alive. But where? And how had he survived undetected all this time? The nagging questions eventually caused a doctor to prescribe daily pills for his nerves, and even those gave him little comfort now.

He poured water from the kettle into an old, tea-stained, white porcelain pot, grabbed his favorite Geisha mug and walked down the lonely hallway. "Where are you, my old friend?" he said aloud to the empty house.

"I didn't know you cared."

The degree to which Max flinched sent boiling water from the spout onto his bare foot. He pulled it away quickly, but stood on the wood floor, gathering himself. He took two cautious steps toward the living room. "Mr. Gardner."

"You sound rather sad, Max."

"Thought you were someone else." Max returned to the kitchen and pulled a second mug off the mug tree. "You could have knocked, you know."

"Would you have answered?" Tal asked.

"What time is it?"

Tal looked at his watch. "Quarter to six."

"No."

"I have three questions. And if your secret smoking-man is hiding behind the curtains, I'm prepared to defend mys—"

"He's not here," Max interjected and sat on the sofa.

"What's ACES and who were the principal members?"

Max closed his eyes and breathed. "How did you hear of this?"

"Ever heard of an invention called the internet? Or perhaps a library?"

"Don't be ridiculous. As if a library would have anything on that. As far as the internet goes, we made sure to remove every trace of material from at least four of the major search engin—"

Tal smiled and nodded.

"Do you have a death wish, Mr. Gardener?"

"That's my business if I do." Tal walked around the room.

"As I recall, you were given a very specific warning about this line of questioning."

"I already know the American Council of Epigraphy Scholars. You and your partner, Mr. Careski, founded it in 1978."

"Oh? Well, if you were smart, you'd realize that my reticence might just save your very life. Go ahead, sniff around, make a nuisance of yourself at libraries, make phone calls impersonating deans of colleges, yes, yes, we know about that."

Tal stopped walking.

"I guess I'd like to know why, Mr. Gardener." Max rose and walked to the foyer. "Why are you doing this? Why have you completely turned your life around for unanswerable questions?" Max opened the front door.

"Because I'm in love with your daughter, and I believe the only way to find her is to pursue the course that began with the Castleman thefts." Tal paced slowly to the doorway. "I want to find her," pause, "so I'm afraid my fate is sealed on this path."

Max shook his head and looked at Tal. "Don't sleep at home anymore," he whispered, barely moving his lips. "Don't use public phones, stay away from your apartment, and do yourself a favor, Mr. Gardner, take yourself target shooting. You'll be needing the practice."

Thirty-Eight

LONDON

Sometimes he liked walking in Harrow. The town center, now one of London's least desirable neighborhoods, Harrow and Middlesex County was nostalgic to him, having lived there as a child, before there were murders and illegal drug transactions and flesh-for-hire. At this point, what could he possibly be afraid of? He eyed the Travelodge and Lindal Hotel on Junction Road and then reconsidered. If they've been tailing me, he thought, they already know I'm here. Okay then, he continued, I could drive up to Windsor or Maidenhead and stay in a bed and breakfast for a few days with a pseudonym. If he had wanted to disappear, there were endless possibilities. Already, he'd been on the run for weeks without really going home for more than an hour at a time. Max told him to hide out, avoid his apartment, and essentially live like a vampire.

"Need a date, love?" came a drunken, female voice. His vision started low with three-inch heels, purple fishnet stockings, and a skirt that hid no more than pubic hair and an inch of thigh.

"Hi, Crystal," he said, recognizing not only her profession but having heard her name called by other girls on the corner. Her expressive gum-chewing seemed to match the degree of paint on her young face. "I've got to g—"

"What's your hurry?" The woman rifled her long fingernails through his hair and put her lips to his ear as she asked. "I think you and I should do some serious talking."

As she stepped back, Tal looked at her, really, for the first time, and smiled faintly to himself. Three fire engines swooped past around the corner followed by two police cars, sirens blazing. He grabbed the woman's arm. "I agree entirely. Do you have a place?"

"Ain't you gonna ask how much?"

He shook his head.

Crystal removed the gum from her mouth and stuck the pink wad to the back of her hand. She winked and nodded for him to follow.

"There's an alley just over there," the woman said, pointing

"No, I want someplace private, but something very close."

She cackled. "Hungry then, ain't you?"

He grabbed her shoulders and shook her lightly. "Where? Where can we go? I can't be seen out here."

She recoiled. "With someone like me, you mean? Your pretty little wife might see us?"

"Someone's trying to kill me, and I need a place … to hide. I'll pay you. Now please, where can we talk?"

Crystal didn't move. Tal took three twenty-pound notes from his wallet and pressed them into her palm. "Please."

Jaw set and without moving her head, Crystal blinked her large, painted blue eyes at a four-story brick building at the end of the alley. "There."

"That's your place?"

"Not exactly."

"Great."

Soundlessly he trailed her, scanning the street and every corner of the alley as he moved ahead. At the other side of the brick building, Crystal climbed concrete steps that led to the second floor - in her three-inch heels. Fumbling behind her, Tal could see a tiny patch of white underwear between her tanned legs.

"What's the matter, love? Not enough physical activity lately? What are you, thirty going on seventy?"

"There's an extra ten quid if you shut up."

At the top of the steps, Crystal leaned sideways and hiked open a wide sash window and folded her legs into the dark edifice.

"Don't turn that light on," he hissed, wondering why the window had been left unlocked.

"May I light a candle, your highness?"

"No." He glanced at the moon's reflection on a dusty bookcase and loveseat with torn upholstery. "Here is just fine."

"For what?" she asked, annoyed, arms folded. She plopped down on the loveseat.

Tal pulled his wallet from his pants pocket and sat beside her. "I need you to do something for me. It'll take thirty-five minutes to get there by cab or Uber from here."

"Your errand girl, eh? Money, love. How much is in it for me?"

"Another sixty."

Crystal watched him pull cash out of his wallet. "What've I got to do?"

"Buy a roll of masking tape and spell *a word* with it." Tal placed the three twenty pound notes on the couch between them.

"What you mean spell a word?" She took the notes and stuffed them in her bra, along with the others.

"Tear off pieces of masking tape in the form of a certain arrangement of letters, reversed of course, to my living room window."

The spidery eyes glided left to right. "Like how big, for example?"

"Make each letter a foot high." He wrote down his address and pulled his spare key from his jacket pocket. "It's near Leicester Square. The flat's on the corner of the building on the left. There's a big courtyard in the center of two buildings. I'm number twenty-five. Second floor. Leave this under the mat when you're done." He stood, and handed her a folded piece of paper. "There's the word I want you to spell."

"You just trust me to leave your key under the mat? No wonder someone's trying to off you."

"I'll be right behind you but I'm going separately."

"Like I said," she yelled after him, "thirty going on seventy. Hey, what's this word mean?"

The next morning Tal disobeyed the rules again and used a phone box. Once again, it was five forty-five in the morning. It took Max Dearden seven rings to pick up.

"Do you watch the *X-Files*, Max?" he asked.

"Mm," Max replied, sighed, yawned, and slowly sat up. "Actually, Fox Mulder taped an X to his window, Mr. Gardner, not ACES."

"But they're both likely to result in the same thing, are they not? I thought it was an excellent attention-getting scam."

"You know, I personally thought your delivery girl was a lovely touch. Andre, however, was not amused."

Tal drew in a breath, and decided that every second of his life had become hinged on lies anyway, so one more leap couldn't be a big deal. "I know things, Max," he whispered.

"Yes, I know, you've been doing your research. What've you learned?"

"That the Institute was founded by your partner to formalize his lifelong quest to, at the time anyway, conclusively discover the first language ever spoken on earth. It was something he searched for his whole career. And that somewhere along the line, he stumbled onto something else, something more ... significant."

Max listened.

"I also believe you're the last surviving member of ACES. All the rest are dead."

Max pressed his lips together. "Yes, well, in my profession I've come to realize that *dead* is a somewhat relative term."

"And relates to Soren Careski as well? You know as well as I do that his death was never confirmed. He went underground, maybe so deep he can't get out. What was it that he stumbled onto that gave him the evidence he needed to go public with his discovery?"

"Put it this way, *what* he stumbled upon wasn't necessarily a *what*."

"A person?"

"A place. Alexandria," Max replied and yawned loudly. "Now, listen to me very carefully, because I'm going to tell you one last thing and then I plan to hang up this phone and go back to sleep for at least another hour. Can I assume that you're dumb enough to be standing in a public phone booth right now?"

Pause. "Afraid so, yes."

"Look around. Do you see a car nearby with four dark-tinted windows?"

Tal's stomach clenched and his palms felt moist. Perhaps he was turning into Fox Mulder after all. Was the smoking-man going to drive a car through the phone booth and would Scully drag him out at the last possible second? His eyes landed on a red car, a Rolls Royce, with dark windows. "Yes, I see it," he replied and glanced around without moving his head to gauge a possible emergency exit route.

"There are three men in that car and they're each holding rifles aimed at your head at this very moment and listening to every word you say."

"Anything else?"

"I'm afraid they're not very well mannered." *Click.*

Outside he saw a Pizza Express on the corner across from the Rolls Royce. Thinking fast, he dialed up the number on the restaurant sign and kept one eye on the car. Without moving his body, he spoke quietly. "Hello, I'd like to order three large cokes and have them delivered to the red Rolls Royce that's parked outside your restaurant right now."

During the pause, he saw a young man in a blue and red uniform come to the window and look out. A moment later, the voice returned to the phone. "Yeah, I see it. You said three large cokes? Are you paying for them or are they?"

"Credit card. Visa all right?"

"Yeah, go ahead."

Tal recited his Visa card number.

"Wait just a minute, I'm filling them up now."

Tal waited and saw no change in the orientation of the red Rolls. He watched their reflection in the phone booth's metal mirror but nobody moved. What were they thinking? What were they about to do? Fear flooded his veins. His fingers tapped the metal shelf in the phone booth. "All right, fine. Thank you, I'll take them out right now."

Now with a diversion, he had less than twenty seconds to come up with a plan. On the corner of Charing Cross and Irving, he tried to remember what was on the next street over. There were no alleys leading off this street, but there was a hotel, Seven Dials, situated three buildings down on the same side of the street. To simulate conversation, he nodded and lip-synched into the phone, turned his body away and ran his fingers through his hair. Meanwhile, a pale-skinned youth with dark hair emerged from Pizza Express carrying a tray of heavy drinks. Skating through traffic, the boy was two steps away, one step.

As soon as the boy's fist made the first knock against the Rolls' passenger window, Tal was out the door and running toward the hotel. It looked to be about one hundred meters from the phone booth and he was already up to twenty. Don't look back, he counseled himself and resisted the urge to do so every three or four strides. He listened for fast footsteps pounding the pavement behind him or shots, but nothing. No guns discharging bullets. He entered the hotel lobby and hid behind a curtain to peek out of a window at the car.

The two front doors of the Rolls were open, liquid was spilled on the windshield … and a boy lay in the street.

Jesus, he thought, please please please don't let him be dead. Tal moved from the front entrance to the most logical hiding place he could think of … the Ladies' Room on the other side of the first floor.

Thirty-Nine

ROME

Alex dreamed about Simone again. Eyes half-closed, he watched the swing of her luxuriant mane shining in front of the moonlit window. In this dream, her hair was wavy for some reason, and shorter on the sides than in the back.

He sat up with a start, scanning the barely familiar hotel room. "How did you get in here? That door was locked," he said into the cool air.

"A ten-year-old can pick a lock, Alex."

Still unclear about his level of consciousness, he assumed he was awake and regarded the intrusion. "Do you also make license plates?"

Mona turned, Soren's diary lay open on the table. "Aren't you going to ask where I've been?" She took three steps toward the bed and sat on the floor in front of him. "I saw my sister at the Angelica Library."

"Isn't that where you were supposed to meet her after you got Soren's email?"

She shrugged. "Yes. Well, it's not that. We were supposed to meet there but it wasn't . . . " she let her voice trail off. "I tried to get part of Soren's code analyzed, and there is someone there who could translate it, an old woman named Terese."

"So what's the problem?"

"I saw what I think was my sister's office upstairs."

Alex rubbed his eyes and got up and went into the bathroom. He left the door ajar. "I thought she worked at the British Museum," he said. "Now she works in Rome?"

"The nameplate on her desk had a different name on it. It said Dr. L. Dearden."

Alex raised a brow.

"Does that name register with you?"

"Soren's partner was Max Dearden." Alex came to sit beside her. "Are you Lily's sister, or her half-sister?"

She looked up, either confused or not listening.

"Do you have the same parents?"

"Of course, why do you— I mean, well, my father was only around till I was about three, and though Lily's older than me, she has very little memory of him."

Alex squeezed her shoulder.

"You think she's Max Dearden's daughter?" she nearly shouted now. "This is getting too fucking weird for me. People disappear and then turn up, dead men rise from the dead to send emails, and nobody is who they say they are. You should have seen Terese's face, the old lady at the Angelica, when I showed her Soren's ema—"

"You *what*? My God, Mona, for Christ's sake you can't be showing that around. As a matter of fact—"

"This piece of paper and the page in Soren's diary that relates to this language are the only things leading us to your wife, and to my sister."

"You just found your sister."

"What aren't you telling me," she asked in a quieter voice, "about the diary and your father?"

"I don't know very much."

"You're telling me you grew up with this guy and never tried to find out all his secrets? That's what we do when we're kids. We rummage around in other people's stuff, reading things we shouldn't, extrapolate and make assumptions and generally unearth things that should be left buried forever."

Alex nodded.

"Look at the facts," she drew in a breath and exhaled heavily. "Your father's supposedly dead. Then out of nowhere you get an email from him, or someone pretending to be him, and some man tries to kill you in your parking garage, shoots at you and kidnaps your wife. Meanwhile, four thousand miles away in Naples, Italy, I find the very same page emailed to me. I tell my museum curator-sister about it, who forces me to fly to Rome and says that my life is in danger. You fly here the same day to look for your missing wife. At the airport, you and I are both kidnapped and brought to the same place. Notice a strange synchronicity?"

Alex filled a glass with water from the bathroom sink. "Not really, no."

"Oh!" she nearly screamed. "And I forgot the most important part. That the very day that both you and I get this email, the two oldest texts in the British Museum are stolen. This is why I brought the email page with me. Don't you see? It either means that Soren's alive and is sending you a message, or that somebody knows the truth about what happened to him and wants to contact you."

Alex stopped walking, stopped moving, and sat on the bed looking at the window shaking his head. "Soren left me a message in one of those stolen books. He must have."

"That's just what I was thinking," she replied.

"It's the kind of thing he would do. If I want to find Simone and if you want to know the truth about your sister, we have to find the Castleman books."

"And this is why I showed the email to Terese at the Angelica. I thought she might be able to translate it, but she was so freaked out when she saw this text she left the room suddenly. That's when I found Lily's office. I did some comparing too, between the email and one of the strands of Soren's diary code. Some of it matches up closely, not all of it though. So if Terese translated the email, I could start translating the diary strand."

"Mm-hmmm," he mumbled, pacing. "Can you find out from your sister the titles of the books stolen from the Castleman Library?"

Mona pulled the folded newsprint page she'd stuffed in the front of Soren's diary. "It's right here, in the London Times," she said, quickly scanning the text.

"That's good," Alex said. "We'll visit the Angelica tomorrow and ask the reference librarian about these two titles, see if they have any other copies of them or a description of what they are."

"What about Soren?"

"Soren was obsessed with one thing all his life and career. He taught, he lectured, he published articles, he traveled, he did research, he made discoveries and received money for them, and in so doing he left an unwitting trail of suitors, jealous scholars, and resentment. He wasn't popular, Mona, he was ... notorious."

"For what?"

"Shaking things up. Getting an idea in his head and burning down forests of history and precedence under the guise of truth. By reputation, he was an epigrapher skilled in identifying and translating the world's most obscure languages."

"But what was he to you?"

"Oh, a treasure hunter. For a long time, that treasure was civilization's mother language."

"Why did he think there was such a thing?"

"He sort of landed on these hypotheses and then ground himself into them until there was nothing left. But based on this theory, he started an organization to find evidence of that one single mother language from which all other languages emanated."

"By mother language, you mean earlier than Hebrew or Greek?"

"He was interested in how some languages influenced others. Like Coptic - ancient Egyptian based on Greek. So he studied the influence of Greece on Egypt in terms of how their languages became enmeshed in this way. And even older languages that weren't even spoken but sort of signed. He had no use for modern languages. He even refused to write in English, as he thought it was a cultural abomination. All his articles were written in French."

"Good Lord." Mona smiled. "Why not Italian?"

"He loved Italy and Italian culture. But the language, French, he believed, was the language of kings, of aristocracy. We've got to follow those missing books, Mona. The answer to our questions is in at least one of them."

"Well, then we're going to Dublin to the Royal Academy because one of the manuscripts was an ancient Celtic text."

Alex nodded. "*The Book of Kells*. Soren was fascinated by it."

"Not exactly - it was taken *from* the *Book of Ballymote*, another Celtic text which, you might recall, is in Soren's diary."

"The Ogham strand of that ridiculous code," he said.

"Right, and the Coptic code read that phrase from the Gospel of St. Thomas, which was—"

"What did you say?" he interrupted.

"The Coptic strand in Soren's encryption code. They were Coptic."

"No, no, I know all that. What gospel did you just mention?"

Mona nodded. "Thomas. The Coptic strand in Soren's code translated to something like 'Lift a stone and you will find me; split a piece of wood and I'll be there.' It's from the Gospel of St. Thomas, whatever *that* is. I'm Catholic and I've never heard of it." She stared now, focused on the haunted look on Alex's face. "Have you?"

He raised a brow. "Somehow, yes."

Alex sat on the wide windowsill and watched heavy rain slap the concrete below. He inhaled and rubbed his face.

"What was the purpose of the organization Soren founded?" Mona asked.

Alex scratched his head and smiled. "ACES. There were only a few people in it, so its mission was safeguarded. Why do you ask?"

"It's written several times in his diary, in several different sections. There's this type of coding, not the braiding encryption but another one that he uses throughout, a very elementary code where he takes a word, moves the last letter to go in front of the first letter and then spells it in reverse. Here, look at this."

Alex fumbled for his glasses.

"Do these look familiar to you?"

... Quick, hide, the soldiers are coming. I hear them! ...

Alex tried to answer her, to speak normal words of English, his native language. But his mind wasn't thinking in English right now.

... *Hinge, that's right. Hinge, because we'll carve the letters into the edge of this 2x4 plank. Now, think about what message you want to leave, assuming the enemy can't read it, which they can't. The enemy? Oh, there were so many back then. Phoenicians, maybe, or other Celts ...*

"Alex?" she was saying, Mona's deep, sultry voice, or was it Simone's now? Had she come back to rescue him from this strange reverie? How had memories of Soren been buried for this long without him knowing?

"Alex? Are you all right?" He felt her arms around his shoulders and her face close. "You remember something?"

"Ogham, the oldest recognized Celtic alphabet." He took a moment to steady himself. "Soren taught it to me when I was a young boy. We'd go off in the woods playing ancient war games, and he taught me how to write messages to him in this secret language, a language the enemy didn't know. It was very well protected. Only one book exists in the world that lists all the variations."

"The Book of Ballymote," she said, nodding.

"Well, a part of it, yes."

"Do you think you could translate it?"

Alex picked up the diary and held it close to his face. He laughed. "He's even got the Ogham encoded. See, there are many variations of the alphabet and he's got ... one, two ... five of them just in this section. No, I can't translate it. But I'll bet the Royal Academy in Dublin can."

Forty

ROME

Alex pictured her, a picture that grew in detail, in movement, in dimension, with every second. Simone, alive, somewhere. He had to keep thinking that, chanting that, replaying that image in his mind. Maybe she was near him at this moment. But regardless of her level of consciousness, somewhere at this moment, Simone was in Rome. That much was clear. He stood in front of the Central Police Station and went over his questions mentally before pulling open the heavy glass doors.

The alarming brightness of morning sun bounced Alex's reflection off the polished glass of the entry, showing his battered face. And, behind the scars, even behind the skin of his raw face, was the image of a blond man – the same man from the parking garage in Herald Square. Alex froze.

Nothing but incoherent thoughts and questions spun through his brain. Stay or go. There were really only two choices. The blond man's face didn't so much as flinch, and it was obvious he knew that Alex had made him in the glass. The man's arms were crossed and he wore sunglasses. No weapons, at least visible ones. Just through the doors was a gray-haired police dispatcher at the front desk. She was close, Alex read her badge. D. Francesca. Okay, Officer Francesca, he thought, let's see what you're made of. He pulled open the doors.

"Buon giorno."

"We speak English here," the officer replied without looking up.

"I have an appointment with Officer Margiolo. And, while I'm waiting, there's a man behind me with blond hair who's followed me all the way from Boston."

The woman's narrow, brown eyes looked him up and down. "A friend of yours?" she asked finally.

The weight of the past two weeks shouldered him suddenly. He rested his elbows on the reception desk and no longer had the energy for conspiracy theories.

"Mr. Careski? Come with me, Officer Margiolo is expecting you," the officer announced.

"I'd like to know your progress on my wife's disappearance."

The officer opened an empty folder and pretended to peruse the invisible contents. Alex observed this display with eerie curiosity. "Your wife was not a resident in Rome, no? A tourist?"

"No."

"Not a tourist?"

"Where is Officer Margiolo? I asked for him personally. I have met with him on two previous occasions regarding my wife's sudden disappearance. He was going to look into it for me and contact me at my hotel. That was four days ago. I've called him every day this week and received no return call. I want to know what's going on here."

"Your wife did not live in Rome?"

God help me, Alex thought. "We've been through this, Officer. My wife—"

"She is from the States, then? Perhaps you should contact your local police first."

"As I have already informed Officer Margiolo, the kidnappers took my wife to Rome. They left me a note. I flew here to try to find her and I was kidnapped at the airport."

The young officer tried to conceal a smile creeping into her lips. She closed the empty folder and folded her hands on top of it. "Do you read the newspapers, Mr. Careski?"

"Fuck you. Oh, excuse me, fuck you, *Officer*."

"The reason why I ask this is because if you *did* read the newspapers, you would realize that there was a kidnapping in Boston, Massachusetts and the prime suspect, you'll be very interested to know, meets your description. So, in your case, Mr. Careski, barging into the police precinct and saying unkind words to an officer of the law is, in your country, referred to as quite a bad idea. Wouldn't you agree?"

Corinna Buchman's phone rang eleven times before her voicemail picked up. Alex replaced the receiver, redialed, and waited. First two rings, then three rings. He knew Corinna, and knew she never picked up the phone without knowing the caller first. But he was the husband of her best friend, and he and Simone knew the code. Now she picked up on the fourth ring.

"Simone? Is that you?" the voice sounded small, almost meek.

"It's me, sweetheart, sorry to disappoint you. Are you all right?" Alex asked, wondering what time it would be in Boston right now.

"Am I all right? Jesus, Alex, tell me something, would you? You said you'd call me last week, I never heard from you, never heard a peep from or about Simone." Her voice caught in her throat. "Why—"

"Take it easy. Have you been to work?"

"Not for two days. I've been, well, a wreck."

"Have you been taking your pills?" he asked, remembering her history of anxiety. "I shouldn't have asked you to deal with the diaries, I'm sorry. I could have asked Kirby to do it for me."

Corinna cleared her throat. "Don't trust him, Alex. I don't know what's happened to him since you left the PD, maybe just age, and I know he drinks too much, or maybe he's seen things. But he's not Tommy anymore. Don't ask him anything and don't tell him anything either."

"What are you talking about?"

"He can't be trusted," she said quickly.

Alex's hands began to sweat. Tom Kirby, his partner in the force, and his best friend for seven years, maybe longer. He was godfather to all three of Tom's children.

"I took," she began, and then stopped. "I tried to … I, yes, found the diaries in the basement and took them to my house."

"And?"

"Alex, tell me where you are right now. You're not safe, and we shouldn't be talking about this. Are you still in—"

"Dublin. I'm in Dublin," he lied, realizing the supreme error in his thinking. "What happened to the diaries? I don't care who's listening."

"There was someone down there when I, I mean, in the basement. I didn't see them and nothing happened while I was down there. I only found two diaries. But I … felt someone. I know it, Alex. I'm not kidding."

"Are you safe right now? Is your front door locked?" he pressed.

"I'm fine."

"And where are the diaries now?"

"Kirby has them."

"What??"

"He tailed me the whole way to your house, I now realize, and he stood by somewhere while I was in the house, but I don't think he was the one down there. I used my spare key to get in. And he caught me going out, pulled me over on Barclay and confiscated the diaries. He seemed to know just what they were and said they were material evidence."

"Of what, for Christ's sake? Does he actually think th—"

"Alex, he was waiting for me. Do you see what I'm saying? How did he know I would come?"

"Back up, please. Kirby said material evidence? He used those exact words?"

Corinna sighed audibly. "Listen to me. Kirby thinks you're responsible for Simone's disappearance. Not necessarily that you killed her but ..."

Alex didn't hear anything beyond the word killed. It made sense now, how no one at the PD in Rome had been willing to help him, and had tried to detain him, visited he and Mona at their hotel. But why hadn't they arrested him, if he was supposedly to blame? And where exactly did they think he had taken her?

"Your house, Alex. I want you to be prepared for what you find when you go back there."

"Did you paint it or something?" he asked, hoping levity might calm his nerves. "You always did hate the color of the upstairs bathroom."

"It was quite the mop up. And I think Kirby's responsible for it. I mean everything."

"Mop up? In what way?"

"As in your living room window has been replaced, every last shard of glass sanitized from the inside of your hallway, your office, the basement, the hallway carpets cleaned. In other words, there's not one single trace of evidence remaining that anything went on in that house out of the ordinary ... other than the police's contention that you killed and buried your wife."

Forty-One

LONDON

Tal took out cash from an ATM and wondered about it being tracked. In line at Alamo Rent a Car, he saw the back of the red Rolls Royce. The exit from the garage parking at the rear of the rental business led to Park Lane which, he knew, joined Piccadilly and the Cavendish Hotel where he'd booked a room under the name of John Smith.

He grabbed a cup of lukewarm coffee from the free stuff in the hotel lobby, and noticed an old man sitting in a corner chair watching him stir creamer into the paper cup. After check-in, he envisioned a clean bed as a place to rest and think. The coffee, which he drank on the way up the stairs and while pulling the curtains, tasted funny. And who was that man in the lobby? And now the carpet near the bed seemed to … almost … move …

Tal was awakened by the clamor of the hotel room telephone set inches from the bed. He turned to his side and saw that it was dark out. How … what...? And taped to his nightstand lamp was a note that read, "Look out of your window."

Tal leaned back with a start, startled by the reality of a stranger in his room and even more startled that it had somehow, without him knowing it, become night. Still in bed, he craned his neck to see out the window, then stood cautiously on the right side and looked down to the street level. A man in a black raincoat with a hood stood with his hands in his pockets. He looked up to Tal's window. Tal instinctively looked behind him and left and right, as if this messenger was intended for someone else. A hand emerged from the folds of the long raincoat and gave a "come" motion.

Raining. Dusk. Tal followed the raincoat down Jermyn, then an alley behind Piccadilly, Sackville, and then into Swallow Street, which spilled into Regent on one side and then back into Piccadilly Circus. Raincoat Man walked quickly, hunched over, medium height.

"Who are you?" Tal called out.

"You don't know me," the raincoat man said as he stopped walking and turned to him. He pulled off the hood to reveal a face Tal did not recognize. A wrinkled, tanned face. But then again, this man felt oddly familiar to him. "Lily's fine, but she's not who you think she is."

"Who are you, and how do you know me?" Tal had to shout over the pelt of the rain.

"Don't you know enough by now to stop asking stupid questions? Don't you know, Mr. Gardner, what you've got yourself into?"

"How do you know Lily Frasier?"

"I watched her grow up, that's how."

"Ah ... the photo on her mantelpiece."

6:00 a.m. Sunday morning, gray sky, light drizzle. Standing outside a working girl's apartment building. My finest hour, Tal thought, pressing Crystal's buzzer for the third time. He'd been thinking about Max's clue, Alexandria. A quick Google search on his iPhone now revealed the second largest metropolitan city in Egypt, the Lighthouse of Alexandria, but more noteworthy was the Alexandria Library, housing civilization's most rare and precious books and the man who burned it down - one of many men who had done so - Theophilus, the twenty-third Pope of Alexandria.

"Whaaaa— who the fuck is it?" he heard from the intercom upstairs.

"It's Daddy Warbucks, get up," Tal replied.

"I'm not taping any more stupid letters to your window."

"You need the money and I need some work done. I can just as easily go somewhere else."

"How much?" the voice replied.

"Sixty quid."

Three-second pause. "Give me one minute."

Tal smiled and, sixty seconds later Crystal arrived downstairs dressed in plain jeans, a white collared blouse, and flat-heeled boots. "Hello, love," she said, grinning at him. "What?"

"Nothing, you look nice."

"For a Piccadilly tart, you mean?"

"You said that, not me." He examined her more closely now. "Bloody perfect, like a college student."

"How about paying me up front then?" she said.

"We're getting to that. Over here," Tal motioned to the bushes on the west side of the building. She followed two steps behind him between two buildings and behind two dwarf cypress trees. "Here's my ATM card, and God help me, I'm giving it to you. Go to the NatWest on the corner and take out three hundred pounds. Keep sixty for yourself, it's what we agreed on. My code is 9-3-9-5."

She stared dumbfounded. "All right. Then what?"

"Meet me back here. I'll wait."

Crystal blinked her only partially made-up blue eyes directly at him, her mouth slightly downturned. "No one's ever trusted me before. I'm a bit touched. For that, you get a kiss." As she pulled the ATM card from his fingers, she leaned toward him.

"Later. Now get moving. I'll see you back here … God willing."

"Ten minutes."

"Don't rush!" Tal turned quickly, not meaning to raise his voice. "Take your time. It's a Sunday morning. You're taking out money to meet a girlfriend for breakfast. Don't behave like you know someone's watching you."

"Someone's watching me?"

"Go. Now. Don't ask questions."

Two hours later, in a rented blue sedan, Tal pulled into an off-the-highway pub with Crystal beside him.

"You know what this is gonna cost you? Having me all to yourself for an overnighter?"

Half of Tal's face smiled at his companion; the other half glanced at the other parked cars, searching for one with dark-tinted windows. Or a suited man holding a handgun. Or an elderly butler who sometimes played the role of wise guy. Or a tall man meeting the description of Max Dearden.

"Hey, sweetheart, pay attention here, we're talking about money," Crystal said waving her hand in front of his face.

"Name your price," he said still eyeing the vehicles.

"Two hundred."

"One hundred," he replied, hiding a smirk on his lips.

"One-fifty."

"Done." Tal pulled out his wallet, wondering if anyone else had been replacing his business cards. He handed Crystal a folded stack of cash. "Dunno if that's enough. Count it." She stared blankly. "Go ahead."

Before she had finished counting the bills, Tal parked the car on the side of the main pub and took three steps toward the back of the building. He looked through a rickety fence at a neon sign, more than likely a shoddy motel at the rear of the pub. He had only known *of* such places in his largely sheltered life, a life that had kept him safe from prostitutes, rogue security guards, and stone-cold killers.

"Get out," he said opening the passenger door.

Crystal fluffed her hair and honed in on Tal's expression. "You all right? You looked haunted."

"Hunted, more likely."

"What?"

He grabbed her arm, wary of what he couldn't see, suddenly. "Let's go." He opened the pub door, surveyed the sedated crowd inside, and turned to leave.

"Aren't you coming in?" Crystal asked, suddenly panicked.

He put an arm around her waist and leaned his mouth into her ear. "Go to the bar, order a pint, sit down and drink half of it, then meet me at the motel. Ask the front desk to ring Picard."

"Picard." She laughed, genuinely at first, then back to panic-mode. "Why don't you just beam me the fuck up from here then?" Crystal sighed and played with the dangling piece of fabric on her belt. "I don't know what I'm doing here. It sounded like fun at first."

"You can go anytime you want to, and keep the money. You owe me nothing. I'll call you a cab right now if you like."

Crystal closed the door to the pub and leaned against the door, watching him. "What did you do? I think I deserve to know that much."

"It's better if I don't. You're taking a risk being here with me, and I'm paying you for that risk, as well as expenses, meals, lodging, and the pleasure of my company."

She widened her light blue eyes, scrutinizing every detail of his face.

"I'm being chased by men who want to kill me."

"Why?"

"I saw a man just before he died, and I know who killed him."

"What man?" she asked.

"A curator from the British Museum. I used to work with him."

The blue eyes blinked again and again. "Why was he killed?"

"For someone *he* saw. Some books were stolen from the museum, and Adrian knew who did it."

"Covering up a cover-up. We're like a bloody spy novel, aren't we? Aren't you a bit like Jason Bourne?" She reached to touch his face, the hair curling down toward his ear. "You even look like him a little."

"We have no more time. Stay or go. But decide now."

"Why?"

Tal took one step from the pub's main doorway into the shadow of the overhanging eaves, then gently pulled Crystal to him and held her with his arms around her waist. Their foreheads were touching, her smoky breath on his face. "Might already be too late. Go now," he said, still looking over her into the car park. "Order a drink, meet me at the motel, sign in under the name of Jones." He saw her now, really saw her, for a split second. "You are far too pretty to be invisible, but do your best."

From the surrounding landscape, Tal guessed that the pub and motel were situated halfway between Bath and Glastonbury. His mother was originally from Bath, they'd taken many day trips there as a child. He still remembered the ghost story about the haunted old relics of Glastonbury Abbey a few miles southwest.

The grounds of The Country Squire motel and pub were clear of visible hit men or cars with tinted windows. Still, he knew better. From the moonless shadows on the western edge of the property, Tal pulled out his cell phone. Still glancing behind him, he waited for what felt like an hour. On the seventh ring, a woman's voice answered.

"Beth? It's Tal. I'm so sorry to ring you at home. It's urgent."

During the long pause, Tal wondered if Beth Leiden had forgotten who he was, and then remembered it had been weeks since he'd seen her at the museum. "Are you still th—"

"I'm here, Tal. What is it? And where have you been?"

Why is she whispering, he wondered. She's in her own house.

"The police have been to the office every other day asking about the missing staff. It's a ghost town down there."

"I'm quite sure Wexler's told them some stories," he said.

"Where are you right now?"

As if waking from deep slumber, Tal sensed the Sea Hag's head rising up out of a sea of velvet blue, watching him now, the dark wrinkly eyes unblinking. Trust your instincts, the voice seemed to say. And his instincts told him that Beth's phone could be tapped. Beth, his secretary, having her personal phone tapped, waiting for him to call. If not, the police could be tracing the call right now. Could she be trusted?

"There's no time. I need you to email an image of one of the Inquisition exhibit paintings to me."

"What? Why?"

"The painting's crooked - it's hard to tell unless you're studying it specifically. And yes, I compared it with all the inventory and delivery logs and there was no mention of a crooked mounting. I need that photograph, Beth. I think it might answer every question we have right now, about Lily, and about Adrian. When it comes to missing persons, all roads generally lead to one place."

Tal heard her sigh, and pictured her small, pointed features analyzing his voice, her fingers tapping the phone receiver in deliberation. "It'll take some time," she replied. "What about the—"

"The security code's on a piece of paper taped on the underside of my desk lamp in my office."

"Call me tomorrow night at this time and I'll see what I can do."

After getting the key to Room 215 from the receptionist, Tal took the lift to the second floor, scanning the long row of tacky, green doors. He looked at his watch – 7:55 p.m. Was no one staying at the motel tonight? Did it perhaps attract a late-night crowd? Not likely, as the Holiday Inn Express was the only motel on this whole stretch of road near Bath. 210, 212, 213, 214. With some relief, his eyes landed on the door to room 215, but relief quickly disintegrated when he saw the keycard still in the door. It was slightly ajar.

Jesus, Crystal, he thought pushing it open gently. "Crystal? You in here?" he whispered.

The room was empty.

Out of both habit and desperation, Tal looked under both beds, in the closet, bathroom, even the shower, checking for her signature scent of cheap perfume and cigarettes. By the looks of it, she hadn't been in here. Had someone approached her in the car park? He'd checked the entire grounds three times before entering the motel lobby. Three quick knocks at the door hastened him out of contemplation.

"Crystal," he said as he opened the door without checking the peephole.

All he saw was the butt of a handgun being shoved up against his nostrils. "Come with us," replied an unfamiliar male voice.

Another black car with tinted windows parked unconcealed beneath a street light in the motel car park. With the pistol still pushed awkwardly into his right cheekbone, the assailant held him from behind and shoved him toward the car. Thrust inside, he landed in a folded heap in the back seat. An older man, whom he didn't recognize, was in the middle of the back seat with someone else on the other side of him - Crystal. Gagged, her frightened raccoon eyes glistened blue with smeared mascara.

Crystal, he thought, I'm surely going to hell for this.

Forty-Two

EIRE

Morning, somewhere in the world. He could no longer keep track of details like country and time zone, and monitor personal dilemmas such as the whereabouts of his father. All he could think of was Simone and if someone had served her breakfast this morning, if she'd been able to soak in the tub the way she loved, brush her hair, and read science fiction for a full hour before bed.

'Every family comes with its myths,' he had said to Mona, diverting her attention, once more, by quick flashes of philosophy or humor. Mona Delfreggio was the only friend he had right now. They had taken a red-eye out of Rome to Dublin and chosen the closest hotel to the airport. Two beds and running water was all he cared about. The Royal Academy opened at nine o'clock the next morning and they would see a young woman named Bernadette about the Ogham written in Soren's diary and until then, there were plenty of demons to keep him company.

Mona, asleep in the other bed, stirred.

"Don't wake up," he whispered.

"Where are we again?"

"Dublin."

"Are you sure?" she asked.

Alex went to the window and opened the curtains.

"See any leprechauns?"

"I don't know, they're invisible."

Mona rubbed her eyes and sat up, then drew the sheet up to her neck. "Are you gonna tell me what Soren discovered and what he's been hiding from all this time?"

Alex sighed. "And what do you charge, exactly, for this ... psychotherapeutic exorcism?"

"How about I tell you a theory."

"Not another one."

"Buried within the folds of *your* brain and only your brain is the link between your wife the translator, your father the linguist, my sister the museum curator, and two ancient books."

"Okay. Soren's sister Rachel died, well, we think, when she was twenty-five."

Mona sat up, her eyes instantly focused in a tacit aha. "Your aunt?" she asked.

"I didn't know her." And then Alex drifted again, his mind, his memory, back to the Boston Herald parking garage, his tiny office with a view of a brick wall, to the scent of Simone's cinnamon coffee first thing in the morning, to the park he and Soren used to play in when he was a boy, where Soren taught him to draw symbols of the Ogham alphabet - the hard marks carved or chalked into the edges of wood. "She and my father were very close, deeply close, but he rarely talked about her." Alex paused. "He used to say I was the only one who understood him."

"Were you?"

"Soren had his quest that propelled him on these chaotic journeys all over the world, and there was no time or energy for anything else. He was doing work that got his name into scientific journals. Coming to my soccer games and graduation was ... superfluous."

"He didn't come to your graduation?" she asked, incredulous.

"Like I said, it wasn't a priority for him. Nothing was, except his quest. So whether I understood him or not is irrelevant."

"What about Rachel?"

He waved his hand. "She was one of his quests, his most important quest. She died or disappeared, no one really knew how, he blamed himself long enough to justify his need to discover the truth about her disappearance. He spent nearly his whole life searching for her, any person who so much as knew of her. It was more than just important to him. He was obsessed by it and I think he felt incomplete knowing that she'd ... I don't know."

"What happened to her?"

"She went to Egypt to excavate some ancient manuscript right before she was to assume a tenured post at Oxford." Alex looked at the carpet.

"She never came back?"

"Soren got something, something Rachel found in Egypt and sent to him," Alex said softer now, "and with it, he discovered a scandal. The truth of it was more than scientific scholars and publishers were willing to bear. And he couldn't go back and pretend it didn't happen."

"Tell me," she insisted.

"I never saw it, but apparently Rachel found a page of an ancient manuscript, maybe one of the most important manuscripts ever written."

"What was it?"

"I don't know."

"So he went underground," she said.

"He had no choice. The existence of this book, or I suppose even the first page of it, must have threatened someone, because after he received it, all the members of ACES started disappearing one by one."

"Threatened who?"

Alex shook his head. "I've pieced this together from just scraps of words and phrases and mumblings. I think Soren and the other scholars on the council were trying to get it authenticated and carbon dated, and as a result, more people learned about it. And people started dying."

Mona knew better than to ask her next question. She had seen his vulnerability and knew now that he'd spent a lifetime involved in his own prolific cover-up. Still, she had to complete the picture if they were to find the missing piece. "Do you know where it is?"

But Alex wasn't listening at that point. His attention had been diverted by another small, white card on the dark carpet just inside the door of their room. He looked back and moved toward the door.

"Don't pick it up," Mona hissed.

Alex stooped and immediately saw another large, calligraphy "I" on the front of the card. He turned it over and again saw the same words scrawled on the back as he'd seen in a similar card left in his house the day of the kidnapping: "I am the Inquisition."

Mona pulled the card from his fingers and went to the window.

"What are you doing?"

She sighed. "Research." She flipped the card back and forth, held it sideways at an angle, then flat, then up over her eyes. "See that?"

"No. See what?"

Mona pointed and moved the card slightly.

"It's a watermark," Alex said trying to make it out. "Two letters ..."

"CZ," Mona replied.

"How did you know to—"

She nodded to his violin case. "The other card that was left for you at your house, same watermark."

Forty-Three

EIRE

Alex locked the room door behind them and they headed to the car park of the Aghadoe Heights Hotel in County Kerry. Mona still had the white card in her hand.

"I've seen roughly forty bed and breakfasts and you got us a room in a hotel. Any particular reason?"

"Because I'm paranoid, that's why."

Mona shook her head. "Of being seen in public with me?"

"No." He watched Mona's face change as he said it, then focused on parking the car on the edge of the muddy road outside a local breakfast spot. "Because we have a lot to talk about and I don't want us to be overheard."

"I know you're worried about being seen with someone my age."

"Meaning what, exactly? How old do I look?"

Mona ignored the question and picked up a menu at a small two-seat table by the back window of The Grill House Restaurant. "What I want to know is why Rachel went to Egypt in the first place. How did she find out about whatever she was looking for?"

Alex took a seat opposite her and slid his elbows on the table. "You'd make a good investigator, you know that?"

"I've thought about it," Mona said without concealing a half-grin.

Alex sighed. "Okay. Soren said Rachel had a benefactor, some older man who had, well, I guess you could say commissioned her to go to these high caves outside of Egypt to find a manuscript buried in a jar underground."

Mona grabbed her journal and started writing.

"No, no, please," Alex said, "none of this will even sound coherent. I'm digging into ancient memories here." He inhaled deeply. "The only time he ever heard from her was when he received something in the mail a few months after she left for that journey."

"A letter?"

Alex tapped his feet. "He described it as a letter within a letter within another letter. It came in a box, and there was a note inside with a sealed envelope in it. Rachel begged him to never open it and to hide it in a very specific place." Alex looked out the window.

"Where?"

Alex looked outside. "Here."

An hour later they were driving on the N71, after a round of Irish breakfast tea, rashers, black and white pudding, eggs, tomatoes, potatoes, beans, and mushrooms. With her journal open, Mona reviewed the new facts.

"'K. 'Strigiformes, BV PC K CK,'" she recited from one of Soren's journals.

"You can keep asking me but I was an eight-year-old when he made me remember it. He used to write it in secret places in the basement where my mother wouldn't see."

"She didn't know about it?"

"She ..." he stopped, "never mind."

"What?"

Alex shrugged. "She didn't want to know."

"Soren never told you?"

"As a rule, Soren didn't answer questions or solve problems. He created them. He was an academic and a teacher, I mean like every second of every day. If we went for a walk, the two of us, the entire time we walked he asked me geography questions that I had to answer correctly. And when I didn't, he'd ask again, three times, four, until he felt I knew the answer. But I remember something else too. He and Rachel used to play when they were little near this old Ogham site and I might know how to find it. My great grandmother lived nearby and she used to let them play outside all day and come home for dinner. Seems like a great way to spend a summer."

"And you think whatever she found in that cave is buried somewhere near this Ogham site?"

"I think Rachel specifically wanted it hidden there to make sure whoever else sought it would never find it. Besides, it's a backup plan in case you can't break the code by the time we get there."

"How long have I got?" Mona looked at her watch.

"Half an hour."

Mona studied the code Alex had written sideways in her journal before they'd left the hotel room: K. Stringiformes, BV PC K CK. "Don't you think it's an odd name, Strigiformes?"

"Sure," Alex smiled, "it's not a name at all, or not a person. Are you online now?" he asked.

"Should be," she said pulling her now-charged iPhone out of her purse.

"Google 'strigiformes.'"

Mona adjusted the display brightness on her phone and slipped her sunglasses onto her eyes from the top of her head. "It's the family name for a bird of prey, owls to be specific." Mona recorded this in her journal. "K. Strigiformes looks like a name and all the other letters are made to look like academic designations."

Alex nodded. "Keep going."

"So if we're talking about owls, the question is where. BV PC K CK. Breaking it apart, does BV or PC mean anything to you?"

Alex raised a brow and shook his head. "Do you know how many times ..."

"So Rachel found a manuscript in a cave," she said ignoring his objection, "and wanted to hide it from whoever was trying to take it from her."

"Presumably," Alex replied.

"Can we assume that her pursuer was not from Ireland?"

Alex shrugged. "Hard to say. Sure, for the moment, why not? He or she is not from Ireland then. What does that imply?"

"So they wouldn't know anything about Irish geography, right?"

"Presumably."

"So Ireland is divided into counties. The last two letters are CK. What if ..."

"Ah. Kerry."

"What?"

"County Kerry."

"Okay, that's possible. Any other counties begin with K?"

"Kilkenny."

"And are there any Ogham stone sites in Kilkenny?"

Alex smiled and turned toward her. "No, but there are plenty of them in County Kerry, also Cork and Waterford are the main ones."

"Okay, so then if CK is County Kerry, could the K also refer to Kerry County? Just looking at the form of Soren's code. "Kerry Strigiformes?"

"Sure, could be."

"Then ..." Mona stopped to study the map, "BV PC K are the other letters at the end of the code. Looking in County Kerry, there's a tourist site called Parkavonear Castle in Killarney in County Kerry."

"Good good," Alex affirmed.

"And BV ..." she had her eyes buried deep in the map.

"Okay," Alex said. "Beaufort Village, of course."

"Do we have it then?" she asked.

"Well, we may have solved the letters in the code, but not answered the larger question of what it means."

"Rachel had her manuscript secreted somewhere near Parkavonear Castle, which is near Beaufort Village in Killarney, Co. Kerry."

"Okay."

"Shit."

"No, you're doing great, don't give up yet. I'm taking us to the site where they used to play as children and I think it's near Parkavonear Castle."

"Will we see it from the road? I love castles," she said dreamily.

"Not that kind of castle. It's more of a ruin and about the size of a house. But ... there was a story of a woman who lived in the castle and was sort of a caretaker of the stones. No idea if she's still alive. She seemed pretty old back then even."

"You met her?"

"I came here when I was five or six, I don't remember much." Alex breathed deeply through the open window. "Except the smell."

"That's it! I see it."

"I told you, not much left of it."

They followed the sign to Parkavonear Castle and parked on the edge of the grass and walked up the slow incline to the two-story cylindrical ruin.

"Is the Ogham stone near here?"

"It should be, just look for a tall, vertical slab of stone."

"So, what are we looking for, specifically?" Mona asked trailing behind him, journal in hand.

"We'll know when we find it."

Forty-Four

EIRE

Alex entered the round edifice, waiting for a chill to follow him, or a strange, cool breeze to brush across the backs of his shoulders, or the flap of wings. Instead, he took in the view of the Lakes of Killarney up ahead and heard footsteps behind him. "Not much to see, I told you," he said.

"I know you," someone said. Alex turned quickly and looked down at a shrunken, wrinkled face, and a woman wearing all white. A nun? There was no cross around her neck.

"I know that face," she said almost as a question, raising her hand to touch Alex's cheek.

Alex bent low and stared at the familiar shape of her jaw, the eyes, something he couldn't put his finger on.

"But you're so young."

"You're Aileen Quinn," he nodded now. "I think you knew my father, Soren Careski, many years ago."

The woman smiled revealing brown-stained, crooked teeth and a smile that somehow still felt luminous.

"And his sister. Such a beautiful girl."

Alex tried to summon Mona with his eyes, but she was already at the broken wall of the castle. "Do you…," Alex said, not quite knowing what to ask.

"Do you still live near here," Mona asked meekly and stretched out her hand. "My name is Mona, and this is my first trip to Ireland."

"Ohhh," the old woman laughed, "welcome to the land of secrets."

Mona and Alex exchanged glances. "Is that what's it called?"

The old woman looked directly at Alex. "For you it is. Come with me."

Aileen Quinn took them across an expanse of tall, soft electric-green grass, and over the next low they saw a small hut; from a distance, it looked more like an outhouse and as they got closer they saw it had many sections added onto it including a lookout loft. Aileen brought them into the kitchen where she set a single cup and saucer, teapot, and boiled water on the stove.

"Have you got the nerve for Irish tea, lass?"

"Try me," Mona replied, setting her notebook beside her. The woman locked eyes with her and placed her hand on top of the notebook and held it there, awkwardly.

"What?"

"You will not write a word in that journal while you're here, not one word about this place, written or otherwise. Your very life may depend on heeding my words."

Mona put her hands up and set the journal back in her bag.

The cabin was made of rough cut wood on the outside and the inside was similarly unfinished, smelling like new construction. But viewing the objects in the room, there was nothing new in here and hadn't been in a very long time. Mona picked up a brass statue of a saint, very small and oddly heavy, and unexpectedly warm.

Aileen spooned two tablespoons of black tea into the teapot and poured water from the dented, screeching kettle over it. She held the pot in her wrinkled hands with only a thin cloth napkin between them and swished the liquid around gently. "You only steep this tea for one minute. It's strong," she grinned.

"So I'll be able to lift up your house and move it a foot closer to the castle then?" Mona joked.

The woman's eyes lowered. "It's close enough thank you ..."

Mona and Alex exchanged glances again.

"You come with me," she said to Alex. "You all right here, sweetie? Milk in the little jug, lemon and sugar," she said pointing to objects on the table and disappeared with Alex.

A round table with two chairs in a small room that more resembled a police interrogation chamber than one of the bedrooms in a remote, Irish cottage. The woman merely pointed and disappeared into the next bedroom and opened something that had a creaky door. Alex tried to stay in the present but some part of him remembered this place and triggered a buzzing in the base of his spine, in this place, this house, the smell of tea, of cigars, and the air thick with unspoken words.

"Do you actually live here?" Alex asked her.

"Live," she said, "what is that exactly? I sleep here most nights, I make tea, I tend the garden. I don't pay money to live here but ohhh, I have paid a much higher price."

Alex listened.

The woman sat opposite him and the atmosphere changed from friendly banter to adversaries. He let the silence form between them and waited.

"You have something for me?" she asked finally.

Alex took the folded piece of paper he'd put in his breast pocket in the car, pulled out the Waterman pen he'd gotten from Monihan on the tenth anniversary of his tenure at the Boston Herald, and wrote on it one word, refolded the page and slid it across the jagged surface of the table.

The woman snickered and passed it back.

"No?"

"Birds of the order Strigiformes, yes, family *strigidae*."

"What does that have to do with my father?"

"Ha! It has more to do with me, a *cailleach* is an owl but in Gaelic it's an old woman, and it was that word that your father gave you to tell you that I was the one holding your family secret."

Alex wiped his sweaty palms on his jeans and opened his mouth to speak, Aileen put a rolled, yellowed, parchment-looking page on the table and let it roll back and forth in front of them. "Go ahead, she said. You have come so far for this and lost so much."

"What about my wife? Sim—"

"She's alive."

"You've seen her?" his voice raised.

Aileen Quinn shook her head. "She's their leverage to make sure you give them this."

Alex wiped his eyes quickly and picked up the sheet and unrolled it. "What language is this?"

"You're smart like your father."

"It's more than one? I see ..."

"This is but the first page of the original manuscript of Origen's *Hexapla*, a compilation of six ancient versions of the Bible, published sometime before the second century AD. There were three English translations published starting in the late 1300s, but this page," she laid her palm on it, "is the first page of the original version from thousands of years ago."

Alex swallowed, afraid to touch the page. "How many people have died because of this?"

The woman shook her head. "Wrong question. Your father's sister Rachel found this, and was sent to find it by her benefactor, a man who sent her letters, drawings, maps, schematics and pictures of where to find this manuscript in the Jabal al-Tārif caves near Nag Hammadi, Egypt."

"Where the Dead Sea Scrolls were found in 1945," Alex added.

"Many things were found there, codices, manuscripts, rolled up and buried in large ceramic vessels."

"Why that way?"

Pause. "Why do you think?" she asked.

"Protecting them."

She nodded.

"From whom?" Alex asked.

"A butcher, a torturer. A man threatened by so much that he killed. Everything. Every day, his whole life."

Alex looked at the page. "Who?"

"Theo. Pope Theophilus of Alexandria."

Alex nodded. "Fourth century. He burned the Alexandria Library, my father spoke of him."

"In the year 391 AD, yes, Theo burned down many libraries, including the Alexandria Library, because he was threatened by any books that challenged the veracity of Christendom. Though the Alexandria Library was burned many times. You recall the witch trials in the States in the last century? Theo also burned heretics, burned heretical books, the families of heretics, churches. After he died, his nephew, Cyril, took up the cause.

"They ..." Alex breathed, "were looking for this?"

The woman blinked back.

"Cyril. And now they'll be looking for me."

"He's already been in contact with you."

"I've … wai … the … 'I.'"

"That's right."

Alex pulled three white cards from his wallet. All were white with a calligraphic "I" on the front and on the back scrolled the words "I am the Inquisition."

"But his nephew, Cyril …"

She nodded. "There have been many Cyrils in that line. This one," she said pointing to the cards, Cyril Zander, "is an old man now, and is a direct descendant of *the* Cyril of Alexandria. He even dresses that way, long dressing gown, black boots, covered by a red velvet cape with a black velvet lining and a long hood."

"So we're in danger."

Aileen laughed. "You're just figuring that out now?"

"Why did my father leave this with you? Wouldn't he know this would put you in danger?"

"I do not fear Cyril. I won't say I fear nothing, but he cannot hurt me."

"But he could take this page from you."

Aileen nodded in agreement. "He could take it, yes, but what he fears more than the existence of this page and the rest of the manuscript that it represents is a lineage of the truth of its existence, of the people who know about it. Your father, Rachel, you, and now the girl who's with you, and everyone any of you might have told."

"Mona and I are only learning of this now, and I doubt Simone knows anything about this."

"Secrets, though, are like drops of water, and water's primary urge is to find other water and burrow its way out to the sea. Even under centuries of ice and rock, it finds a way."

Alex shook his head. "But this is only the first page."

"How else would someone, even a linguistic scholar like your father, be able to conclusively identify a manuscript that had six different translations of the Bible, or anything for that matter, without seeing the cover page? Otherwise it would be gibberish and impossible to authenticate without a very large sample. This page brings authenticity to the rest of the *Hexapla* manuscript. Look here," she pulled out a tiny flashlight and shone it on the top right part of the page. "Origen, that's the author. You can see here the different languages and names of the translations here."

"Has this—"

"Yeees," she read his mind, "the page was carbon dated many years ago and by many people, and by your father no less."

"How did he get this?"

"Rachel, his sister, was smart. She found the cover page and managed to separate it from the rest of the manuscript and, one way or another, Cyril never discovered it, and she found a way to mail it to your father."

"He told you this?"

She nodded, soberly.

"What does this page have to do with the Ogham stones? If we're correct that Soren's alive, I think he's been leaving me messages in *hinge Ogham*. There was a message carved on my violin case while Mona and I were still in Rome."

Aileen waved a hand. "Well, that's all speculation at this point. There weren't many languages in existence back then. Some variations of Ogham could be that old, certainly yes. And Ogham scripts and the alphabet were used by the Phoenicians, who were able navigators, watermen and world travelers. They could have traveled to the Middle East, there are relics and evidence supporting this, but whether that evidence is authentic and tells the real story, there's no telling. I think your father chose this site, this castle so close to an Ogham relic, because of its symbolism to a lost, ancient language, Ogham, and because this page in front of us relates to other lost, ancient languages."

"Do you know what the six languages were in the *Hexapla*?"

"Well, none of them were Ogham if that's what you're asking. For the most part, they were all variations of either Greek or Hebrew."

Alex rose from the table and opened the door. "Mona …"

"What are you doing?" the old woman asked.

"Mona!"

"Listen to me. You must be very careful what you do next. We are likely being watched at this very moment. Cyril, Cyril Zander, that is, has many eyes and a network of underground followers of his mission."

Alex took out his phone and unrolled the page. "Please, hold this," and he took three pictures of the page with his phone.

"Why photograph it? What will that do?" she asked, confused.

"Because I want you to keep this."

"No. I've held onto this long enough. You must take responsibility for it now. I have done so for forty years and at great risk and great loss. She rolled the page up, fastened it, and handed it to him. It is yours to do with what you will."

Alex took it in. "You have done my family a great service, I thank you. And now I must ask you one final question."

"He's alive," she nodded.

Alex closed his eyes.

"Why did he never come to me all these years?"

"To protect you, of course ... you and your wife."

"Simone," he said under his breath. "And Rachel?"

"You'll find all the answers to what your heart is asking soon."

Where's Mona, Alex thought, realizing now that when he'd called her, no one answered and Aileen had quickly changed the subject. He tore open the bedroom door and Mona was no longer at the table. Not again, he thought walking around the dining table. The front door was cracked ajar. She was outside and came through the doorway toward him.

"This was on the car seat," she said handing him a tourist flyer for the Killarney Whiskey Tour. Mona flipped it over and pointed to writing on the back.

"Murphy's," Alex said aloud.

"It's a pub in Beaufort Village," Aileen said, standing behind them. "It's time."

Alex held the rolled manuscript awkwardly in his open palms, and Aileen Quinn shook her head slowly. "It's yours now. Use it to buy what you want of your future, or let it go. It's up to you."

Forty-Five

EIRE

"Are you going to tell me what's going on here?" Mona demanded, getting into the car.

"Eventually, yes. Right now we're going to get a pint."

Mona looked at her watch. "It's ten in the morning."

"Welcome to Ireland."

Mona sighed. "Right. Looks like we get back on the Upper Lewis Road toward Lewis Road to College. Should I assume our car has been bugged?"

"Probably."

"So if I know you by now, I think you left the manuscript with that woman because whoever's following us would assume we were taking it with us."

Alex looked directly at her. "In other words, now that you think our car has been bugged, let's definitely talk through all the details?"

"For heaven's sake, they probably already know. I need to understand what's happening here. And how will that woman protect herself from whoever wants it or thinks she has it?"

"Do you know what the code word was that I gave her?"

"Strigiformes?"

Alex rolled his wrist.

"Um, strigiformes is the taxonomic order of owls."

"And …"

"Owls, Irish owls, the Gaelic word for owl is …"

"*Cailleach,*" Alex replied, turning onto Lewis Road, instinctively looking in his rearview mirror every five seconds. "What do you make of that?"

Mona paused, thinking, remembering the connotation of owls and their connection to otherworldly powers and the occult. "You think she's a witch?"

He laughed. "That wasn't the word I would have used, but yes, a *cailleach* in Gaelic folklore is not just an owl, and not just slang for a wise old woman. Owls have power, more than other animals, and not just physical power. They have the spiritual gift of vision beyond just the ocular. Aileen Quinn has a kind of vision too, and a power beyond what you'd normally see in a seventy-five-year-old woman. I'm not afraid for her, and she's not afraid of Cyril."

Mona looked at him.

He nodded. "We'll get there."

"There it is," she pointed to Murphy's Pub on the left in front of them. They parked on the street in front of the bar, already crowded with young men, old men, singles at the bar, women seated at a round table in the corner. Alex noticed that his hands weren't sweating now, and his heart felt oddly neutral at the thought of seeing Soren after all these years, alive. He immediately recognized his large shape at the bar - a man in a black pea coat and a fisherman's wool cap.

"What do you go by in these parts, Paddy O'Rourke?"

"You got the surname right anyway," the man turned around and replied, stone-faced. "It's William, or Willie as some call me."

Alex watched his father, Soren Careski, emerge into the glow of morning sunlight and swivel his seat toward them. He extended a hand to Mona. "Introduce me to your young friend."

Alex tried to suppress a roll of his eyes. "This is Mona Delfreggio, a traveling companion from Rome."

Soren lowered his head. "William. Nice to meet you, young lady. Let's find a table." Soren rose and lumbered slowly to a table near the back windows, brightly lit.

"I thought vampires were afraid of sunlight," Alex commented. He sat down then pulled his chair back a few inches from the table.

"Nice to see you too," Soren replied, folding his coat over the back of the chair.

"Maybe I should go and get us some—" Mona interjected.

"No, stay right here, you're a part of this … conversation," Alex replied.

"Is that what it is?" Soren asked.

"Is this where you've been holed up all these years, Willie? Let me guess, you're a commercial fisherman now, who's married to a young librarian half your age, you have seven children ..."

Soren nodded. "It's all right, I expected this."

"You did? Well, let me ask you then. Did you also expect that Simone would be kidnapped and our very lives would be split apart by the secret you weren't willing to deal with yourself?"

"Good morning, folks," said a cheery dark-haired woman, setting down three huge glasses of beer.

"Wait," Mona said, "I didn't order—"

"Welcome to Ireland," Alex smiled.

"I did deal with it," Soren replied, leaning his shoulders in to Alex, who sat opposite him. "I stayed away all these years, away from you, Simone, my job, my work."

"Yes, to protect us, I'm sure that's what you've told yourself all these years, but you left all your diaries in the basement, didn't you?"

"Why not? They're worthless."

Alex sighed. "They're thirty years of research from you and your partner."

"Max," Soren said, sadly.

"Yes, I remember him, Max Deardon. What you and your partner uncovered after all your trips around the world, all your manuscript authenticating, your lecture circuit, your papers, the book you never finished—"

"I finished it. It's been finished for ten years. I just can't publish it."

"Why not?" Alex probed.

"You've been to see Aileen Quinn. How can you ask that question?"

Alex took two sips of beer. "You wrote a book about ...?" Alex raised his brows.

Soren nodded.

"What? The page we found, the page Rachel sent you that you hid up here in an old woman's house for the past four decades?"

"About the man and the family that's been trying to get it back since the fourth century AD."

"Cyril Zander," Alex said.

Soren sighed. "That's one man's name, yes, along with a whole network of radical disciples of his who all believe that the book, the *Hexapla*, threatens what the modern world believes about the Christian church."

"Does it?"

"Certainly, yes."

"And you finished this book while you were up here?"

Soren nodded and took another sip.

"So, where is it? Carved in Ogham on the edges of wood and trees?"

"It might surprise you to learn that I'm more adaptable than that. I've got the manuscript broken up into twenty segments and stored online on twenty different servers across three countries. There's no way to wipe out all of it. With one single command, it's been programmed to compile into one single file and automatically sent to three universities, along with newspapers, literary agents and publishers. The modern world loves blood, gore and violence. And this story makes *Game of Thrones* look like *The Little Mermaid.*"

"And these men you speak of, they know about this?" Mona asked.

Soren shook his head. "It's possible, but I doubt it. My research in cryptography has helped me protect my work. Even if they did access one of the servers, they'd never find it intact." Soren moved closer to Mona. "Using the *Hexapla* as a model, I broke my manuscript up into six pieces, and each piece has one hundred forty-four parts that require a specific encryption key so it can be read by human eyes."

"So what happens if they steal back the—"

"The page you're carrying? Nothing. It's been photographed, scanned, embedded in the manuscript of my book and radiocarbon dated by several different scholars."

"Including you?"

"Me, yes, as well as Cambridge University, Oxford, and University of Leiden."

Alex sat back, taking it all in. "I admit I'm impressed. You never wanted anything to do with email the last time I saw you."

"I still don't because I'm paranoid. Email is as unsecure a communication method as talking face to face in a bar.

Anyone within earshot can hear what we're saying, and any hacker with minimal experience can hack an SMTP server. But if you're suggesting that I'm a linguist with no knowledge of computers, you're mistaken. Binary is the fundamental language of computers and, therefore, the basis of our modern digital age. And I'm using it to my advantage, believe me."

"Okay," Alex sighed and moved the glass aside to put his elbows on the table. "Okay," he repeated. "Why is this all happening now? Simone's kidnapping, the man shooting at us in our house, ransacking the basement looking for ... what ... this?" Alex tapped the bag on his lap.

"Cyril Zander is over ninety years old, and he's near death. He never married, has no children or offspring to pass on the legacy from his thousand-year-old bloodline. So he wants to destroy as many of the remaining texts that threaten the second-century conception of Christianity as he can before he stops breathing. That includes, or in his mind anyway, what you've got with you now, as well as the two books stolen from the Castleman Library at the British Museum."

"My sister!"

"Yes, well, your half-sister, Lily Frasier," Soren corrected, "with whom you share a mother but whose father is my partner, Max Deardon."

"My sister's been missing since the day after the Castleman theft and I found her—"

"There are other books too he's after, from other libraries," Soren continued. "He's got his minions working for him, who can fulfill assignments, steal, rob, kill when they're asked to, but no one that feels the pulse of the work he's been obsessed with all his life, no one who feels or understands the urgency. The quest dies when he does. The rest is just a crime story, good guys, bad guys, all running around trying to kill each other."

"What about ACES and the institute you started?"

"That was my original mission, what Max and I set out to do so many years ago. It was a research center to hunt down the first language ever spoken on earth – the mother language, if you will, from which all other languages evolved."

"And did *you* find it?"

"Well, it was different back then. So many discoveries have happened in the past decade and, to be honest, my quest changed ... everything changed when I got that page in the mail from my sister. For the first twenty years or so, I was obsessed with proving she was still alive. I felt she was alive, I knew she was."

"And now?"

Soren lowered his head. "She was one of Cyril's victims. If he had no reason to keep her alive, he wouldn't have. So then my mission was to uncover the larger picture of that manuscript, who was protecting it and what they feared enough to kill my only sister."

"Dad," Alex said finally, "where's Simone?"

He nodded. "Right. The matter at hand. She's being held by three of Cyril's men, and so far they haven't harmed her."

"How do you know, and if you know that, why haven't you gotten her?"

"To answer your first question, let's say I have my own 'minions.' And it's not my place to charge in there and rescue her. She's a pawn intended to trade what you're carrying in your backpack."

"Well, facilitate the trade then, for God's sake!"

"Doesn't work that way. They'll contact us."

"How?" Alex demanded.

Soren snickered. "Believe me, we'll know."

Forty-Six

EIRE

"Follow me."

Soren drove a black SUV across Killarney to an old, thatched historic cottage at the end of Killarney Bypass toward Kerry Airport.

"The spare bedrooms are all upstairs," he said grabbing the bags. "Take whatever ones you want, there's a bathroom up there too. Make yourselves at home. I'll start the tea."

Mona walked up the creaky stairs and Alex followed with both of their bags.

"So are you and that woman ..." Soren began with a half-turn.

"You really don't know me at all, Dad," Alex replied and went up the stairs.

Ditto, Soren thought.

They ate Irish stew, soda bread and Guinness.

"Well, between the three of us, can't we think of something to talk about? I can't remember the last time anyone's eaten with me here."

Mona looked around the room, then back at her place.

"How did you get involved in all this?" Soren asked her.

"Oh, cut the crap, en," Alex said.

"Don't call me that."

"It's your name isn't it, or one of them, or it used to be. You sent the image of the *Hexapla* page to Mona to avoid museum security, knowing she would tell her sister about it. You also sent it to me from your ghost email account."

"I was sending you and your sister," he added to Mona, "a message."

A shot fired through Soren's front window just then, and went straight out the back. "Get down!" Soren shouted.

"Looks like we've just been sent another one," Alex said.

"What is this?" Mona asked with her hands covering her head.

"The reckoning."

Forty-Seven

ROSS CASTLE, KILLARNEY NATIONAL PARK

"Where do we go?"

"Don't do anything, don't say anything," Soren answered. "They're watching us and they can hear us. Just wait. You okay back there, young lady?"

"So far."

A car parked opposite them flashed its lights on and off once.

"That's it," Soren whispered and opened the driver's side door. "Alex, come with me." And to Mona, "Please stay here, it's the safest place for you right now."

Soren led Alex toward the other car and stopped at the halfway point.

"How do you know what to do here?" Alex asked. "Is this how you conduct all your communications?"

"These people don't waste any time or energy on things that don't matter," Soren answered without taking his gaze off the car in front of them. "Do you hear me?"

"Got it."

"You have the cylinder in your bag?" Soren asked.

"The one you gave me, yes."

"The page is in it?"

"Well, the page you *put* inside it, yes. Something tells me—"

"Quiet," Soren warned.

"Do you see Simone?"

"She won't be in the car."

"Where is she?" Alex demanded.

Soren shot him a hard stare.

"All right, all right," Alex nodded, "sorry."

"She'll be in the castle, probably in that entrance over to the left, held by someone." Soren turned to look directly at Alex. "Whether she lives or dies will depend entirely on what happens in the next five minutes. Do you understand?"

"What did you put in the cylinder?" Alex asked.

The car lights flashed in front of them again. "Mr. Careski, I should say the elder Mr. Careski, come forward, please," called a British, educated voice from the entrance of the castle fifty paces away.

Soren turned to Alex and took the backpack from him and set it over his right shoulder and moved forward a few steps.

"Closer, please, we don't bite."

Soren gave an exaggerated nod so whoever had watched him in binoculars would see his intent of compliance. He took ten more steps, then slowed to look ahead.

"Very good. You can come straight up to the car."

The car was empty, as he'd thought. Soren hoped, *prayed* Alex would stay glued to the spot of earth where he'd left him and not come charging forward. He told him that telepathically, through a type of Ogham that was both unspoken and unwritten. It had worked when he was a small child. Would he still remember?

"Place the whole backpack on the front seat of the car, the window's open. We only want the contents of the cylinder, you'll get the backpack returned."

Soren obeyed, unsure if the backpack was zipped or unzipped, and slid it off his shoulder, through the car window and let it fall onto the passenger seat. He put his palms in the air and took several steps back and stopped.

"Very well. Return with the younger Mr. Careski to your car and wait a moment."

Soren turned his back to them, a bold move purposely reinforcing his desire to comply and be vulnerable to their directions. Close to Alex, he nudged his head in the direction of the car. Alex followed.

"Get in," Soren said to Alex. "I'll wait out here for further directions."

Alex sighed, looked up at the castle in a moment of indecision, then opened the car door and stood in the open door jamb. They watched as a man in a black suit and light hair emerged from the castle's entrance and moved to the open car window.

The blond man! Give me strength, he thought.

The man looked ahead and without taking his eyes off Soren's car, pulled the backpack out the window, and retreated toward the castle. Soren saw the man pull out the cylinder, hand it to another man, who handed it to someone else who opened the container.

"Will they be carbon dating the page right now?" Alex asked.

"Accelerator dating it, yes, probably, though the results are not judged to be terribly accurate. Gas counting or liquid scintillation methods take a few hours, and I'm sure they'll do that too eventually."

Alex counted down from one hundred as a way of distracting himself from the certitude of their impending death. Eighty-seven, eighty-six ... a motor started and then the lights of a different car emerged from the castle, and the car rolled slowly forward, then accelerated toward the road behind them. With all heads turned back to watch this display, something told Alex to look ahead of them.

"Oh my good God, Simone," he barely whispered and held his breath at the sight of her, wobbling unsteadily on bare feet, her mouth gagged and her face bruised and bloody. He didn't dare move for fear that it was a trick and she'd be shot en route. Tears spilled from his eyes and time slowed, barely able to pull air into his lungs.

"Mona, get in the front seat, please," Alex said calmly moving to the back seat and opening the back door so Simone could get in. He didn't try to hide his sobs at seeing up close what they'd done to her beautiful, delicate face and worse, her spirit. He helped her into the back seat and held her thin frame, barely able to breathe. "You're okay now, sweetheart. You're okay," he whispered. "Are you okay?" he asked, burying his face in her hair. How he had missed that hair.

Simone looked back at him with hollow eyes, but they blinked back, communicating from some deep place. She was alive and breathing, that's all that mattered right now.

Two men emerged from the castle's entrance, one carrying the cylinder, the other carrying Alex's backpack.

Backpack man walked assuredly toward Soren's car and stopped at the driver's side and handed over the backpack. This couldn't have been Cyril, the face belonged to a man barely forty. Smooth skin, clean shaven, the face seemed less threatening than Soren had imagined all this time. "For your sakes, I hope our paths never cross again," he said.

Forty-Eight

LONDON

"Where the hell am I?" Crystal moaned, rolling on her left side.

Tal stood over her at first, then sat on the edge of his bed and dabbed the bruise on her forehead with an iced gel pack. "In my flat, you're safe. Keep resting."

She sat up and glanced around the room.

"They're not here, you're okay. Please, lie down."

"What, how, I don't remember how I got here."

"Do you remember the car, the back seat of the car we were in?" She nodded slowly. "The driver must have lost control and the car drove into a stone wall. I grabbed you and took off and found a cab around the corner dropping someone off. They took us here."

"My head," she said. "Am I?"

"You're okay, no broken bones, not even bleeding," he reassured. "You'll be sore for a few days and you can stay here."

While Crystal studied his face, Tal grabbed her hand and held it gently, broken off by a sound at his front door. "Stay here, I'll just be a minute."

He looked through the peek hole and saw only the wall across the hall. So he picked up the bag of trash by the door and unlocked the latch

"Oh, so sorry," Tal stammered, repositioning his bag of garbage and staring at the woman outside his door. "You startled me."

Lily Frasier rebalanced herself on uncomfortably high heels and retrieved Tal's bag of recycled paper, which she'd caused him to drop.

"Thank you," he said pulling the bag from her arms. "What are you doing here?" He hadn't meant for the question to sound irritated, or worse - accusatory. But he knew it had. So it begins, he thought, motioning for her to go inside.

They stood in awkward silence for a full minute, Tal setting down the bag, Lily crossing and uncrossing her arms. "I heard you've been busy since the theft."

"Mainly wasting time trying to find you." Tal watched Lily's face redden and noticed that almost everything about her seemed different now. Was she different, or was it he who had changed? Her hair, previously strawberry blonde and wavy, was now longer, straighter, even darker. She wasn't wearing the same kind of makeup either tonight, but she had on an expensive suit and absurdly high heels. "You look nice, off on a date then?"

Lily sighed, set her suitcase-sized handbag on Tal's sofa and slid out of her Burberry trench. "Have you eaten?" she said in a friendlier voice.

Tal stared for a moment, incredulous that she was asking about something as trivial as a meal. "Did you steal the Castleman books? Is that why you vanished and ran out on the coppers that night? And how exactly did you get away with that?"

"I didn't," she said quickly. "I was arrested and I've been sacked. That's what I've come over here to tell you." She leaned on the back of the sofa. "I was released," she said raising her brows, "for what it's worth, yet still sacked because of how this theft apparently reflects on the museum community and how in some way, I am being held responsible for allowing it to happen." Lily examined her shoes. "I've worked there for ten years. It was my first job out of college."

Tal pulled out one of the dining chairs and turned it slightly to sit semi-opposite her, not facing her directly, and understanding the significance of this detail. He was facing the living room windows and looking at the floor. "I must say your father's turned out to be quite a surprise."

"Yeees, he and underworld friend Andre Doyle are something right out of *The French Connection*. He has a few redeeming qualities, though."

"Like what?" Tal was interested, now.

She shrugged. "He's a scholar ... who knows other scholars. He set up the connection for me with the

Angelica Library in Rome, got me my own office there whenever I had a reason to visit. As a result, we set up a trust to facilitate book exchanges."

"What I still haven't figured out is what their interest or connection is with the Castleman books."

Lily sighed. "My father and his partner, who may be dead for all I know, have been looking for this old manuscript, actually just a fragment, for more years than I care to count."

"And they think that manuscript page might be, what, in one of the Castleman books?"

"I don't think so, no. I think Max and Andre think whoever stole the Castleman books is the same person who's been trying to hunt down that missing manuscript page for thousands of years."

"So, what then, an immortal book thief? A vampire perhaps?"

Lily turned now to face Tal. "What's the centerpiece of the Inquisition exhibit?"

Tal knew exactly the piece. Did she? And had she been the one to leave the clue pointing to Max? "It's an oil painting, Pope Theophilus of Alexandria."

"Right," Lily nodded.

Tal waited for the rest of it. "And?"

"Well, what's his legacy? You do actually *read* the copy I write for the exhibition catalogs?"

"No offense, but everything you write reads like a Ph.D. dissertation."

"Right, thanks for the compliment. Theo, or The Trimmer as he was also called, was basically known as a destroyer. Initially, of course, of any books or legacies that threatened the quite narrow definitions of Christianity, but eventually he burned entire libraries, including of course the Alexandria Library, but many others, just because they held books, old books that he felt represented a past that Christendom did not support."

"Okay. Theo hated pagans and old books. Got it."

"Well, some books survived those fires and one, in particular, may or may not have burned but there may have been several copies."

Tal crossed his legs and suddenly craved a cup of tea to help clear the clutter in his mind. "Earl Grey?" he asked rhetorically and went into the kitchen. "So The French Connection believes that some distant relative of Pope Theophilus is now ..."

"Cyril."

"Who?"

"Saint Cyril of Alexandria was the nephew of Pope Theophilus," Lily said, "so we could be talking about the umpteenth great-grandson of Cyril."

Tal spooned tea into a large, white pot. "And you're thinking this—"

"My father thinks," she corrected.

"Right. That this modern destroyer is responsible for the missing Castleman books and is also looking for the secret manuscript that escaped the Alexandria Library fire in, hold on, the fourth century?"

Lily snorted. "Well done, yes. And I never said the manuscript escaped – it may have indeed burned, but there may have been more than one copy in existence."

Tal returned to the living room and set a tray on the table. "So what is this book?" he asked and watched tension instantly form around the corners of Lily's mouth. With no response, he poured the tea. "Do you think my apartment is bugged or something? I mean, isn't this just basic history? What's so clandestine about it?" Tal passed a cup and saucer to Lily, took his, and returned to the dining room chair. "How about I just keep asking you questions and maybe at some point you'll answer me?" He took a sip.

"The *Hexapla* and it was written in the third century by Origen of Alexandria. Its original incarnation was said to be 6000 pages, and the text is significant because it contains six different side-by-side versions of the Bible, in different languages and dialects, different translations and is said to include some of what the modern world calls the lost gospels."

"And that was threatening to the Christian church?"

"Theo burned anything worshipped by pagans," Lily said after sipping the tea. "Temples, books, statues, anything they worshipped and revered, he openly destroyed. And of course, the term pagan had pretty wide definitions back then, like communists in the McCarthy era. Theo's world was very black and white."

"So Max and his partner spent all their lives looking for this manuscript, or looking for who was hunting it?" Tal asked.

"Neither. The story, as I heard a long time ago, was that Soren, Max's partner, had a younger sister who was an archaeologist. She went to Egypt early in her career on a commission to find a missing manuscript. No one really knows who sent her, but she never returned from that trip. Apparently, she found the manuscript, but was intercepted by someone who shot and killed her guide, stole the manuscript and took her with him. One way or another, this woman managed to stow away the cover page of this manuscript showing the title, the author, the contents and sent it to Soren before she died."

"*If* she died," Tal corrected. "Anyway, where is this page now?'

"Not sure if anybody knows. It's notorious, responsible for so much death and suffering. I almost hope it's not found."

Tal's stomach growled. "What are you going to do now?"

"You mean with my life?" Lily laughed and shrugged. "I don't know. Mainly I was thinking about dinner."

Crystal, he thought. "In a minute. I've got a friend staying with me that I need to check on."

Forty-Nine

ROME

Cyril Zander stood like an old statue at the west window in his loft, which had a perfect view of his old friend, the clock tower, in the central piazza of Montagnana. The espresso cooled in the tiny demitasse in his right hand, but somehow, today, he could not bring himself to drink from it. He'd craved structure and regularity in his life, all his life, and demanded this same perfection from those around him. But today, there was no order in the chaos of his mind and heart. Part of him wanted to open the window and toss out the cup and saucer, lean forward and wait for the clinking jingle of porcelain crashing against the ancient cobblestones eighty feet below.

How long would it take, this fall, of a cup that weighed maybe two, three ounces? And how long would it take him to fall, plunging his old bones out of the open window to fly with the pigeons and crows that circle around dead rats in the shadowy corners below?

Marta pulled a loaf of bread out of the vintage oven and, while it cooled on the stove top, she moved down the hall to her bedroom. To rest. To think. To prepare. She sat on her bed and took in the view of an entire wall of books. Anthropology, archaeology, rocks, bones, ancient cultures, as many as she could collect, gather, borrow from the school down the street, and read, the only thing she had ever loved doing her whole life. She pulled the dusty beige suitcase out of her closet, and the much newer, shinier carry-on, travel stickers covering nearly all four sides and the edges of the original RC still barely detectable in between them. How long would it take to pack ten years' worth of a life into two vessels?

Back to the kitchen, she sliced and buttered the bread, sliced three ripe tomatoes, drizzled olive oil on them and poured a fresh pot of coffee, all arranged neatly on a wooden tray with two, not one, linen napkins.

Marta knocked twice; he knew it was her. Quietly, but with enough pressure to be heard within the large room.

"Yes," the man called.

She would open the door now, walk in slowly and softly and set a tray on the credenza against the wall opposite the window. "I'm tired, Marta."

"I know," she replied with her back to him.

Zander walked around the room, his hard shoes loud on the polished floors. He turned to her and removed the red cape and let it fall to the floor. "I'm tired of the clothes. Do you hear me? I'm tired of upholding someone else's work. A curse! That's what it is now, a curse."

"Yes," Marta said, still without turning around.

Zander unbuttoned his dressing gown and pulled it over his head. "I'm tired of being someone else, of carrying on for someone I never knew." He bent down and pulled off his high black boots, leaving them to decorate the impeccable floors with a heap of ancient costume, a weight he was no longer willing to bear.

"But your work," Marta said in a soft voice. "It has defined you. Defined your family. Your lineage."

"I took so much from so many and have nothing left to give, even to myself." He stood, in his stocking feet, a pair of sleep pants and a white undershirt, in the center of the large room, twelve-foot ceilings towering over him.

Marta poured cream in the coffee, and gently spooned in two tiny heaps of sugar, and stirred. She felt his eyes on her now, wondering about her, standing vulnerable in the center of the floor without shoes or dignity. "Are you hungry?" she asked, sliding a small vial from under the second napkin and emptying it into the demitasse cup. Then she stirred. "I made poppy seed bread."

"I'm afraid," the man found himself saying, even before he'd had a chance to review his thoughts and edit the words. "I feel unwell today, Marta, please, stay with me up here." The man moved to the bed and put his heavy brown robe around his shoulders.

"I must leave soon. I'm taking the six o'clock train."

"What? Where?"

"To see my brother, I told you. Now please, eat, so I know you've at least done that before I go."

Zander sat on the edge of the ridiculously large bed, too large for a newlywed couple, let alone a man with ninety-year-old bones. He stared at the window now and wondered.

Marta took the napkin-covered vial and tucked it in the pocket of her robe, leaving the tray on the sideboard.

"Marta! Why must you leave me?" Zander moaned.

Marta, with one hand on the doorknob, turned to the man who in her lifetime had been her sponsor, her kidnapper, nearly her killer, and then forty years later her employer. "My name ..." she said in clear, resonant voice, "... is Rachel."

Fifty

EIRE

Soren Careski stood before the long mirror on the inside of his bedroom closet door, appraising his looks - hair scantly covering the shape of his skull, chin cleanly shaven, donning the only suit he owned, freshly dry cleaned, too tight around the middle, too large in the shoulders, matched with a pressed white shirt and ridiculous yellow tie.

His quest had started with Rachel, and so this was the most fitting end to it, wasn't it? What people would call full circle.

He drove his car to the other end of his property because it was raining today and thirty-five degrees, and he was wearing his good suit. With rubbers over his shoes, he walked without an umbrella but with an auger in one hand and a plastic bag in the other and stood in front of the tall stone he had ordered online for the empty grave of his still missing sister. It read:

RACHEL DARBY CARESKI

BELOVED DAUGHTER, SISTER AND FRIEND

INTREPID SCHOLAR, PRESERVER OF HISTORY

GOD BLESS YOU, REST IN PEACE

It was polished marble, the most expensive they offered, and he visited it once a month and planted a fresh pot of yellow asters each time, her favorite color. He took off his suit jacket and laid it on the ground, knelt in front of the stone, and dug the auger into the ground to the left by about six inches. He turned the crank and dug it down about twelve inches, pulled it back up and dug it down again and again, until there was a hole in the earth the diameter of a small fist. He pulled the small cylinder out of the plastic bag and held it front of the stone.

"This is why you went to Egypt so many years ago, why you sacrificed the best job any woman could get at that time in history, and I've brought it home and am returning it to you, where it belongs." Soren thought about opening the tube and eyeing the manuscript page one last time, but the rain would no doubt damage it. This way it would be buried back in the earth, where it had lain thousands of miles away for thousands of years. He slid the tube into the earth, and filled in the dirt and mud around it, pushing it down below the surface about four inches. Then he took the four-inch plant, pressed it out of the plastic pot and buried the fragile roots in the damp earth, where he knew the sun and rain would help it bloom. Where the light of Rachel Careski, some part of her, would always bloom.

"Until next time, my dear," he said and bent down to kiss the headstone.

Fifty-One

BOSTON

"Damn," Alex whispered, squinting at the folded, coffee-stained and refolded New York Times. "Eight, nine, dammit."

He heard Simone stifle a snicker in the next room, where he knew she was preparing *soba* for a special dinner. "What?" she asked.

"Tombstone territory, eight letters."

"Arizona?"

"That's seven."

"Graveyard?"

"Nine," Alex replied, secretly enjoying the almost unfamiliar feeling of leisure. Lounging in pajamas at ten-thirty on a Sunday, hearing Simone moving around in soft steps across the kitchen floor, remembering the feeling of her warm body next to his. His vision clouded momentarily, at the same time that Simone started humming something.

"Did Soren say when he's coming to visit?"

Alex waved a hand in the air. "Summer," he said. "Question is, which summer."

Simone stood in the kitchen doorway, dish towel in hand, studying him. She always knew the messages of his heart even before he did. What is it, her face seemed to ask him.

"Can you ever forgive me?"

Simone shook her head. "Why are you blaming yourself?" She moved to him and sat on his lap, crushing the newspaper, purposely, he knew. "Could you have stopped it? I mean, unless you had magic powers?"

"I might ask myself that question for the rest of my life."

"I can think of better things to do with your time," she smiled and raised her lips to his face.

"Oh, really? You mean, like, watch a movie for example? There's one starting in five minutes." She moved closer. "Is it true that translators hate watching movies with subtitles?"

"Not necessarily. Some languages are … universal."Start

About the Author

© Lee Towles

Lisa Towles' 2017 thriller, *Choke* (Rebel ePublishers) won a 2018 IPPY and a NYC Big Book Award Distinguished Favorite in the Thriller category. Her other published books (published as Lisa Polisar) include *The Ghost of Mary Prairie, Blackwater Tango, Knee Deep,* and *Escape: Dark Mystery Tales.* Lisa is an active member of Mystery Writers of America, Sisters in Crime, and International Thriller Writers.

Lisa was raised in New England, lived in New Mexico for many years, and now lives in the Bay Area. She has an MBA in IT Management and works in the tech industry.

Learn more about Lisa at
http://lisatowles.com or
https://digitalraconteur.wordpress.com

Please turn the page for a preview of her thriller, *Choke.*

Choke

Chapter One

"Castiglia? Do you have it?" The whisper came in the hushed darkness of San Francisco General Hospital's ICU recovery ward. Nurse Alice Redfield gave an insistent stare as she awaited an answer.

Certified Nursing Assistant Kerry Stine steeled herself against the jabbing pain in the side of her head and gestured toward the bed in front of them. "Right there. And what do you mean 'do I have it'?" She wondered, afterward, if the migraine had colored the tone of her words.

Redfield had already moved on to the next patient. "It's not there," she said without looking up.

Kerry Stine picked up the medical chart from the slot at the bottom of patient Rosemary Castiglia's bed. "Emergency Evacuation Procedures – Part I" was the title on the front page of what should have been, and clearly had been less than an hour ago, Castiglia's medical chart, containing a summary sheet, doctors' notes, lab results, etc. She shook her head and glanced in Redfield's direction. "Who would steal a medical chart?"

Nurse Redfield glared at her over wire-rimmed glasses. “That’s the first thing you think of if it’s missing?”

This question reminded Kerry that she’d only been a CNA for six months and most of her classroom training she’d found completely inapplicable to hospital reality.

Nurse Redfield marched toward the exit door and paused. “If you wanted to steal a patient,” she whispered, “the best way to do it is to steal their chart first.”

Kerry stared at her supervisor. What a strange thing to say, she thought.

“Sure,” Redfield went on, “ the chart’s got the patient’s labs, schedule of tests, which then tells you when the patient is likely to be ... unattended. Get it?”

“Not really.” The door closed behind Redfield, and Kerry glanced back at the semi-cadavers in post-op recovery – five of them crammed into a small, dark, uncomfortably chilly room purposely set to the temperature of a meat locker for infection control. To her, it felt more like a morgue, except the patients were technically still breathing. Through ventilators.

Rosemary Castiglia, the oldest patient on the ward, was the only one breathing on her own. Miraculous, and no one understood it. Still, with enough morphine to choke an elephant, all the lines she’d previously seen on the patient’s face were smooth now – her forehead and eyes looking a decade younger. Sleep, Kerry thought, memorizing the patient’s facial features, again acknowledging the pounding in her head. She looked at her watch – ten minutes left on her shift.

"Miss Stine?" The man paused. "Can I see you please?" Hospital Administrator Mark Ferri stood just outside the ICU entrance beside Nurse Redfield. As Kerry approached, Ferri gestured. "In my office." She hated how Ferri talked – pausing at odd times to inject extra importance to his words.

"How's your training class going?" Redfield asked, looking suspiciously at Kerry. Kerry ignored her and followed Mark Ferri into his large office. Every wall contained a piece of matching chocolate-brown leather furniture. Two stiff-looking chairs, angular sofa, and an oversized ottoman she was sure had never been touched.

"I'm glad to see you taking advantage of our training programs. That's one of the things I'm working to revitalize here." Ferri gave her a 'good work' nod.

She shook her head. "I haven't enrolled yet. I need to stack up as many hours as I can right now. They offer that course again in six months."

The pounding in her temples had morphed into a vice-like squeeze. She felt an almost bouncing sensation when she closed her eyes, as if her head were vibrating. Despite the pain, she was unable to stifle the yawn that crept into her mouth as she sat down.

"Am I keeping you up?" Ferri was in front of her now, leaning back against his desk. She knew the body language – arms crossed to symbolize authority and their distance from each other in the hospital food chain, head lowered to signify interest, even intimacy.

You're not my friend, she thought. "My head ... I'm sorry. I've got a killer migraine."

"Let me give you something for it. I get them too." Don't trust him, her inner voice counseled. "Fiorinal, Imitrex, Motrin with Codeine ... if you ever need anything, help yourself." Now he looked straight at her. "I know what it's like." Ferri handed her a sealed sample packet of Fioricet. She just shook her head and looked at it. "Anyway," he went on, "you're probably wondering—"

"What's there to wonder about? A chart goes missing on Redfield's watch, so naturally blame it on the CNA. I understand the concept of hierarchy. Sir."

Ferri stared, eyes slightly wider.

She crossed her legs and arms, settling deeper into the uncomfortable chair. "Rosemary Castiglia's chart was there at 7 pm, I—"

"You looked at it?"

"No, but I saw it."

"That means you looked at it," Ferri said.

Okay, so you're a freaking homicide detective now. Note to self: watch what you say around him. Kerry rose and walked toward the door, wondering now if he'd secretly locked it. "If you're asking me if I physically picked up the chart and pulled it out of the holder, no. I visually confirmed that it was, in fact, her chart, checked the patient, checked her levels, saw that she was sleeping and moved on." She opened the door.

"Miss Stine, I wouldn't leave right now if—"

The door slammed behind her.

CPSIA information can be obtained
at www.ICGtesting.com
Printed in the USA
FSHW020946250519
58437FS